THE QUIET ONES

JEFF DEPEW

SURTR
BOOKS

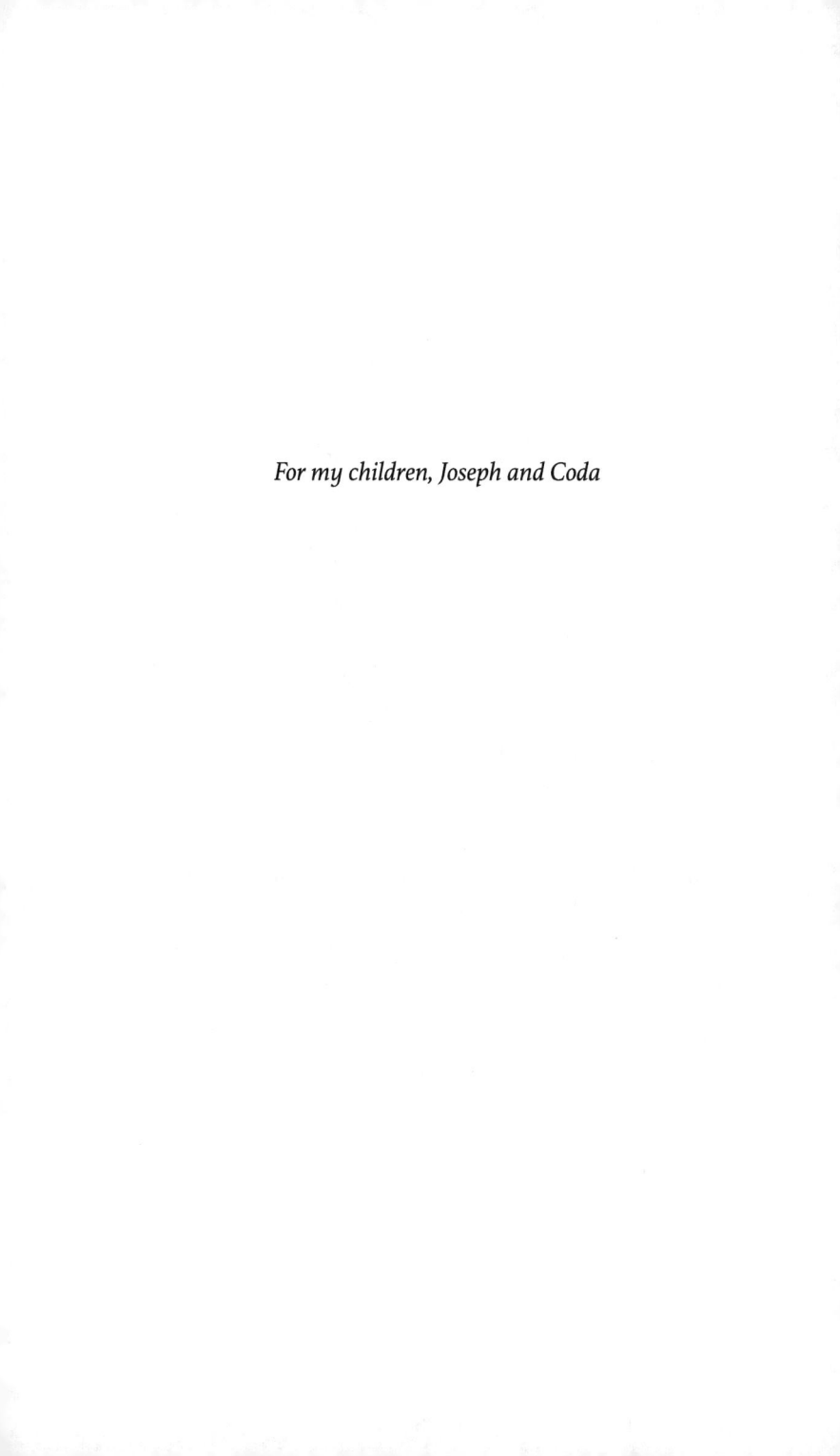

For my children, Joseph and Coda

ACKNOWLEDGMENTS

I would like to thank Mary Beth, who believes in me more than I believe in me sometimes, as well as Missy Ryan, Juliana Bahar, and Tara Geever for reading my manuscript and giving me the honest criticism that only English teachers can give, and to anyone who has read my work and asked if I have written anything else they could read.

The most merciful thing in the world, I think, is the inability of the human mind to correlate all its contents.

H.P. Lovecraft

NOW

A young man in a blue plaid shirt and dirty green apron staggered past Callie, less than five feet away, without even looking at her. His left eye was swollen shut and crusted over with yellowish ooze. He opened and closed his mouth like a hungry goldfish, his lips and tongue forming silent words.

Callie watched carefully as he passed, to make sure he kept moving. She wasn't afraid he would hurt her, but she would rather have him in front of her than behind her.

Like all the other Quiet Ones, the only sound he made was his unsteady shuffling footsteps, scraping along the empty street.

He staggered slightly, swaying from side to side like a drunk. His hands hung down; his fingers stiff. He hip-checked a parked car, nearly toppled over, but stayed on his feet.

She watched him until he turned a corner and was gone. All the while his mouth opening and closing, speaking words no one could hear.

Where was he going? Where were they all going? And what was he saying?

It was rare to see them so early in the day. Maybe that was a sign they should find a place to hole up for the night. Nighttime was different. At night there were things that could hurt you.

She looked over at her brother, his blank stare mirroring the man who had just passed them. He took a shuffling step forward, pulling on the leash until it was taut. She tightened her grip on the strap, wrapping it around her hand a couple of times to pick up the slack.

She looked down at the baby in the stroller. He looked up at her and she grunted. He was probably getting hungry.

She gave a little jerk on the leash, placed her hands on the stroller handles, and continued on.

They had a long way to go.

1

BEFORE

For Callie Hawthorne, the world ended on a Saturday.

Not that the days of the week mattered much afterward. But there was a certain irony to the idea that on Saturday, out of *all* the days, on Saturday, the best of all days (the last Saturday before school began, in fact) the world ended.

She had been in a foul mood since her dad woke her up at seven. Seven. On a *Saturday.*

"Get out," she mumbled, burying her head beneath her pillow. He flicked her light switch, nearly blinding her.

"Let's go, "Dad said, his voice too loud and too cheery for this early. "We need to be out the door in half an hour."

"Why do I have to go?" she said. "Why can't I just stay here?"

"You know why," Dad said. "Half an hour." And he closed her door.

Callie was grounded for not calling or texting last Thursday night when she went to the movies with Jessica. But she felt it was also because her mom didn't like Jessica. Mom hadn't wanted Callie to go in the first place. She thought Jessica smoked, even though she didn't. At least Callie didn't think she smoked. And even if she did, so what. Callie didn't smoke. It was gross.

Mom had relented though and allowed Callie to go. On the condition she would text them when she got to the theater, and when she was on her way home.

And now her parents were angry because Callie didn't return any of their calls or texts. How could she when the phone battery died? And how was that even her fault?

But Mom and Dad didn't want to hear "that excuse." But how is it an excuse when it's true? They were waiting for her when she came home, sitting in the good chairs in the living room. That had not been a fun conversation.

"Do you know how worried we were?" and, "You should plan ahead," and, "Borrow someone else's phone," stuff like that. It didn't matter that she was in high school. It didn't matter that she was almost sixteen. All that mattered was that she didn't answer her phone. So she was grounded. She couldn't leave the house at all. The last weekend before school began. No movies, no friends' houses, no friends over, no nothing.

"There are consequences when you break rules," her dad had said. *Gee, thanks, Dad. Can I write that down?*

Except, of course, parents were allowed to break rules whenever they wanted. Her mom hardly ever answered texts until way later. And Dad...forget it. He left his phone on the kitchen counter most days, even when he was at work. She sometimes wondered why he even had a phone.

Callie was grounded, not supposed to leave the house, but because her brother Jake's soccer game was today, and they didn't want to leave her home alone, so they dragged her along. She was "reverse grounded" as her dad called it. *Ha ha, good one, Dad.*

Even though the game started at nine (which meant they had to get there by eight) it was already warm, which was unusual for central Oregon, even in August. Fortunately, some big shade trees were lining the field, so that's where they set up their chairs. The same old group of dopey soccer parents began chatting about the same old parent stuff: their kids, soccer, this heat wave, the chances of Jake's team making the playoffs...

A dog barked. Callie jerked her head around and saw some lady in a bright pink warm-up suit and oversized sunglasses walking her big yellow goofy-looking dog. It was pulling on the leash, straining toward the field, and barking at the players. Callie made a face. She hated dogs. *Hated* them. She always had. They were stupid. Stupid and mean.

A neighbor's dog had bitten her on her elbow when she was three. She could kind of remember it, at least certain images, flashes, really: the terror, the blood, the dog's muzzle latched onto her arm, and the screaming, from both her and then her mom...

She still had the scar. She looked down at her arm, at the shiny C-shaped mark just above her right elbow. Stupid dogs.

Callie watched until the woman and her mutt walked away before she put her earbuds back in.

She didn't pay attention to the game. She had no interest in soccer. Running around kicking a ball for two hours? No thanks. Softball and baseball were her favorite sports.

Jake played well, based on all of Mom and Dad's screaming and carrying on and Dad high-fiving the other dads (which was so cringeworthy Callie actually moved her chair a few inches away.) But Jake always played well. His league team, his high school team. He would probably get a scholarship at Oregon State, which is where he really wanted to go. He was a senior, so this was a big year for him.

Mom glanced over after Jake had scored his second goal (or maybe it was his third?) and scowled at Callie, who still had her earbuds in, bobbing her head and scrolling through her music.

Mom reached over and smacked Callie's knee with the back of her hand and mimed removing her earbuds.

Callie rolled her eyes in that exquisite way that only fifteen-year-old girls can, without a wasted movement, pointedly plucked an earbud out, held it up, and raised her eyebrows at Mom. *Yes?*

"Can't you even *pretend* to pay attention?" Mom asked softly, but with meaning. Her eyes narrowed, staring so hard that Callie shifted her gaze away. She looked at her feet.

"I didn't even want to come," said Callie. "I'm supposed to be grounded, remember? You didn't say anything about watching the game."

Mom started to say something but glanced around at the other parents. "We'll talk when we get home."

Callie shrugged, palms up, mouth open, shoulders raised, the universal *What did I do?* gesture. Mom shook her head and turned back to the game.

2

When Callie thought back, down to the exact moment, she wasn't sure of the time *It* happened, but she knew it had to be after one o'clock. They were home after the soccer game (apparently, he scored three goals and came close to getting another, so that was cause for celebration). Mom made tuna melts for Callie and Jake, and she and Dad were going to go run some errands. Jake was getting picked up by his friend Nick, bound for who knew where. *And who cares?* thought Callie. *He can do whatever he wants.* She could listen to some music and watch some baseball on TV. The Mariners were playing a day game.

At least she would be alone for a while, away from her jerk family.

Lunch conversation consisted mainly of Dad and Jake sitting at the kitchen table recounting every moment of the game, with Mom chiming in, smiling proudly at Jake, and rubbing his shoulder when she refilled his water glass. Callie ate by herself, standing at the counter, leaning over her plate, not joining in the conversation.

"Cal, why don't you come sit with us?" Dad asked.

"I'm fine," Callie muttered.

"She likes being a cool emo loner," Jake said.

Callie opened her mouth, ready with a nasty response, but her mom caught her eye.

Fine, she thought, shaking her head. *Jake can say whatever he wants. The golden child.*

She dumped the rest of her sandwich in the kitchen trash and slid her plate into the sink.

"*In* the dishwasher," Mom said.

Callie sighed, took the plate out of the sink, and put it in the dishwasher with more force than necessary. She stood up and looked at her mom. "Happy? Anything else I'm doing wrong?"

Mom ignored her. Another thing that parents could do but you couldn't. If you ignore them, it was "disrespect," but when they did it, they were making a point. Uggh.

"Can you take my plate, too?" Jake asked, holding out his plate. He smiled at her, smug and secure in his place as the current favorite child.

Mom and Dad were talking to each other, so Callie shot Jake a quick bird and went and flopped on the couch.

Jake burst out laughing as he got up and put his plate in the sink.

It was hot. Too hot for anything except going to the beach or hanging out inside and watching TV. Some of her friends were going to the pool at the rec center. Maybe go to the movies? So many options. But not for Callie. She was grounded.

She lay on the couch texting Erica, her best friend, one eye on her phone and the other watching the Mariners playing Oakland. Callie was looking forward to school starting so she could get back into playing softball. She had been playing for three years, usually catcher, and liked it;

the competition, the camaraderie with her teammates. All the good stuff. She wondered how excited her parents would be if she got a scholarship.

She was getting bored, though, because it was only the bottom of the second inning and the A's had already scored three runs and had the bases loaded with no outs.

Dad was out in the garage, calling for Mom, ready to go, while Mom scurried around the kitchen, looking for something. Jake was taking a shower. At least that's what he had said he was going to do. More likely, he was sitting on his bed, playing on his phone.

"Callie, have you seen my keys?" Mom was always losing her keys. Last Christmas, Jake and Callie gave her one of those key-finding devices you put on your key ring so if you lose them you can call your keys with your phone. When Callie had asked her why she never used it, Mom had said she "lost" it. Well, she told them she lost it, but Callie secretly believed that Mom was kind of insulted by the gift as if they were telling her she was absent-minded. It was probably on a shelf somewhere, still in the box. Meanwhile, here Mom was, looking for her keys. Oh well.

Callie spoke without looking up. "Nope."

Her mom stopped, lifted her sunglasses, and looked at Callie. "Would it kill you to get up and help?"

Callie shrugged. "They're your keys. I don't ask you to help me find my stuff."

"Oh?" Mom laughed a not-at-all amused laugh. More of an incredulous laugh. (*Incredulous* was one of Callie's vocabulary words last year. Someone who was incredulous was unwilling or unable to believe something.) Mom stepped forward. "What about—"

Her father called from the garage. "Marie, let's go! What's the holdup?"

Mom turned and called out: "I can't find my keys! Are they in the car?"

Her dad laughed, "*I* have them! We're taking your car, remember? My car's in the shop."

Mom slapped her forehead. "That's right. I completely forgot."

She looked at Callie. Her mouth was tight, her eyes hard. "Remember, we're going out to watch the meteor shower tonight. All of us. Including you. Dad and I should be back by five. And remind Jake."

Callie turned back to the TV. "Yeah, I'm so excited. A meteor shower. How fun."

Mom spun. "You know what? Maybe if you had a little more interest in this family, you wouldn't—"

"Marie!" Dad again.

Mom glared at the back of Callie's head, turned, and was gone.

Callie sighed. Sometimes her mom was such a— great. On the TV, one of the stupid A's just doubled home three runs. Five to nothing now. Maybe there was a movie on. She began channel surfing.

She heard the low rumble of the garage door lowering. Caught a glimpse of her mom's white SUV driving past the front window. Then they were gone.

She never saw her parents again.

3

Sometime later, not too long though, because the game was only in the fifth inning, Callie was texting with Erica about which band shirt Erica should buy with her birthday money when she felt a low rumble. Definitely not the garage door. Deeper. Stronger. Callie sat up. Dishes rattled in the kitchen cabinets.

Earthquake?

Jake shouted from down the hall, "What the hell was that?"

She texted madly. "did u feel that???"

Another jolt, this one more powerful. Something crashed to the floor in the living room.

Frightened, Callie stood up to go find Jake, when a wave of sound, louder than she could ever imagine, swept through her, almost lifting her off the floor in its intensity. She took a wobbly step, then her legs collapsed from beneath her and she fell on the carpet. Her head flopped back against the couch. She moaned. The sound was not just in her ears, but in her *mind* as well.

The sound went on and on. A deep, high-pitched

metallic grinding, as if a gigantic shovel was being dragged across an immense concrete parking lot. A God-sized bird crying out in anguish. A sentient star exploding, screaming its name to the universe.

The windows were vibrating in their frames. The walls were shuddering. Glass shattered. She covered her ears, closed her eyes, but there was no escape. It was everywhere. The sound was everywhere. It was everything.

Gasping, sobbing, Callie crawled up onto the couch and pulled a pillow over her ears, fists jamming it tight up against her head.

But the sound, relentless, continued. Callie's stomach churned and she fought back the urge to vomit.

The sound continued. Another rumble, followed by a solid jolt. She felt the house around her shudder. She heard, just over the sound, something shattering. She pulled the pillow tighter over her ears. The sound continued.

Then the lights went out.

Callie wasn't sure if she had fainted or not. She never had before, even when they drew her blood last fall at the doctor when she was really sick. So she really wasn't sure what fainting was like. In the movies, it looked just like sleeping. Admittedly, she felt groggy and slow, the way you sometimes moved in a dream.

Her ears rang and her head hurt. Really hurt. She put a finger in each ear, looked at it, checking for blood. All clear. The ringing persisted.

Callie carefully stood up, leaning on the back of the couch for support, and looked around for her cell phone. There. On the floor beneath the coffee table. She must have dropped it. Maybe she did pass out. So weird. *What* was *that sound?*

She texted Erica: hey did you hear that??? what wuz it??

She waited, but no response.

Again. "erica you there??? pls."

She hit the phone icon and put the phone up to her ear. After four rings, Erica's voicemail picked up. Callie hung up without leaving a message. Erica would see the texts. But why didn't she respond?

She hesitated, fingers poised above her phone's screen, then tried her mom's number, but it went straight to voicemail. Same with Dad.

The ringing in her ears had faded a bit.

She glanced at the TV, did a double take. It was still on, but the picture was weird. There was something wrong. The camera was just showing the floor. Gray concrete. A soda cup lying in a pool of dark liquid. There was part of someone's foot in the lower left corner. The camera wasn't moving, and neither was the foot.

Callie picked up the remote and changed the channel. Cartoon, commercial, a sports news program—but the camera shot was off center, and the hosts looked like they were asleep, unconscious, or something. They were slumped in their chairs. Not moving. Eyes open, but unfocused, just staring. Callie sat on the couch, eyes on the TV. What was this?

A man came in from the side. He wasn't a host; he was wearing a baseball cap and a tee shirt. He had a headset on and held a clipboard. He walked unsteadily to the broadcast desk. He said something too soft to hear. He poked one of the hosts, a bald man with glasses, who slid off his chair and fell bonelessly to the floor. The man with the clipboard

♦

looked at the camera, his face panic-stricken, and stumbled back out of the frame.

Callie clicked the remote and checked more channels, but they were all the same. Any live programs just showed the hosts or newscasters lying on the floor or slumped over their desk. Everything else was just movies or commercials or dead air.

What was going on?

Callie set the remote on the coffee table and went to the front window and pulled the curtain aside. Her eyes widened and she swore quietly as she looked out in her front yard.

There was a car on their lawn. It had driven right over the sidewalk and smashed through the low picket fence and only stopped when it ran into the big maple tree outside the living room window.

She reached to her right, and without looking away from the window, locked the front door. *Should I call 911?*

Callie went to her phone, picked it up, punched 9-1-1 and waited. It rang. And rang. And rang. Nobody picked up. But it was 911. Someone was always supposed to pick up 911 calls.

She moved to the kitchen and picked up the phone that sat beside the ancient black answering machine that their mom refused to get rid of even though the only ones who called them were telemarketers. There was a dial tone, and she repeated the process. Again, nobody answered. Callie placed the phone back in its cradle and walked back to the front window.

She looked more closely at the car. There was somebody behind the wheel, but it was hard to make out because of the glare. *What if they're drunk?* That would be scary, to be sure. Then, more insistently: *What if they're hurt?*

She moved to the front door, unlocked it, took a deep breath, and pulled it open. The car was just a few feet away, and she could hear the engine running. Cautiously, Callie moved closer. Her foot slipped on a loose brick as she moved closer to the car.

The driver was just sitting there, behind the wheel. Not moving. Just... sitting. Like the people on the sports show. He was an older man. She could make out his white hair through the glare of the windshield. His glasses were sitting down low on his nose. He was staring straight ahead. So was he okay? *He's sitting up.* The engine rumbled beneath the dented hood. The front of the car was dented, and some shiny liquid was leaking onto the lawn.

She looked past the car at the rest of the neighborhood.

Something was really wrong.

4

Callie walked down the driveway and stood on the sidewalk. Someone had rear-ended the neighbor's SUV parked along the curb across the street. The car was angled with its rear end out in the street. Like the car in her front yard, it too, was still.

Callie turned her head as movement caught her eye. She watched, half-amazed, half-horrified, as down the block, a blue SUV bounced up the sidewalk, drove slowly across a lawn, bulldozed a bush, and slammed up against the front of the house, shattering a large picture window in a shower of sparkling, broken glass. She heard the crunch of impact and the glass break from way down here.

She stepped farther out and scanned up and down the street. Where was everybody? Didn't people usually go outside after an earthquake, and stand around and talk about it? That's what they did in the movies. But all was quiet. So still. Just some car alarm in the distance. And somewhere she could hear a baby crying.

Black smoke billowed skyward from several blocks over,

and as she looked around, she noticed smoke in at least three other locations.

Her mind whirled. She slowly turned around.

Oh! There's Mr. Phillips.

He was a friend of her dad. She'd known him forever. He was standing in his driveway, two houses down, kind of... wobbling.

Callie ran toward him, her heart hammering in her chest, but also, relieved, safe, in a way. Somebody she knew. An adult. "Mr. Phillips! Hey! Mr. Phillips!"

He made no sign that he had heard. He stood beside his car, wearing khaki shorts and a blue Corona Beer tank top. A bucket of sudsy water sat at his feet. A yellow sponge lay on the ground. Callie picked it up and held it out to him. Nothing.

"Mr. Phillips?" Her voice sounded frightened. *Well,* she told herself, *I AM frightened. This is scary.*

She spoke softly, slowly, the way you do to a child or a very old person. "Mr. Phillips? Please, do you know what's happening? Are you okay?"

She reached out and tapped his arm and he shuddered. She noticed a thin stream of blood leaking out of his right ear. His lips moved but he wasn't saying anything. He let out a loud sigh and collapsed as simply as though the bones had just been removed from his legs. He landed hard on the concrete, knocking the bucket over. The soapy water flowed down the driveway, flowing to the gutter and away.

Callie dropped the sponge and backed up.

She whirled around, looking for someone, anyone, who could tell her what was going on. Someone who could help her.

A woman lay on the sidewalk three houses up, a small

dog beside her. The dog, still on its extendable leash, was sniffing at her face.

Callie hurried over and knelt beside the woman. She was wearing pink track pants and a pair of oversized headphones lay cockeyed on her head. She could hear the music. A pop song. Callie felt a strange, out-of-place urge to straighten the headphones.

 The dog, a little black and brown something-or-other with a red bow, kept its distance. It moved as far away from her as the leash would allow. Callie reached out to touch the woman, but she couldn't bring herself to do it. And she didn't want to get too close to the dog.

The woman's eyes were open, and her chest was faintly moving, so she was alive. *But what's wrong with her?*

"Are... are you okay?" she whispered.

The woman's eyelids fluttered, but other than that, there was no sign that she had heard. She was bleeding from her ear. A thin stream of blood ran from her nose. It joined the blood coming from her ears, where it pooled stickily beneath her head. The dog whined and Callie glanced at it. "Hey, buddy," she said automatically, her voice husky and thick with panic. The dog growled unconvincingly and backed away until the leash was completely taut. Callie glanced down at the woman again.

The familiar whine of a jet airplane caught her attention and she rose and looked up. The sun was still blazing, and she shaded her eyes with a hand. An airliner, off in the distance, spun slowly as it headed earthward at a dangerously steep angle. She watched, not breathing, until it disappeared from view behind the tree line, and even though it was miles away, she heard it impact the ground.

Callie put her hand to mouth. *All those people...*

The car alarm continued, unabated, and beneath it, the crying baby. Callie looked around.

Why doesn't somebody help it?

There were none of the normal neighborhood Saturday sounds she was accustomed to: lawn mowers, cars driving by music blaring from somewhere, kids shouting. None of that. And in some ways, that was the worst part of everything that had happened. People were loud; people made noise. Silence was...lonely.

Callie started. *Jake!* She had forgotten about Jake. He was home!

5

Callie flew over the sidewalk, across two lawns, and bolted through the front door (stopping to close and lock it first) and down the hall.

"Jake!" she bellowed, swinging into his room, and stumbling over one of his cleats. His room was empty. His dirty soccer uniform in a heap on the floor.

She found him in the bathroom, standing in front of the mirror. He had changed after his game and was wearing his favorite Real Madrid jersey. His dark hair was wet and slicked back. The faucet in the sink was running. She automatically turned it off and looked up at Jake. He was staring at himself in the mirror. But not really. His eyes were... unfocused, kind of glazed over. Like Mr. Phillips. *Please, no,* she thought, and reached out and cupped his chin in her hand and turned his head down to face her.

"Jake?" she whispered. "Jake, are you alright? What's wrong?"

His eyes were blank, staring straight ahead. There was no recognition, no warmth. This was Jake, but at the same time, it wasn't. He was empty. Like part of him had been turned off. Shut down. Like a computer. But how?

"Jake?" Callie's voice was barely audible.

She tried to fight back the tears, but it was no use.

She hugged Jake, her brother, her family, and held him close. He didn't topple over, like Mr. Phillips had. In fact, he was pretty steady on his feet.

After several minutes, she composed herself and wiped her eyes. She grabbed some toilet paper and blew her nose. She wanted to go check out the TV again. Maybe now something was on that would explain all this. And they couldn't stay in the bathroom all day.

She took one of Jake's hands and gently tugged. She was expecting him to fall down. Instead, he leaned forward, almost lost his balance, then slid one of his feet toward her. She pulled at his hand again. Just a little. He moved the other foot.

He could still walk. She felt a thrill of excitement flutter in her chest. So there was *something* there, inside him. Some shred of Jake.

Step by step, slowly, methodically, she led him out of the bathroom, down the hallway, to the living room, and sat him on the couch.

Something had changed. After countless millennia, it stirred and roused itself from its endless sleep, miles below the ocean's surface.

It was awake.

Sitting on the couch, switching from channel to channel of dead air and old movies, Callie held tight to Jake's hand. She had been crying off and on all afternoon. The feeling of his hand in hers gave her comfort. Human contact, even just holding his hand, was something. But she couldn't sit here all day.

She closed her eyes and counted to ten. Forced herself to stop crying and take stock of her situation. She slowly looked around. That's when it caught her eye. In the kitchen, a blinking red light.

The answering machine!

She released Jake's hand and raced through the kitchen to the phone and pressed the "Play" button.

A robotic voice announced the time the call had come in; about an hour ago, when Callie had been outside.

Then her grandmother's voice: "Marie? Marie? Call me as soon as you can! Something... incredible has happened! Please! I need to talk to you!"

Callie tugged her phone from her back pocket, scrolled through her contacts, and hit "Grandma."

It rang three times before a message began. "This is Kathleen. I'm not able to come to the phone right now, so please leave a message and I'll get back to you when I can. Have a blessed day."

Normally, Callie would have smirked at such a corny message. "Have a blessed day." Yeah right. Sure, some days might feel blessed. But not today. Today was extremely "unblessed."

"Grandma, please it's Callie! Something happened! Mom and Dad are gone, and there's something really, really, wrong with Jake! Please call me. I'm so scared!" She hated how weak she sounded, like a little kid, but under the circumstances, who could blame her? She thumbed the Hang Up icon, then tried her mom again. Straight to voicemail.

She crossed over to the front door, opened it, and stepped out onto the porch and looked around. Nothing had changed. The car was on her lawn, the engine idling more roughly now. Mr. Phillips was still crumpled in his driveway. Still so quiet. A bird twittered nearby. A thin trail of black smoke drifting lazily upward in the distance. But that was it. She went back to the couch and sat beside Jake.

For the rest of the afternoon, Callie alternated between crying, going to the front door, and looking out, and desperately changing TV channels hoping for... what? Something normal? Someone or something to explain what was happening? But it was all the same: preprogrammed movies, kids' cartoons, or what was supposed to be live programming, but was now either an unwavering shot of a studio floor or an awkward camera angle of a TV set with silent, collapsed, comatose hosts with perfect hair.

Is that what it is? They're in comas? Callie didn't know anything about comas. *Only*, she thought, looking at Jake, *only that sometimes people come out of them.*

Even though Callie was exhausted, she was restless, and went to the door again, out to the porch. The car was still there, the engine making an unhealthy knocking sound now.

The sun was on the horizon, lengthening the shadows, making everything seem so much worse. *Night. It's gonna be dark soon.* The very idea of spending the night alone, like *this* terrified her. *How can I sleep? Where is everybody?* But she thought she knew.

The baby was crying again. But it sounded different. Shriller, weaker.

Callie glanced at the car on her lawn. Then to the woman across the street. Her dog had somehow gotten away. The leash was gone as well.

The woman and Mr. Phillips and this old man in the car were still alive but would soon die. No food, no water. They wouldn't last long. Any of them.

Callie had avoided thinking about it, because she had her own family to worry about, her own problems, but the thought had been nagging her. If she didn't help, who would?

She had never been one to volunteer for anything, especially at school. She preferred to sit in the background and let others take the lead. She was quiet by nature, except around her friends and family. Now she wished she was more of a go-getter. Her mom wasn't afraid to try something new or voice her opinion...or help people who needed it.

Should she help these people? Could she? But how? There were so many of them. Not just the ones out in the street, but in all the houses, too. All up and down the block. How could she possibly help everyone?

And if she didn't help, what did that make her?

She looked over at Jake, who sat placidly on the couch, gazing at the TV without watching. A movie about sexy teenage vampires.

She opened the front door for what seemed like the hundredth time that day and stepped out onto the porch.

The old man in the car. Mr. Phillips. The woman on the sidewalk. The baby.

"I can't," she muttered, shaking her head, close to tears. "I can't help them all."

The infant's cries pierced the perfect silence.

Callie cocked her head and listened. *The baby. Maybe I can help the baby.*

6

She peeked in on Jake, made sure he wasn't going anywhere (*Haha*) then strode purposefully into the street, avoiding looking at the driver of the car, the woman on the sidewalk, and Mr. Phillips, who was now being soaked by his automatic sprinklers.

She followed the baby's plaintive wailing. Two houses, then three. But now it was quiet. Callie stood, waiting, listening. The car alarm in the distance, sounding weaker and more desperate.

She tried to remember if she had ever seen any babies in the neighborhood. It was difficult. She'd never really paid much attention to her neighborhood. They'd moved here three years ago from California. She never walked to school. Either Mom drove her or she took the bus. So she really didn't know the neighborhood that well. Most of the kids were either older or way younger. But had she ever seen any babies...? She couldn't recall.

She walked up the brick steps to the nearest house and paused, then knocked on the door. *I can just walk inside someone's house now.* Then a thought. *What if someone answers?*

But of course there was no answer. With shaking fingers, she tried the knob. It turned easily.

She pushed the front door open. A black and white cat greeted her, rubbed a figure eight around her legs, chirped once, then darted outside and disappeared in the shrubs along the driveway.

Callie stepped farther inside the house. She was in a tiled entryway. A closet across from her, to her right, a shadowy living room. It was getting dark. And Jake was alone. She needed to hurry.

There was a faint, high-pitched humming coming from the left. She followed the sound and stepped into the kitchen. White counters, bright chrome refrigerator and dishwasher.

A woman lay on the kitchen floor. Her dark red hair was thankfully covering her face, so Callie didn't have to stare at another pair of empty eyes. On the counter above her, an electric mixer was spinning mindlessly in a mixing bowl. A box of cake mix and a carton of eggs sat beside it. Callie peered into the metal bowl that was slowly turning. The batter inside looked unnatural, too fluffy, and somehow bloated. It looked gross.

She reached out a tentative hand and flicked the lever. The motor whined down and stopped.

The refrigerator hummed and the ice machine clinked behind her. Other than that, all was silent. No crying baby.

Maybe I'm in the wrong house?

Without thinking about why she grabbed the egg carton and put it back in the refrigerator. Milk, yogurt, some beer, and *there it is*—a half-full jar of baby food.

A high-pitched cough from behind her and she simultaneously cried out, jerked up, and slammed her head on the refrigerator door frame.

She grabbed the back of her head and staggered away, blinking back tears as she scanned the kitchen. No one was there. But her head hurt. It really hurt. She pulled her hand away, looked at her fingers. No blood.

"Waugh!"

There it was again. She spotted a white plastic baby monitor on a shelf above the sink. A green light winked on and off as a baby's voice sputtered through the tinny speaker.

She walked through the deathly-silent house, down a narrow hall, peeking in each room. An empty bedroom with a king-sized bed. Folded laundry lay on the bed. Towels and sheets, it looked like.

An office, the desk covered with manila folders and papers that would never be read.

A bathroom, with a little yellow baby bathtub in the corner. It smelled faintly of flowers. Shampoo?

And finally, at the end of the hall, a half-closed door.

She entered quietly. Light blue walls, a crib to the right. A window on the left, the curtains blowing gently. The mother must have left it open to cool down the room. Lucky. If the windows had been closed, she never would have heard the crying.

A baby lay in the crib. It looked up, its face red and tear-streamed, and blinked at Callie.

"Hey, sweetie," she said.

Callie had a little experience with babies. Her cousin, Samantha, was only eight months old, and last time she and her mom had gone up to Portland, Callie had played with her all afternoon. Babies were a lot of work, and she knew this (whatever this was turning into) was going to be hard, but what could she do? Leave it to starve to death?

She picked up the baby and it began to cry. The diaper

was full, bulging and barely hanging on, and boy, did it stink. She set the baby on the changing table and commenced her first official solo diaper change. She gagged at least three times, went through a dozen baby wipes, and learned that the baby was in fact, a boy. He calmed down a little bit, although he must have been hungry. She held him to her shoulder and moved away from the disaster she had left on the changing table.

"It's okay, buddy. It's okay."

But it wasn't okay, she thought, gazing at the red-faced, whimpering baby, who had now become her responsibility.

It might never be okay again. That was a depressing thought, so she pushed it far down.

She found a stroller in a corner of the living room and placed the baby in it. It was sturdy and had lots of pockets and space for stuff. She wheeled the stroller back to the nursery and loaded the pockets with clothing and diapers and wipes. She didn't know a lot about babies, but she knew they needed wipes. Then she left the baby in his stroller in the living room and went into the kitchen and loaded up on baby food. She avoided looking at the woman on the floor.

Ten minutes later she rolled the stroller up her front steps and into her house. Jake was sitting on the couch, just as she had left him. She glanced at the baby, then at Jake.

What now?

Callie decided that they should all stay in the family room. It would be easier to keep an eye on both of them, and the TV was here as well. If anything happened, she would know right away. *If anything happens.*

7

Jake slept on the couch. Callie had brought in an air mattress from the garage, but by the time she had blown it up with the pump, Jake was fast asleep, slumped sideways on the couch. The baby was asleep in his stroller. At first, she wasn't sure what to do with him but then she figured out how to lower the back of the stroller so he could lie down.

She'd fed the baby. It was harder than it looked, and much messier. He ate an entire jar of mixed squash and plums, and then she let him have a couple of graham crackers. He held one in each little fist and went to town on them.

Then it was time to feed Jake. She walked him to the kitchen table and sat him down and put some food in front of him, but he didn't react. Just that same blank stare. She held a graham cracker up to his mouth and he opened his mouth a little bit. She pushed a corner of the cracker in and he bit and chewed and swallowed. She didn't want to give him too much, for fear he would choke. She gave him another bite. He chewed and swallowed. She held a plastic cup to his lips and gently poured. Most of the water went on the table, and he began coughing and sputtering. Her heart stopped for a moment; afraid he was going to choke. But he calmed down and went back to staring at nothing.

She tried to get him to drink with a straw, and that worked a little better. He didn't get much water, but at least he didn't spill it all over the place. So, in this way, step by step: bite, chew, swallow, sip; repeat, she fed him. It took over an hour.

It occurred to her, as she was struggling to change the baby's diaper (only wet, fortunately) that at some point in the very near future, she should also change Jake. And soon. She couldn't let him walk around in his same dirty underpants.

With the baby settled, she led Jake to the bathroom, and managed to get him on the toilet. *Maybe he'll go, the same way he figured out how to eat?* He did go, which was a tremendous relief. When he finished, she walked him to his room and changed him into a pair of PJ pants and a tee shirt. It was uncomfortable, and she managed to do it without looking directly at...him. It was still awkward, but what else could she do?

When it was all done, and both Jake and the baby were asleep, Callie called her mother's cell again. At the sound of her mother's recorded voice, she burst into tears.

"Please, please, Mom, if you get this, please call me. I'm scared. I'm so scared. I don't know what to do." She slid down the wall until she was on the kitchen floor, staring through bleary eyes at her mom's contact photo in her phone. "I'm sorry," she said. "I'm sorry."

She sat for a long time, looking at her mother's picture, reading some of her recent texts.

"At Trader Joe's. burritos for dinner?"

"can you text me, please? worried"

"Call me when you're on way home. Love you."

Callie smiled through her tears, closed her eyes, shut her phone, and stood up. She didn't have time for this. What were they going to do?

She dialed her grandmother's number again. This time it didn't even go to voicemail. There was a click, a strange whining sound, and then a dial tone. She hit "redial," but this time, all she heard was just static. She thumbed the disconnect button. At least Grandma had survived. She was still alive. Alive and still... turned "on." Like she was.

Callie wasn't tired, although she *was* exhausted. She just didn't want to go to sleep. She was scared.

She slid open the back door and stood in the backyard, staring up at the night sky. The meteor shower was tonight. The one they were supposed to watch together.

The stars were bright pinpricks in the dark velvet night. A white line flashed from right to left. A meteor, Callie thought miserably. Her mother would get so excited. She would have made cocoa and cookies and they'd load the car with chairs and blankets and drive away from the city lights.

Callie had to admit, meteor showers were pretty cool. Of course, she'd never told Mom that. She'd huffed and puffed and rolled her eyes like a spoiled—

What was that?

Something had crossed the sky above her, briefly blotting out the stars. A plane?

Callie's first thought: *There's someone else out there!*

She stepped out into the yard and scanned the night sky. She turned her head from left to right. There! In the distance, stars winking out and then on again as something flew beneath them. Whatever it was, it was too big to be a bird. And it was moving fast. It had to be a plane.

Then: *If it was a plane, why aren't there any lights? And no sound?*

The air seemed to turn cold. Callie hugged herself and went back inside, making sure to lock the door. She pulled the curtain closed.

She shut off all the outside lights before going to bed.

Callie lay on the air mattress, a blanket pulled up to her chin, and stared vacantly at a cartoon playing on the silent TV. She realized that she hadn't eaten anything since lunch. She needed to eat, she knew that, but she wasn't hungry. She was exhausted. And frightened. But most of all, she thought, listening to her brother's rhythmic breathing, she felt alone. *Maybe tomorrow he'll wake up and be back to normal. And he'll know what to do.* And with that thought, that wisp of hope, of something better, she drifted off to a restless, fitful sleep.

Callie dreamed.

She was at the beach. Lincoln City? Florence, maybe? It was calm and looked like it was late afternoon. The sun was just setting over the far horizon, turning the water blindingly red and orange. Flashes of gold on the waves.

Then something changed. The air grew cold. Callie gasped, feeling goosebumps rising on her bare arms. The wind picked up, whirling, howling now. She could see her breath.

It became dark. Not dimmer. Not darker. Dark.

Just like that. The sun was gone, replaced by something massive, something completely black, void of light. Something huge, on the horizon. She gazed out at the malevolent blackness that was alive somehow... and two immense red eyes opened.

Callie awoke with a start. She looked around, her eyes wild and frightened. Her face was slick with sweat. *What is that?* She'd heard something. Had someone said her name? Was it that dream? That weird dream. With that thing.

There. She heard a sound again. And it was close. The TV lit the room with a sickly blue light. The baby was out; fast asleep. She could see his face, so mouth slightly opened in repose.

"Mom?" Nothing. She pushed herself up on her elbows.

The sound again. Something moving. Callie turned toward the sound and exhaled in relief. It was Jake. He was asleep, but his lips were moving, his head rocking from side to side. His arms fought to free themselves from his covers. She slid closer to him.

His mouth opened and closed, as if he was speaking. Callie crouched beside him, waiting to hear what he was saying, but it was quiet. Just the sound of his breath and his body moving beneath the blankets.

She put a hand on his shoulder. "Jake?"

His mouth closed and he rolled over, facing away from her.

Callie sat beside him. *What was that all about?*

8

The baby woke her up early. He was fussing in the stroller, squawking, and rocking back and forth, trying to free himself. Callie blinked and rubbed her face. She stood up and stretched, picked him up, changed him on the floor, and carried him out front. It was still dark out, the sun just beginning to lighten the sky, fingertips of pink and soft red stretching out over the trees to the east.

She turned away from the rising sun, staring through the houses, the neighborhoods, the city, down the country highways to the coast, and thought about her dream.

The car was still on the lawn, but the engine wasn't running any more. She avoided looking inside it, keeping as far away as possible as she crossed her front lawn.

She froze, not daring to move.

Two dogs trotted down the middle of the street. One looked at her as it passed, but they didn't slow. They turned the corner and she exhaled.

She raised her face and sniffed. Smoke. Something was burning. *That can't be good.*

She moved to better see what she could see. There.

Where the airplane had crashed, a thick cloud of black smoke rising into the air. She told herself that it would be okay, that the fire was pretty far away. The dogs were heading away from the fire...or was that just a coincidence?

She checked the sky. No clouds. No rain today. And it was already warming up. Another hot one.

She walked out to the sidewalk and looked up at the street. Looking for, wanting to see, any sign that something had changed... that she wasn't alone.

She did see something.

Mr. Phillips was gone. The bucket was there on the driveway, still on its side, and the sponge. But no Mr. Phillips.

A flash of hope. Maybe he woke up and went inside.

Callie hefted the baby up to a more comfortable position on her hip. He gurgled and squirmed, but she held tight. *I have to figure out his name,* she thought. *I need to call him* something.

Callie walked up the sidewalk toward the Phillips' house but paused and looked back at her house. Jake. Could she leave him? She vacillated, even stepping one way, then the other. Finally, she turned and headed up the street. If Mr. Phillips was there, she could run back and get Jake. If not— *there's no "if not"* she thought. *He'll be there. He'll be there and he'll be okay and he'll help me find Mom and Dad and everything is going to be fine.*

She started up the sidewalk toward the Phillips' house. They had two sons, both in college. She'd never really met them. She'd seen them, coming in or going out of the house. Said hello at a Christmas party. But they were older, out of her and Jake's social orbit.

Mr. Phillips and her dad were pretty good friends. They watched football and drank beer together (and one time Mr.

Phillips got *really* drunk and his wife came to walk him home and she was *not* happy). Once in a while, the Phillips' and her parents went out to dinner. Callie had only been inside their house a handful of times.

She knocked on the front door. No response. She rang the bell, and heard it echo hollowly through the empty house. She tried the handle. Locked. She knocked again, harder.

"Mr. Phillips!" she called. "Mr. Phillips! It's Callie! Callie Hawthorne! From up the street!"

Nothing.

Still carrying the baby, who was getting heavier every second, she moved around to the side of the house. She peered in the dining room window, the kitchen window, and the living room window. No sign of anyone.

Where could he have gone? The baby began to really fuss now, so Callie headed home.

On the way back, she noticed the old lady was still on the sidewalk. *She* wasn't going anywhere.

The smell of smoke was getting stronger.

After feeding the baby, she sat him down on the floor and then dealt with Jake. She woke him gently and together they walked to the bathroom where she put him in the shower and changed him. Soccer shorts seemed to be the easiest to put on and take off, and fortunately he had a lot of those. She sat him down and fed him, led him back to the couch and channel surfed for a while. Most of the channels were just blank, a blue screen or just a shot of the studio. But there were still some cable channels showing movies, and she stopped when she noticed a scene from *Moulin Rouge.*

Her mom loved that movie, and just a few months ago they had sat together and watched it, snuggled beneath their blankets, a bowl of popcorn and a box of tissues between them.

Callie's throat ached and her eyes burned. She wanted to cry again, but she couldn't. She had to stay strong for Jake, and for... *I don't even know his name.* She sat beside the baby and ran her hand down his back. He was gnawing on one of Callie's old stuffed animals: a zebra that she had gotten as a gift years ago.

She got up and walked into the kitchen and hit the "Play" button on the answering machine. Her grandmother's voice repeated the words she had already committed to memory. "Marie? Marie? Call me as soon as you can! Something... incredible has happened! Please! I need to talk to you!"

What to do? If Mom and Dad were okay, then why hadn't they called or come home? Were there other people like her and the baby? People who... hadn't... been affected by whatever had happened? There were other people, right? The baby. And that guy on TV, with the clipboard. There had to be more. Right?

I should stay here and wait for Grandma to call or Mom and Dad to come back. We're safe here. We have food, and shelter. We're safe.

It felt good to reach a decision, like she had accomplished something.

The baby was playing happily on the floor, rolling around on his back with one of the zebra's feet in his mouth. Jake was sitting on the couch. She slid the slider open and stepped out into the back yard. The smell of smoke was stronger out here. *Is it getting closer?* She wondered.

As she stepped through the doorway, there was a thunderous crack, followed by a deep rumble from beneath her, so powerful that she was jolted back a step. The crystalline sound of glass breaking from within the house, the windows rattling in their frames, and in the distance, more car alarms.

Another earthquake? She hurried inside. *Not again.*

Jake was still where she had left him, on the couch, oblivious. A picture frame had fallen from a table beside the TV. She picked the baby up and moved him to his stroller and went to the kitchen for the broom. She swept up the broken glass and the broken frame and bent down and picked up the photograph. She smiled. A picture of the family. She was little, and Jake looked like he was maybe nine or ten, so it was about eight years ago. They were at a beach, *maybe Lincoln City?* And her cheeks were bright red and her smile was endless. Mom and Dad behind them, beaming. And Jake, covered with wet sand, a big gap in his smile. So happy. So proud. And now... she lifted her gaze to Jake, his eyes fixed on... what?

What was going on in his head? Anything? He could walk, he could eat, but he didn't react to her or anything else? Why was the baby *normal? And me?* she thought, but Jake wasn't? And Mr. Phillips? At the thought of him, a wave of guilt swept through her again. If she saved Jake, she could save the others. Could she? Should she?

The baby squawked, looking like he was getting ready to fuss, but she gave him the zebra and he calmed down. She would have to get more supplies for him: clothes, more toys and food. And diapers. Lots of diapers.

In the back of her mind, the fear of another round of

that horrible screeching sound that had caused this—is that what had happened? That crazy-loud noise turned every-one... off? Just shut them down.

She considered her options as she swept up the glass and the frame. She could go back to the baby's house and get some more of his things, but the thought of walking back into that house with the dead woman in the kitchen frightened her. *But you don't know that she's dead. You might be able to save her*. Callie shook the thought out of her head as she emptied the dustpan into the kitchen wastebasket. The wastebasket was almost full. It was her chore to empty it into the garbage can and then wheel them out to the street for pickup. But there wouldn't be any more pickup. *No more chores,* she thought, but then remembered Jake and the baby. She had plenty of chores.

Callie returned to the baby's house the next morning, leaving him in his stroller and Jake beside him in the entry-way. She had debated about leaving Jake at home on the couch, but the fire was making her nervous. She knew, although she didn't want to admit it, that at some point in the (*very*) near future, probably sooner than she wanted, they would have to leave. The smoke was getting thicker, which meant the fire was getting bigger, and closer. *So much for staying put.*

She wore her new school backpack, after first dumping all her unopened school supplies on her bed. Highlighters, mechanical pencils, notebooks. She wouldn't need them anymore.

So with one hand on the stroller, and the other holding one of Jake's hands, they had slowly and awkwardly made their way up the street. Jake slowed and stopped every few steps, almost like a toy car that loses momentum until she gently but firmly tugged his leash to get him moving again. He would follow as long as she was pulling him. That was fine, until she realized that when she stopped, he would keep going. He knocked into her twice.

It was difficult to guide the stroller with one hand. She wasn't strong enough, and really needed both hands to keep it moving in a straight line. She had to stop and redirect it every few feet, which meant that Jake would also stop, which meant she would have to tug him in the right direction to get him going. What should have been a five minute walk took twice that long.

Once she was in the house, she left the boys just inside the front door and, staying as far away as possible from the kitchen, headed straight for the baby's room, where she yanked open his little white dresser and loaded the backpack with clothes and toys and the few diapers she had left behind last time. A diaper bag hung on the back of his door, and she crammed it full of lotion and toys and more clothes. Then, a strap over each shoulder, she headed back to the living room.

There had to be a portable crib around somewhere, but she couldn't find it. Not in the little hall closet.

Another door opened to the garage, and she found a Pack and Play, which seemed to be a portable crib, folded neatly on a shelf. That would work. But it was so big. There was no way she could carry it *and* push the stroller and pull Jake. *Maybe we should move in here?* she thought before the image of the woman on the kitchen floor flushed that notion right away. She knew she couldn't go back in there.

And the thought of disposing of the body ... she shook her head in disgust.

She did, however, find a bigger backpack in the garage. There was also a tent and two sleeping bags on the shelf as well, which she left, but mentally filed them away. Maybe she'd need them later...?

She transferred everything from both her pack and the diaper bag into the big backpack. It was a camping back-pack, with a metal frame and plenty of room. She looked at her empty backpack, the one she had picked out when she had gone school shopping with her mom at Target and stuffed it into the backpack. She'd need it later.

There was a car in the garage, a four-door sedan, with a baby seat in the back and as Callie was transferring all the stuff, she had a thought. If they had to leave (*when they had to leave,* insisted the rational part of her mind), how would they travel? Walk? Just the short trip up the street had taken far too long. How could they possibly walk hundreds of miles?

The thought of traveling farther than a quarter-mile or so was crazy. Could she... could she *drive* if she had to? Her ill-fated permit test came back to her, but she knew the basics. The laws, at least, not that they mattered anymore. But she'd been in the car enough times, and she had sat on her dad's lap and steered up the street when she was younger. How hard could it be? She knew the key started the car, and you pushed pedals with your feet to make it go and stop, but that was about it. Could she even reach the pedals—she was distracted from these thoughts at the sight of a heavy-duty jogging stroller, with three larger bicycle tires, much more durable and easier to handle than the other stroller. It hung neatly from the rafters above her.

That would definitely make pushing the baby easier. But what about Jake? She needed a hand free to pull him along. The thought of walking with both hands occupied bothered her. She had to keep him close. Otherwise, he would wander off. Who knew what was out there? Dogs, for one. But what else?

Callie found a stepladder, and after a few minutes, had the jogging stroller locked and loaded. She went back into the house, pushing the jogging stroller, and transferred the baby and his stuff into it.

As she was leaving the garage, she was struck by inspiration and opened the driver's door and looked around until she found the garage remote. She could just come back into the garage for the playpen. No need to walk past the kitchen.

Then, leading Jake with one hand and pushing the stroller with the other, they made their way home.

With all her thinking and musing in the garage about how they would travel, and what mode of transportation would be best, one question remained unasked: exactly where were they going?

After settling her two charges for the night, Jake back on the couch and the baby still in his stroller, but with a full belly and a pacifier, she hurried back up the street and got the playpen out of the garage. With a half-fearful, half-wistful look at the car, she lowered the garage door.

As she walked down the sidewalk, lugging the playpen, she wiped the perspiration off her forehead. It had been another unseasonably hot day, and it was still warm. The trees rustled in a warm breeze. Other than that, there were no sounds, nothing around. Nothing but silence and the smell of smoke.

9

So it went on. Two days, then three. Feeding the baby, feeding Jake. Changing the baby, changing Jake, playing with the baby. Talking to Jake. Taking them both for walks around the neighborhood. She still didn't know the baby's name. She supposed she could go back into his house, look around in his room for something with his name on it, but she didn't want to.

She imagined returning in his room, searching through his dresser, only to feel a hand on her shoulder, and turning, staring into the milky-white eyes of his dead mother, the dried blood stiff and brown on the side of her head, her red hair sticky and matted. "Where's my baby?" she would croak, her voice raw and hollow.

∿

Friday (or was it Saturday?) night, something strange happened. She wasn't sure how to feel about it. On one hand, it was hopeful, a sign of progress, but on the other hand, it was scary.

She was fast asleep on the couch and jolted awake to a loud banging.

She sat up, terrified, and saw a shape at the sliding door. Her heart pounding, she sank farther down into the couch. *Someone is in the house.*

She reached out for Jake, on the air mattress below her, but he wasn't there. Her fingers touched cold rubber.

The figure banged into the sliding door again, rattling the frame. She looked more closely as her eyes adjusted. She turned on the lamp beside the couch.

It was Jake. He was trembling, rocking back and forth, bumping into the glass door. Beyond it, the yard, and the starry sky. *He's going to break the glass.*

Callie jumped up and went to him.

"Jake? What are you doing?" She put a hand on his shoulder, and he shuddered and seemed to shrink in his skin. He stood still now, his open hands splayed on the slider. She turned him so he faced her.

"Jake? What are you doing? Are you okay?" He looked through her, his eyes unfocused. She led him back to the air mattress and he allowed her to lay him down. She lay next to him, a tentative hand on his chest. Her heart was still racing. What did this mean? Was he getting...better? Or was it something else? And if so...what? She left the light on.

Callie stood on the back lawn, watching the thick black smoke billow into the sky. The fire was spreading and was much closer now; about two blocks away. It was no longer an "over there" problem. It was "here." The entire outside smelled like smoke, and little flecks of ash and cinders danced through the air on the hot summer wind.

That was another thing. It was still hot. Callie had kept a hope in the back of her mind that it might rain soon, but the sky remained blue. A couple clouds, but they were white and wispy and far away.

She walked into the family room (an apt name now, considering her little family spent all their time there) She brought Jake out into the front yard to let him walk around and get him some exercise. She set the baby down in the shade, sat beside him, and watched him crawl over the grass, which was getting so long now.

She avoided looking at the car. Yesterday she had used a blanket to cover the windshield of the car on the lawn. She didn't want to see the dead man.

She pulled Jake down and sat him beside her. "We have to leave here," she said. It helped to say it out loud, even if only to Jake. It made it more real, like she had made the right decision. "I'm not sure where we should go, but that fire's getting too close. We'll find another house. A nice one. What do you think?" Jake gazed through her. No reaction. A gleam of spittle on his lower lip. She reached out and pulled up the collar of his shirt and wiped it off.

"I'll take that as a yes," she smiled.

The shrill ringing made no sense.

"Wha—?" Callie jerked awake at the first ring, but couldn't comprehend what the sound was, what it signified. It was so foreign; it had been days since a phone had rung. *The phone!* She scrambled out of her sheets, made her way through the dark family room. The baby was stirring in his playpen and even Jake was sitting up. She could see him silhouetted against the wall.

She picked up the phone on the fifth ring.

"Hello?"

Static.

Louder this time. "Hello!"

"... Callie? Is that ... fzzt?"

Grandma! Relief spilled over Callie. Without realizing it, she began weeping, her voice raw and husky. "Oh my God, I'm so glad you called. Please, come and get me. Get us. I don't know where Mom and Dad are and Jake is really sick, and I found a baby now and I'm just so...scared."

The connection was bad. So much static and line noise; it was hard to hear, but Callie could tell that her grandmother was crying as well.

"Oh, sweetie, I know. I am... fzzt...so sorry. We didn't...fzzt..." she trailed off.

Callie's mind was a maelstrom. "Sorry"? What did Grandma mean? What was she sorry for? Everything that had happened...or something else?

"Grandma? Hello? Grandma?"

"...there. But you're going to have...fzzt...brave."

A loud burst of static that evolved into a high-pitched whine. Callie winced and held the phone away from her ear and shouted into the mouthpiece.

"Grandma? Grandma? Are you there?"

Her heart was racing. Had Grandma said "there?" Was she coming to Callie? Hope, something Callie hadn't experienced in days, poked her head out from her cave. Maybe everything was going to be okay, after all.

"Listen, Cal... fzzt. I don't have ... fzzt... much time. But I can't come to you. We have too...fzzzt...You have to...fzzt...here...fzzt...facility!"

Wait. Callie opened her mouth and couldn't think of anything to say. Grandma couldn't come get her? *But...*

"What do you mean? How can I get to you?"

"...fzzt..a way..."

"Do I have to?" Callie asked, lowering her head. Her voice was soft. Weak. She hated it, but at the same time, she felt angry and petulant. Grandma was the adult. She was supposed to take care of Callie. *It's not fair.*

"...fzzt..to San Diego..."

"... fzzt... have to find a way. Something is...fzzt..."

Callie closed her eyes against the flood of tears that threatened to inundate her. "I... I don't know. It's so far..."

Grandma was harder to hear. She was beginning to break up. "I n—... can't leave. I'll explain when you...here. Stay   off   the   freeways   and   open...--ces. It's...fzzt...dangerous..."

"But..."

"...hide at night."

"But..."

"...at night...watch out for...—" The line went dead.

"Grandma! Grandma!"

No response.

She listened. Nothing. No dial tone. No background noises.

How was she supposed to get to Southern California? What about the baby? What about Jake?

And what did Grandma mean when being careful at night? *'Don't trust' who?*

What's out there?

Callie sank to the floor, her back against the kitchen cabinet, phone in her hands. She stayed there staring at nothing, thinking about nothing and everything at the same time until eventually the baby began to stir and fuss. She glanced over at him but didn't stand up.

When he began crying, she stood with a sigh and stretched. It was still dark

Callie carefully placed the receiver back in the cradle. She walked over to the baby, leaned in, picked him up and changed him on the floor. She put him back, leaning in whispering and stroking his back. He was asleep in minutes.

She went to the couch and sat beside Jake, who was still sitting up, staring into the darkness. Callie leaned her head on his shoulder and pulled his arm up so it wrapped around her. She felt him tremble for an instant, but he settled back into the cushions. They stayed like that until morning, Callie nestled up against her older brother, like she had done when she was little.

She thought back on the abbreviated conversation. Her grandma had mentioned some type of facility. Callie wasn't exactly sure what her grandmother did for the Navy, but she knew she worked in a lab down in Loma Linda, in San Diego. Maybe the Navy knew what was going on? But San Diego...that was so far.

The call was the motivation she hadn't realized she needed. She knew they would have to leave at some point. Her parents weren't coming back. Nobody was going to save her. And the fire was getting closer every day.

10

The automatic garage door made its creaky, squeaking way up its tracks. Callie rolled the stroller into the garage, out of the sun. The plan was to walk down the street to her house, load up anything else she might need, and, what—head to California? But first she needed to know how to get there. A map.

She had looked up the distance to Miramar on her phone last night. It took a while to get a signal, but her data still worked. But then she lost the signal. How much longer would she get any signal, even GPS? That's why she needed a map. Most people kept maps in their glove compartments, didn't they? She tried the driver's door, but it was locked. *Who locks their car in the garage?* She slammed her hand on the window, angry at herself, frustrated, frightened of what was next.

Shit, she thought. She would have to go back into the house.

Callie wheeled the stroller into the entry and pointed it away from the kitchen. The baby was awake and struggling to get out of the stroller. Maybe he recognized his house?

She knelt down and gave the baby a couple of graham crackers. One for each fist. That should keep him busy for a while.

She backed Jake up against the garage wall and wrapped his leash around the door handle. She was still in the entryway. She took a cautious sniff. The smell was getting bad. It wouldn't be pretty in the kitchen, but that's where she should look first. Whenever Mom had forgotten where she put her keys (which was daily) she always *claimed that* she had left her keys in her purse, and her purse was usually in the kitchen. But she really hadn't. She left her keys wherever she happened to put them down; the kitchen table, the living room, the counter, and once even, in the refrigerator. Moms usually kept their purses in the kitchen, right? Callie couldn't remember if there had been a purse on the counter or not. Or even a rack for keys.

The air was thick with the sweet and unwholesome stink of rotting flesh, and she could almost see a fog in the house, a fog made of blood and death and... *Keep it together.*

Gagging, she grabbed a fistful of her shirt and pulled it up over her nose. It helped. A little. She poked her head in the kitchen, swept the room with her eyes. There. On the table. A brown leather purse. Callie slid over, snatched it up by the handle, and backed out of the room. She hurried back to the living room where she had left her boys and opened the front door. She sat on the porch step and opened the purse. Some makeup, a pair of sunglasses, a stack of coupons paper-clipped together, a pink wallet, but no keys.

"Shit!" Angry, frustrated, she dumped the purse upside down and shook it. Coins, a pack of tissues, a couple of pens fell to the ground. But no keys. "Shit!" she said again. "Why can't anything be easy?" she asked the universe, putting her face in her hands.

The universe, if it was listening, declined to answer.

She stayed like that for some time. Not crying, but not (*not*) crying. She wanted to be strong. She had no choice. It wasn't even a possibility. The rattle of Jake's leash brought her out of her misery. She wiped her eyes and looked at him. Jake. Her older brother. On a leash.

Oh my god. I have my brother on a leash. Hysteria began to rise, but she took a breath. Then, more sensible, but *what's the option?*

Callie sighed and stood up. She could always try another car, she thought. But no, she was here now.

Back inside, she glanced at the baby, who was still hard at work on his crackers, and she headed back into the kitchen. But this time, she had a twisted-up tissue in each nostril. It helped—kind of.

She tossed the purse back on the table, stopped, and glanced down at the woman's body on the floor. The blood had dried and blackened the linoleum around her. She was wearing jeans. And jeans have pockets.

On one of her bone-white ankles, just below the cuff of her jeans, Callie saw part of a tattoo. Blue and red ink. Something curvy and feminine.

Callie swallowed, took a deep breath, let it out, and dropped to one knee beside the woman's body. She closed her eyes and turned her head away and reached down and felt around. The woman's shirt, then lower, her jeans. The flesh beneath the clothing was cold and hard and yielding, like clay. She ran her fingers under the body, over the denim, feeling for lumps in the pockets. There. Something hard and thin. Her fingertips traced the shape. Definitely a key. One problem, she knew.

She looked down at her hand. It was beneath the corpse. Callie was going to have to turn her over.

No time. No thinking. Just do it. Callie squatted down, reached beneath the woman, and heaved. She lifted her up, up, but the body just arched, the back bending, arms flailing, almost hitting Callie. The dead woman's shirt slid up to reveal a bluish-white belly, and Callie let go and slumped back down.

She widened her stance, spread her arms out, and lifted again, grimacing as she reached farther beneath the corpse, and rose to her knees. The woman's cheek pulled away from the dried blood with a sucking sound, and her head flopped disturbingly, dead, sunken eyes staring up at Callie.

You stole my baby.

Callie lifted and rolled her on her back, dropping the body harder than she intended. She fell back against the cabinet, gasping. Bright color out of the corner of her eye. She grabbed a dish towel with a flowery pattern and draped it over the woman's face.

Okay. Get it together. This is far from over.

Callie wiped her eyes, nodded, and reached into the woman's pocket and pulled out a key ring. A shiny pink metal disc (it looked brand new) that proclaimed "World's Best Mom" and three keys, one which had a large black plastic tab with a silver "H" above several red buttons. She got to her feet, a bit unsteadily, and went back out to the entryway. The baby's eyes met hers. She couldn't look at him. Not right now. Jake was sitting in a folding beach chair staring into space. Callie smiled a smile she didn't feel.

"Okay, she said. "Let's do this."

She hit the unlock button and the car beeped and the lights flashed once. Callie opened the front passenger door and slid in.

She popped the button on the glove box and the door fell open. Napkins, some folded papers, a dirty screwdriver, a thick book with a black cover, and there, at the back, a folded map. She grabbed the map, turned it over to see the cover. "The Western United States." Perfect. She set it down and shoved everything back in the glove box and slammed it shut.

At her kitchen table, she pored over the map as day turned to dusk. On the table beside her sat her school notebook, a couple of pens, and a pack of yellow highlighters. She pored over the map, tracing her finger west and then south, highlighting, jotting down names of towns and distances on her sticky yellow pads, and writing notes in her spiral notebook.

She continued long into the night, after she had put down the boys. The acrid smell of smoke permeated the house, and along with everything else, added a new sense of urgency.

11

They left at first light. It was cool, which was a nice change, and toward the east, the rising sun was partially obscured by clouds.

As they walked past her house, she didn't dare turn her head. She told herself it was because she needed to get moving, but the real reason was it would be too hard. All those memories, all her stuff. She had packed food, clothes, and a couple photo albums in the trunk, but nothing else from the house. At the last minute, she had torn a sheet of paper from one of her notebooks and written a note in black Sharpie and taped it to the front door.

"Mom and Dad. I have Jake. We are going to Grandma's house. We are doing good. Please call me. I love you, Callie."

Maybe the fire won't reach our house. Maybe we'll come back in a couple of weeks. Maybe.

She turned left at the first intersection The freeway, she knew, was to the left. The coastal road which would eventually take her to freeway I-5 was to the right. But what had Grandma said? "Stay off the freeways?" Stay off the freeways? But why? Wouldn't the freeways be faster?

That word she had used. *Dangerous...*

She walked past a pickup truck that had crashed into a light pole.

The next street over wasn't as bad. It looked like after It (she had taken to thinking of the actual event, the sound, the earthquake as in "It" with a capital "I") had happened, most of the cars had kept going until they ran up on the curb, someone's lawn, or slammed against other cars. As they traveled on, she looked around at the neighborhoods. There were not too many corpses on this street, but she did see a cat sitting on the hood of a car, leisurely cleaning itself. It gazed at her as she passed, unimpressed, in typical cat fashion.

Who's taking care of the animals? She wondered. *What are they eating—* She tripped over something, stumbled, and looked down, horror-struck, at the corpse of a young boy. She averted her eyes and moved on, limping slightly. She had twisted her knee when she stumbled, but it didn't seem too bad. She'd had worse playing softball. As she continued, it hit her. *If I get hurt, who will help me?* Her eyes moved up to the rearview mirror and she saw the baby's face, looking around, confused but excited by the big bump. *Who will take care of them?*

The streets ahead were littered with stalled cars. There was one car that was nothing but a blackened, burnt-out shell. Most had run into the curbs, trees, or light poles. A delivery truck lay on its side, half in and half out the front window of a restaurant, debris and broken glass scattered all over the sidewalk. She turned and gazed up the street. More cars. Every intersection was a jumbled mass of cars. An occasional body on the sidewalk. Smoke rising from several points in the distance. Nothing moving. No living people. Only her. Her and her two companions.

A chirp from the stroller. The baby. He was probably hungry, and judging by the smell wafting up to her, he needed a change.

She turned to Jake. He kept pace with her, staring straight ahead at nothing.

"Yikes! Do you stink!" she said, more brightly than she felt. The baby lay on his changing pad on a yellowing lawn that was overdue for a mowing. Callie gazed around at the neighborhood. Similar to hers, but a little more run down. Smaller houses, older cars. The windows are dark and mute. All quiet and empty. *Only they're not empty*, she thought. *Not really.*

She smiled down at the baby. *I really have to name him.* "What do you think? Where would you like to spend the night tonight?"

It was at that point that the first raindrops landed on the sidewalk beside her, leaving dark spots on the white sidewalk. Just a few drops, but Callie was not ready for rain. The baby squinted as a drop landed on his forehead. She picked him up and stood up and surveyed the neighborhood.

The rain began to fall faster and harder. Callie put the baby back in his stroller and looked at the front of the closest house. Peeling white paint, single story, dark windows. But then she saw that the front door was open just a bit, and in the dim light she could make out an arm or a leg on the floor just beyond the entrance.

"Let's keep looking," she said, and tugging Jake, moved across the street.

A dog barked. Another answered. Callie looked around nervously but didn't see a sign of any dogs. The last thing she wanted right now was to run into a hungry dog. And that thought frightened her, because there must be hundreds, thousands of hungry dogs out there. She quickened her pace.

The next house was badly burned, black fire damage around the front door and the big window that faced the street.

Next.

This house was a little better maintained. An American flag fluttered weakly from the porch. A VW Bug in the driveway with an Oregon State bumper sticker in the rear window. Callie approached the front door, tied Jake's leash to the stroller and turned the door handle. It opened easily.

She pushed it open and cautiously set one foot on the hardwood floor. "Hello?" she called. "Hello?" Louder. "Is anybody here?"

Her heart thudding, Callie stepped all the way into the house. She reached out, flicked a wall switch up, and a ceiling light instantly filled the entryway with a comforting glow.

She wished she had a weapon of some kind, but what? A gun? *Yeah, right.* A knife? Could she stab someone? Why would she have to? She took a deep sniff. Waited. It smelled okay. Kind of stale was all. She made a quick circuit, moving quickly. Straight ahead into the kitchen. All quiet.

The garage was also empty, but smelly. Living room, three empty bedrooms, and two bathrooms. Nobody home. But looking through a bedroom window into the backyard, there was... something... on the grass beside a lawn mower. Callie pulled the blinds without looking closer. She shut the bedroom door and went to get her boys.

She was getting used to death, she realized as she backed the stroller in through the front door. It was impossible not to get used to. It was all around her. *What will his world be like?* She mused, looking down at the baby's pudgy little face. He puffed his lower lip out and crinkled his brow, a sure sign he was getting ready to fuss.

"Gotcha, buddy. Just give me five minutes," she said, going out to retrieve Jake. She led him inside and sat him on the couch.

The rain was coming down full force. It drummed on the roof and the windows, pattering on the branches and leaves outside. Before, rainfall at night had been a comforting sound, reminding her of warm soup and cocoa and fire in the fireplace, snuggling up on the couch watching TV. But now it was a sad, almost forlorn sound. It reminded her of home, of her family. Intensified her loneliness.

She laid the baby down, and only gagging once, changed him. She was getting better. She took Jake to the bathroom, helped him do his thing, and changed him. It was still awkward changing Jake.

"When this is all over," she said, "You're going to owe me big time."

She found some spaghetti and an unopened jar of pasta sauce in the pantry, pulled out a pot, and dinner was ready in a little bit. She gave the baby some cooked pasta to play with and (hopefully) eat while she fed Jake. She had to really chop his food up, but it, like everything else, was getting easier.

After she ate and brought the dirty dishes back into the kitchen, she debated about whether or not she should wash them. It was silly, she knew. In the end, she compromised and just rinsed them and left them in the sink.

The three of them slept in the master bedroom. She went into a cramped walk-in closet and came out with an armful of sheets and blankets. She replaced the pillowcases and sheets and piled the used ones in the corner. It was bad enough sleeping in a stranger's bed, but not with their dirty sheets. Yuck!

She and Jake shared the king-sized bed and the baby slept in a dresser drawer that she had removed and emptied. She pulled the drawer beside the bed and crawled under the blanket. She was so exhausted, and the big bed was so comfortable, that she was out almost as soon as her head hit the pillow.

12

She had the dream again.

The beach was serene and placid, the sun slowly setting. The air going from warm to freezing in an instant. Then the sudden darkness, the overwhelming feeling of terror, and the red eyes. The impossibly huge eyes staring...at her. Looking for her?

Callie woke up. Something had happened. A sound. Something shook. *Inside the house?* She couldn't identify it, but it had been loud enough to wake her. It was still night; she didn't feel as if she had been asleep very long. She lay still, her heart pounding. The rain had lessened, but the house still creaked and groaned, as unfamiliar houses do in the dead of night. She reached over and turned on the bedside light. Jake sat up, ramrod-straight, beside her, his eyes wide open. He blinked a couple times in the bright glare of the light.

He began mumbling again. He struggled to get out of bed, his limbs stiff and awkward.

Callie slid away from him. *What is he doing?*

"Jake?" Her voice soft, like a frightened child.

Jake stumbled out of bed, off balance, staggering. His

arms flailed as he kept his balance. He turned and walked toward the door. He was doing it on his own. But where was he going? And what did this mean?

He hit the door frame and backed up. He stepped to the left and moved through the doorway and down the hall.

Callie leaped out of bed. She made her way through the hall, fascinated and somewhat horrified. *The way he's moving. Not like Jake at all.*

Jake stood by the front door, his right hand struggling to turn the knob. His fingers were splayed out, making it difficult to grasp the knob with just his palm. His left hand at his side clenched and unclenched.

She slid between him and the door, grabbed him by the shoulders, and looked up at him. "Jake? Jake? What are you doing?"

He stiffened and struggled against her grip. His mouth opened and closed, speaking a silent language. She hugged him, putting her face against his chest. He rocked back and forth, struggling to keep his balance. He didn't fight her, but didn't give in, either. They slammed against the wall, knocking a picture frame to the floor.

Callie held him, wrestling to keep him still, and moved him away from the door. She spoke to him, held him, loved him, until he stopped struggling. They sank to the floor. Callie didn't let go of him. Her chest was heaving. She didn't realize how hard she was breathing. Her shoulders were sore. She released her grip and looked at Jake.

"Jake? Buddy? You okay?"

No response. He was back to "normal." Just sitting and staring at nothing. But he had gotten out of bed without waking her and walked to the front door. So, something was working in his head.

They sat like that, on the floor, until she was satisfied, he was okay. She helped him stand and led him carefully past the broken glass and—a loud crash from outside. The windows rattled and the entire house shook.

Oh God, what now? Callie thought. She waited for whatever was coming. Almost ready to just give up. It was so hard. How would she make it all the way to Grandma's? They had barely left her neighborhood.

Callie slid to the side and turned to the window. She lifted the blinds and peered outside. She could make out several figures in darkness and rain. They staggered in the street, moving in the same direction she was heading. There were at least four of them stumbling along in the darkness. One of them was crawling atop a parked car.

Callie ducked back down and hugged Jake. She waited for what felt like an eternity until she was sure they were gone.

Nothing else happened. The only sound outside was the incessant tattoo of rain on the roof. She led Jake back to bed. He looked so peaceful, sleeping there. *But...*

Feeling guilty, she tied the leash around one of his wrists. She looped the other end around a leg of the metal bed frame. She pulled on it to make sure it was secure. Even if Jake woke up, he couldn't go anywhere. And it would wake her for sure.

Even after double-checking all the doors and windows, she decided to leave the hall light on.

Her eyes were drawn to the closed bedroom door at the end of the hall. The one that looked out into the backyard. Had the rain masked the sound of a window sliding open? The wet, slimy sound of a cold, sodden figure slipping over the sill and landing, with a thud, on the floor? Crawling across the floor, leaving a trail of mud as it reached up for the door...

Stop it! She shook her head, trying to get the image out of her mind. She slipped back into bed.

But Callie didn't get any more sleep that night. Eventually, at 4:35 AM, according to her phone, she gave in and got up. Jake was still fast asleep.

With the bathroom door open and all the lights on, she took a shower. The first in what felt like weeks. She meant to take a quick rinse, as her mother had called them, just in and out, but the warm water felt so good, so relaxing, that when she finally turned off the water, the bathroom was completely filled with steam.

She wrapped herself in a towel and went to the mirror, wiped a circle clear.

She looked at herself. Not too bad. Green eyes. Her mother's eyes, people had told her. Dark brown hair, down past her shoulders. It was getting long. She'd have to cut it herself.

"Callie Hawthorne," she said. She pushed her hair out of her face.

"Calista Jane Hawthorne." Jane. That was a lame middle name. For Jane Austen, her mother's favorite author.

She looked so young, her face fresh and pink after the hot shower. Too young for all this. She turned away from the mirror.

She found a fluffy robe in the closet and wrapped it around herself, went to the kitchen, rummaged through the cabinets, and made herself a cup of tea. She sat at the table in the quiet (too quiet) kitchen. Her mom used to make chamomile tea for her when she was sick or had trouble sleeping. Mom would sit on Callie's bed, talking softly and stroking her hair until she fell asleep. Sometimes Mom would even lie down with her. But she hadn't done that in a long time.

And it sure as hell wasn't happening again any time soon. She wondered where her parents were right now. Was it wrong to leave the house the way she had? Should she be looking for her parents? Where had they been going? What if they come back to the house? She felt like crying but realized she had no more tears left. She was all cried out, it seemed.

Callie stood up, stretched, and headed back into the bedroom. She had seen something in the closet when she was getting the sheets. It was weighing on her mind.

She went through the master bedroom and into the walk-in closet. She stood on her tiptoes and pushed a stack of blankets to the side. Something back there. Black metal. She reached in carefully and pulled out a holstered handgun.

13

Callie sat at the kitchen table, looking at the gun. A box of bullets sat on the table. "Elite Performance Ammunition" was written on top in big bold letters on both the top and the side. Sure. Like she would know an elite bullet if she saw one. She opened the box and pulled out a bullet. What looked like brass and gray metal. She thought bullets were supposed to be made out of lead. She looked at the gun, then at the bullet. *Where the heck do you put it?* Was the gun even loaded? And if not, could she do it? She could probably find a website that would show her how. Although, every day, it seemed like fewer and fewer websites were working. She supposed it was only a matter of time until the internet stopped working altogether, then the electricity.

That was a depressing thought. No lights.

She picked up the gun and turned it around in her hands. Flat black, metal. Dangerous looking. Not like in the movies and TV shows, where guns were cool. This was deadly.

She held it with both hands and aimed it at the wall. It was heavier than she would have thought, and she had to concentrate to hold her arms steady. It made her feel... strong, not so weak. Not so scared. She squeezed her left eye shut and tilted her head and put her finger on the trigger.

She opened her eye, looked at the gun, and carefully placed it on the table. She opened her hands and put them on her lap. *What am I doing? I don't know how to shoot a gun.*

She stood up and moved away. She turned off the kitchen lights and went back to bed, leaving the gun on the table.

Callie climbed back into bed beside Jake and lay down, facing away from the door at the end of the hall, away from the thing that might or might not be in the backyard.

She slept for what felt like five minutes, sat up, and looked around. Jake was deeply asleep, but the baby was stirring in his makeshift crib.

It was morning, but barely. Weak gray light fought its way through the curtains. She leaned over to the window and slid the curtain aside. It was overcast, but the clouds weren't as dark and menacing as yesterday. She definitely didn't want to walk in the rain.

Something had been niggling at her mind just before she went to sleep, and she thought she knew what it was. If the power did go out, then how would she charge her phone? No phone, no GPS. No way to contact Grandma. She sighed. A pleasant thought for another probably shitty day.

Callie got up, dressed, and made herself some frozen waffles (there was cereal, but the milk was bad, so she poured it down the sink) and some orange juice. It was still uncomfortable eating and sleeping in someone else's house (a stranger's, no less) and practically stealing from them. But the food would go to waste, so what was the difference?

She dumped the dishes in the sink and went to the table and picked up the bullet and put it back in the box. She carried the gun and the box of bullets into the bedroom, where she wrapped the gun carefully in a tee shirt and put it in an outside pocket of her backpack. She stuffed the box into the bottom of her backpack.

The baby was stirring, and Jake was sitting up. He did that sometimes in the morning. He never got as far as standing up, but he would push himself to a sitting position. She decided to take another look around to see if she could find anything useful.

She found a winter coat that would be a little big for Jake, but would do, and also a backpack. He could carry stuff too, right?

After rifling through the kitchen drawers, she discovered two portable phone chargers, which she added to her stash. She stepped into the garage with the intent of looking for more supplies, but the stench of something really foul and sweetly rotting drove her back inside. It was probably old garbage, she thought. Probably...

She got the boys ready, cleaned, dressed, and fed, loaded up the stroller and backpack, got Jake set with *his* backpack, and headed out the front door. Another day in paradise.

14

The stroller tires made whizzing noises in the damp street. Jake followed along, always passive, always docile. Callie kept them walking in what she hoped was the right direction. South. Then through downtown and west toward the coast.

The rain had let up, the sun was coming out, and each step took her one step closer to Grandma. *But that's a hell of a lot of steps,* she thought. Once again, doubt swam through her mind, some thoughts small and innocuous, others heavier, more threatening. Maybe she should go back home and wait. Wait for what? It's been more than a week, and --.

A woman stumbled out from in front of a parked car and lunged across the street right in front of her. Callie squealed and backpedaled rapidly, tugging at Jake's leash, and pulling the stroller with her.

Callie's mind raced. *Maybe she's...normal. Maybe she's like me. Just scared, like me. Maybe she didn't see me.*

"Hey!" Callie shouted. "Hello!"

Then she noticed the woman was only wearing one shoe.

The woman didn't pay any attention to her. She lumbered up on the sidewalk, almost fell, and continued through an open gate in a side yard.

Before Callie had time to think about what she was doing (the desire to see another person, to talk to another person, overrode her fear and caution) she turned the stroller and followed the woman, up over the sidewalk, through a low wooden gate and around the side of the house.

There was a body on the ground, just inside the open gate. A young man, wearing jeans and a yellow hoodie. He was barefoot. The bottoms of his feet were torn and bloody.

Callie stopped and wrapped Jake's leash around the handle of the stroller. She turned and grabbed Jake by his shoulder and met his eyes as best she could. "Stay here," she said, "I'll be right back."

She followed the woman around the back of the house. The woman was on all fours, digging in the dirt, throwing clumps of plants and soil behind her.

Beside her, a man was also elbow deep in the lawn, tearing out chunks of soil and tossing them aside, although his movements were sluggish and jerky. A second man was crawling in a slow circle across the lawn, clawing at the sod.

Another corpse lay off the side, headfirst in a shallow hole. Dead while digging.

Callie was horrified. What were they doing? What did this mean? The woman turned and gazed at Callie, with hollow, blank eyes, a pale green that seemed somehow wrong, then turned back to her mindless digging.

Callie turned and stumbled back to the front of the house, the sound of bloodied hands scraping the dirt soiling in the quiet afternoon. She was careful to step around the body of the young man, so she didn't notice that the fingers on his right hand had grown unnaturally long.

They made good progress the rest of the day. In the late afternoon, a family of deer crossed their path, not five feet away: a doe and two babies. Callie stood in the middle of the street. She put out a hand on Jake's chest and stopped him beside her.

The doe glanced at them but didn't seem bothered. The three deer walked up the sidewalk and hopped over a short white fence into a flower garden and began eating. One of the fawns had a bit of trouble with the fence, hesitant to jump over, pacing back and forth before taking the leap and hopping over it with ease. Callie smiled at the cuteness of it. She couldn't help it. Despite all that had happened, all that *was still happening*, cute was cute.

She watched them eat for a few minutes. *I could probably walk over and touch them*, she thought. Things had changed. Humans were no longer a threat.

They stayed mainly on the sidewalks, as the streets and intersections were filled with one collision after another. Some were bad; broken metal and glass littered the streets, and in some cases, there had been fires, leaving blackened skeletons of cars (and passengers as well) but thanks to the rain, nothing was burning. Callie didn't get too close to the cars; she didn't want to see any more than she could avoid.

They came down the crest of a hill and as the streets became wider as more storefronts and shops appeared. Callie could see the tops of distant buildings over the trees. *Tomorrow. Or maybe the next day.* That's when they would reach downtown Portland. The thought of walking through the dead, silent city made her nervous.

The houses were thinning out as more commercial buildings took their places. In some areas, you couldn't even tell that anything at all had happened. Cars parked in driveways; sidewalks clear.

In others, it was obvious.

The burnt-out shell of a Mexican restaurant across the street.

The back half of a city bus sticking out of a used clothing store.

A paint store where the lights from inside flickered madly like a strobe through the front windows.

And strangely, and somehow disconcerting, a small hardware store where the front window was smashed in. Tools were scattered on the sidewalk and parking lot, along with a half dozen bodies. One of the dead bodies was still clutching a hammer. Like there had been a fight.

She passed a supermarket where they had shopped so many times. The parking lot was full (*It had happened on a Saturday, after all*), and Callie didn't even have to think twice about avoiding it. All those people inside the store. She would look for food somewhere else.

For lunch, they sat at a picnic table in a park beneath a massive oak and ate saltines, raisins, and bottled water. She didn't give any raisins to the baby. He could choke. She knew that much. There were several small corpses of children over by the playground, (*Where are the parents?*) but Callie turned so she sat facing away from them. She was tired of seeing death everywhere. But what else was there?

She glanced down at the baby, whose full attention was on the broken, drool-soaked cracker he clutched in a death grip. She smiled, stood up, and stretched. She took off her shoes and socks and walked in the grass. Ahh. Walking barefoot in the grass always made her feel like a little kid.

Her feet were sore. She needed better shoes. So did Jake, probably. She shaded her eyes and gazed at him, sitting peacefully on the bench. Staring at what? What did he see? She knelt in front of him, grasped his head gently on either side and gazed into his eyes.

"Jake? You in there, buddy? Anybody home?"

He blinked, opened his mouth— *he's going to say something!* — shot through her mind, but he only smacked his lips together a couple of times and continued his thousand-yard (*more like thousand mile*) stare.

They found a sporting goods store that afternoon. One of the doors was propped open, and the familiar big red bright CHUCK'S SPORTING GOODS sign was surprisingly welcoming.

The body of a young man wearing a green sweatshirt lay in the parking lot. A dark stain, shiny on the damp concrete, created an iridescent halo around his head.

Beside him were several shopping bags, their contents scattered around him. The wind, probably.

If Callie had looked more closely at the dead man, she would have seen that something had been at him. Part of his shoulder was gone.

15

Chuck's Sporting Goods was one of those, "We have all the sporting goods you could ever want - but not really good quality" variety. Callie had been there before with her dad and Jake, mainly for his soccer equipment and cleats. She played soccer for one year, way back when she was in third grade. The only thing she remembered about it was the snacks after the game. The games themselves? Lots of running around and parents yelling. The snacks? Awesome. Softball was her sport now. It was more fun, but the snacks weren't as good as she got older.

Two more bodies, piled on top of each other by the front counter. She looked over the counter at the space between the two registers, but it was clear. Nobody there. She wheeled the stroller in and guided Jake. She set Jake's backpack down in front of the stroller. The baby was looking around, eyes wide. Jake was staring into space. She put her hand on Jake's shoulder and guided him to a sitting position on the floor. That would keep them both in one spot while she "shopped."

The store didn't smell too rank, thankfully because of

the open door. Another body, this one an employee, over by the sunglass counter. He was face up, his grayish-green face gazing up at the ceiling.

The shoe section was in the back. On the way, she grabbed a sweatshirt and a Mariners ball cap. A tent display caught her eye, and she walked down the camping aisle. Another body. This one a child. Maybe four or five. Callie stepped over him without breaking stride, avoiding looking too closely.

She pulled a backpack down from a shelf. A *real* backpack. Bigger than the one she was using. Metal frame and everything. It would be large for her, but she could wear it. She could transfer all the crap from hers into it after she got her shoes.

She walked along the back wall, looking at all the shoes. Running. Basketball. Cross trainers. Hiking boots or walking shoes? She wasn't sure which ones she should get. She leaned a hand against a counter and balancing on one foot, pulled her shoe off. She looked inside. Size eight.

She knelt and scanned the shelf stacked with a variety of shoeboxes. "Eight, eight, eight..." she said softly, moving from box to box. *Aha!* She pulled a box holding walking shoes off the shelf. She sat down on the plastic bench, opened the box, and slipped her foot into the shoe. She began to untie her other shoe and froze when she heard a sound from the front of the store. A jangling. She stood and looked over the rack of shoes toward the front of the store. *Oh shit.*

Three dogs trotted down the main aisle. One was small and harmless looking, a white, scruffy thing, but the other two looked mean. They wore heavy dark collars, their tags jangling. The first was black with a ragged, torn ear, and the other, the bigger one, a pit bull, was brown with black ears.

The dogs looked thin, ribs showing through their sides. But they were still dogs, and dogs were dangerous, especially now.

Callie stood perfectly still. If they kept going the way they were headed, they would pass her one row over. The black one with a torn ear sniffed a display of exercise weights, turned around, and peed. Callie wrinkled her nose. *Gross.* The little dog went over and sniffed the pee.

A noise from up front. The baby squawked. The pitbull growled and turned toward the front of the store. The little white dog perked up its ears and turned back toward the front door. Where Jake and the baby were waiting. Helpless.

Without thinking, Callie shouted, "Hey!"

All three dogs turned, saw her, and as one, began barking and running at her.

Oh shit, she thought, and backed up, stumbling over the bench, and almost falling. The dogs came closer, faster, their barking somehow angrier. Callie turned and began climbing up the wall-mounted shelf, kicking away the shoes on the display until she was as high as she could get. The dogs were right below her now, in a frenzy, barking and snarling, jumping up at her. The little one was running back and forth, yipping and growling, like a coach encouraging his players.

Callie climbed up as far as she could. She was sitting on the top of the narrow shelf, pushed back against the wall as far as she could go. She twisted around and realized she was holding her shoe. She chucked it as far as she could, but the dogs didn't even notice. They continued to growl and jump at the shelves, scrambling to get to her.

Callie squirmed around and got her backpack off one shoulder, slid it in front of her. Now she could move back a little more. Her back hit the wall. This was it, as far as she could go. Her feet scrambled for purchase.

The dogs' rage increased. Their eyes were wild, rolling in their bony heads. Their mouths were foaming, the jaws chomping, teeth white, sharp. and shining in the fluorescent glare.

They wanted her. The pit bull was incensed, jumping, snarling, snapping at the other dogs.

Callie barely breathed as she unzipped her backpack and carefully reached in and unwrapped the gun. One of her feet slipped and her heel sent a black cleat tumbling to the floor. The black dog snatched it up, and snarling, shook it like it was a rat.

Moving slowly, so slowly, Callie held the gun, two-handed, and extending her arms, pointed it at the dogs. She swallowed, closed her eyes, and pulled the trigger.

Nothing happened. The trigger only pulled back a little. She opened one eye and looked at the gun. The shelf shook as the black dog leaped up even higher, knocking an entire row of shoes to the floor.

As the dogs busied themselves tearing the shoes to pieces, Callie, still pushing herself back against the wall as best she could, glanced down at the gun, and turned it so she could see both sides. "P-220" written on the handle. A little lever above the trigger. She slid it and it turned on a tiny hinge. *This is the safety.* She wasn't sure how she knew that, but she did.

For the second time, she pointed the gun, arms extended toward the dogs, squeezed her eyes shut, and pulled the trigger.

An explosion of force and sound. Her arms jerked up and back, causing her to lose her balance and slide sideways. She reached down to steady herself and dropped the gun, heard it (through ringing ears) clatter dully on the tile floor.

When she felt secure, she looked down. The three dogs were sprinting through the doorway, the little one in the lead.

Without thinking, Callie leaped down, scooped up the gun, and ran after them, shouting. By the time she reached the front of the store, the dogs were halfway across the parking lot. ("Now it's a barking lot" her dad's voice echoed in her head).

She kicked the wooden shim out from beneath the door and yanked it shut. She looked through the glass. The dogs were still running, but slower now, on the sidewalk. The little white one looked back at the store. Callie pushed the door open, stepped one foot out, raised her hand, and fired the gun into the air. She felt the force up to her shoulder. But it worked, and the dogs took off.

The baby was whimpering. Callie slid a shopping act in front of the door and went around the counter and knelt beside him.

"It's okay, buddy, it's okay. They're gone." She picked him up and snuggled him, kissing his head and whispering. Once he was settled, she put him back in his stroller.

She scooted beside Jake, and they sat like that until nightfall.

They slept in the store. Sleeping bags, air mattresses, thermal blankets; everything they needed. Callie used a jump rope to tie the front door shut. They had more crackers for dinner, and jars of baby food (the baby had one jar and Jake had three) and for a treat, Callie gave them some lukewarm sports drink from a cooler by the front door.

Before turning in, she checked her phone for any

messages, but there were none. Her reception was getting spotty. She plugged in her phone, along with the portable chargers before settling in for the night.

She kept the gun beneath her air mattress, within reach. *How many bullets are left?*

Callie lay awake, listening to Jake's breathing, thinking about the gun and the ugly black hole it had made in the tile floor. It had saved them, and she didn't even know how to use it. *I sure don't know how to load it.*

She took the walking shoes after all, and a pair of hiking boots. She selected a pair of shoes for Jake, and some thick socks as well. Fall was approaching, and soon enough it would be winter. Callie took several packs of long underwear, thick socks, gloves, a couple of beanies, and the Mariners cap. She stocked up on batteries and flashlights and sleeping bags as well. She climbed over the glass display counter in the firearms section and rooted out two boxes of bullets that matched the one she had taken from the house. She wasn't sure how to load it, but what the hell?

She upgraded the jogging stroller after noticing a display. They had a model made for twins, which gave her more room for storage. The extra seat could hold a sleeping bag. A roomy pocket behind each seat, and another storage area underneath. The baby stroller could carry more than their backpacks. She chose a dark blue one over a yellow one. Less conspicuous. No sense in standing out. Besides, yellow was obnoxious.

She looked at the price tag before tearing it off. Over five hundred dollars. She shook her head. Who knew strollers were so expensive? But it had to be good, right?

By mid-morning, they were ready. The sky was clear, cloudless and it was actually warm, and best of all, the dogs were nowhere in sight. It was now or never.

Jake and Callie both wore larger backpacks, and the stroller was overflowing, every pocket full. protein bars, water, spare clothing, and even a couple of packs of peanut M&M's from a candy rack by the front register. Those were her favorite candies.

Before heading out, Callie checked her phone once again for messages, texts, or anything new. There were no new messages. She was only getting one bar, and no internet. No more GPS.

She texted, "Grandma we are on our way." She paused, then: "I love you."

16

She knew she was closer to the freeway than she had been yesterday, and she felt better about walking instead of driving. She could cut through some neighborhoods and then maybe find a car where there was more room on the roads. She still didn't *want* to drive, but she knew it made the most sense. California was a long way off. And considering it was her first-time driving, she hadn't done so badly, all things considered. At least until the car had been stolen.

She looked over the bikes in Chuck's. A bike would be good, except for all her stuff. But they had baby trailers you just connected to the back of the bike. It didn't look that complicated. That would take care of her and the baby, but what would she do with Jake?

So, she walked. The stroller was ahead, and Jake was a little behind. She kept her eyes out for the dogs. She opened a pack of beef jerky to throw if they showed up again. She thought that might slow them down. They looked hungry. What about all the pets still in the houses? She couldn't think about that. All she had to worry about was those three dogs.

And of course, she had the gun.

The next couple of days were peaceful and they made good time. No more earthquakes. No crazy dogs. Just the occasional bark in the distance.

She saw two other people, but they weren't like her. They were like Jake. One of them, a woman in a bathrobe, was walking through the middle of the street, occasionally bumping into a car. If she saw Callie and Jake, she gave no sign. Just kept walking and silently talking.

Around noon she saw a young boy, wearing a pair of shorts and no shirt. His feet were bare. Callie was coming out of a gas station mini mart, where she had managed to find several jars of baby food and a Portland Street map, of all things, tucked behind the counter.

The little boy stumbled across the street and turned the corner. She called out, but he didn't respond, and by the time she had gathered Jake and the stroller and reached the spot where she had last seen him, she couldn't tell where he had gone. He could be in any of these houses.

She didn't want to leave Jake and the baby, so she let him go. But she thought about that little boy for the rest of the day. For some reason, he made her sadder than all the others she had seen. He was all alone.

Other than that, their travels were uneventful. And quiet. It was eerie how quiet it was. Leaves rustling in the breeze, birds chirping, occasional dog bark. But no human sounds. No cars, no lawnmowers, no music. She missed music, although she would have been glad to hear any human-made sound, even those ear-splitting fire alarms they used at school. Anything that showed that there were people around.

The most unusual thing that happened, (which wasn't

really so unusual when she stopped to consider the past couple of weeks) occurred just as it was getting dark late one afternoon. Callie saw a flicker of movement up ahead and she stopped and stepped further into the street so she could see.

An old man stood in his garage, standing amid boxes, furniture, and other clutter. He was staring at her, his face not friendly, not even surprised. Callie opened her mouth to say something (she wasn't sure what) when he reached up and grabbed hold of a red cord and pulled down the garage door. It banged into place with finality, echoing around the street.

She stood there, confused, frightened, and a little angry. *What the hell is his problem? Do we look dangerous?*

She considered going up to his house but thought better of that. He obviously wanted nothing to do with them, and for all she knew, he could have his own gun.

They spent the night in an apartment motel. She picked up a keyring from the parking lot, beside a dead woman. On the third door they tried, the key worked, and thankfully, so did the shower. The apartment was small, stuffy, and empty. She opened the windows to let in some air.

Callie spent too much time getting them all cleaned and washed before settling down for a night of restless sleep. Tomorrow they'd reach downtown.

Early the next morning, they stood at the crest of a hill, looking across the Willamette River toward downtown Portland.

The pedestrian bridge appeared to be the easiest way

across the river. Callie had been across it once before, on her bike with her parents and Jake, a few weeks after it opened. After crossing, they rode along the lake shore and stopped for ice cream at a shop. The ride back across the bridge had been difficult because she was so tired, pedaling hard to keep up with her parents, trying not to cry. Jake had teased her, zooming ahead and then letting her pass him just so he could pedal past her again.

She scowled at him. *Jerk.*

But not really. He wasn't much of anything now.

The road they were traveling on merged with the freeway onramp which would take them to the closest bridge across the river. But she could see from here that it was totally packed with cars all sandwiched together, one after another, the bright metal and chrome gleaming in the sunlight. Some were sideways, across two lanes, and other cars had plowed into them, completely blocking the bridge all the way across the lanes.

By herself, it would be tough, climbing over and around all the cars. And all that broken glass and twisted metal. What if she cut herself?

With Jake and the baby, no way. She would have to lift the stroller over more cars than she could count, as well as helping Jake climb across hoods and roofs and trunks—*and forget it.*

None of that on the pedestrian bridge. It was completely free of cars. There were, of course, all the dead pedestrians. And bikers. She stood at the entrance to the bridge, looking at the bodies. She counted them. When she got to twenty, she decided to walk back the way she had come, then over through the train crossing and walk across the center of the bridge, where the light rail train traveled. She bumped the stroller up so that one bicycle wheel was on either side of one of the gleaming metal rails, wrapped the leash around her wrist a couple of times, reining Jake in. She didn't want him stumbling into the rail.

The smell from the bodies was bad, but bearable, especially considering some of the houses she'd been in. She couldn't really see over the concrete barrier at the corpses on the other side of the walkway, and she was fine with that. Instead, she walked deliberately, facing straight down, focusing on keeping the stroller straight and moving forward.

There was a break in the barrier and quick movement caught her eye. She turned and recoiled in horror. A dead woman, lying on her back, was moving. Well, her sweater was moving. Callie took a step back. Then she shrieked as a rat poked its pointed snout through a hole in the material. Now she could see more rats, crawling around and over the bodies.

She retched and turned away.

She stared at her feet. Left. Right. Left Right. Keep walking.

The baby squawked.

"It's okay, buddy. It's okay." Her voice sounded rough and hoarse to her ears. How long had it been since she'd spoken?

How long had it been since someone else had spoken to her?

Through the chain link fence, she saw a small red and white boat drifting slowly down the river. It was sideways, moving slowly, with no direction, no purpose.

She moved closer to the fence and looked more closely at the boat. The front was dented in several places. Nothing moved aboard it. A body lay splayed on the front deck.

She stood watching as the boat continued its aimless

journey until it disappeared beneath the bridge. Where had it come from, and where had it been headed?

After they crossed the river, she found a nearby coffee shop, and they sat down at a metal table outside and ate lunch.

As the baby dozed off and Jake stared at the water, Callie unfolded her map. She had marked the route with a high-lighter, and she had a general idea of where to go. She needed to get to the freeway on the southern end of the city. If she followed the river and walked along it as best, she could, she could probably keep it in sight.

"All right, boys," she said, getting Jake up and turning the stroller toward the nearest road. "Let's do this."

Once she got a few blocks in, the smell hit her. A musty, rotten fruity smell, that she knew wasn't fruit. She knew that smell, all right. She was getting used to it. She pulled her bandana over her mouth and nose, and it seemed to help. Jake didn't seem to mind.

She saw a man walking away from her, a couple of blocks over. She watched him, for a bit, ready to run, then noticed the tell-tale shuffling gait. He was one of *them*.

Callie moved with a sense of purpose. If she hurried, they might be able to get through the city before it got dark. She didn't relish the idea of spending the night surrounded by thousands of corpses. She much preferred some house a bit away from the city. It was hard though; weaving through the streets, and at the same time, tugging Jake, slowing to make sure he could step over a curb or make his way around a car stuck on the sidewalk.

The apartments and office buildings loomed above her

as she led her boys through the dead streets like cliffs of concrete and glass. The windows, like empty eyes, stared down at her, dark and pitiless. There were bodies scattered here and there on the sidewalks, the streets, and cars snarled with each other or sitting at odd angles in the street, clogging the intersections, and sometimes even the side-walk. She saw a few rats and avoided walking too near sewers and trash cans.

They walked steadily, only stopping for a brief diaper change. They all had some water, split a can of fruit cocktail, and got moving again. But it felt like they weren't getting anywhere. They were making progress because she checked her map twice. But so slowly. The streets all looked the same. Everything looked so much closer on the map.

It was later in the day; the shadows were getting longer, and the baby was really fussing. Callie began to face the fact that they were probably going to have to find a place in the city to sleep that night.

An apartment? Maybe a hotel? A fancy hotel? That might not be so bad. They had passed one a while back. She remembered stepping around the uniformed bellman on the sidewalk, dressed kind of like one of those English guards in his shiny red coat. It would be hard though if there wasn't any power, but anything was better than spending the night out here. In the open, with all these bodies. And the quiet, the absolute stillness, was beginning to get to her too. She was in a city—a city, surrounded by stores and offices and restaurants and cars and trucks... and the only sound was her footsteps. Creepy.

She looked around, trying to get her bearings, looking for a hotel or something, but not really familiar with the layout of the city. A building up the street looked fairly new and shiny. She made out the word "Hotel" on the marquee. Maybe they could stay there. Newer hotels would probably be near nicer buildings, right? She picked up her pace a bit, moving past the half-eaten body of a police officer (*don't think about it*), when a voice called out, "Hey kid!"

17

Callie screamed out loud (which frightened her even more) and spun around, trying to see where the voice came from. She grabbed Jake's leash tightly in her hand, yanked him toward her, and pushed the stroller, headed for the nearest building to find some kind of shelter. She bumped the stroller up over the curb and felt the leash tense as Jake stumbled over the curb. She turned in time to see him fall forward, but he put his palms out so he landed on his hands and knees. She stepped back and grabbed his collar and yanked him to his feet and pushed him against the nearest building. She slid along the building toward a door marked "Delivery Only." She reached out and tried the handle. It was locked. Of course.

The voice called out again, "Hey, hey! Girl! Calm down. Calm down. It's okay. We ain't gonna hurt you."

Callie crouched against the side of the building, shoving Jake into the doorway, shielding him and the baby as much as possible. She dug one hand in the backpack, scrambling for the gun. She felt its deadly, familiar weight wrapped up in a tee shirt and pulled it out and unwrapped it. She held it, two-handed, her heart pounding in her chest. She let out an enormous gasp and realized she had been holding her breath.

"I have a gun," she shouted, her voice shaky.

Callie leaned forward and looked down the street both ways but saw no one. She squatted down and tilted her head and looked underneath the cars across the street. Nothing.

"Up here," the voice called. "Look up here."

Still squatting, Callie looked up and then over, and there, across the street on a balcony, about five floors up, was a young shirtless man with dreadlocks and a big smile on his face. He held up his hands high over his head. "Don't shoot!" he called, not losing his smile. "Sorry, man, I didn't mean to scare you."

Callie stared at him. She said nothing. The baby began to cry.

"Hey, you hungry? Come on up." The guy was leaning on the railing, getting a closer look.

She eyed the front door of his building, below the "TOWER WEST" sign, half expecting someone to come rushing out. She did not lower the gun. She stood up slowly, holding the gun away from her, making sure he saw it.

"Hey, is that a baby?" the guy asked, pointing.

Callie didn't respond. She moved a little closer to the stroller, not taking her eyes off the guy. She put a hand down, and ran it over the baby's head, trying to soothe him. She felt his tears and his little hands grabbing at her fingers.

The guy was still watching, still smiling. If he was alone, how long would it take him to get down here? Should she run?

The guy on the balcony held up a hand. "Hold on a second, okay?" He turned and spoke to someone behind him, and a moment later an older woman came out to the balcony railing and looked down at Callie. Callie felt a surge of relief. *An adult. A woman.* A normal adult. Someone who could give her advice and help her decide what to do.

The woman, swaying slightly, wore a bathrobe and held a glass of wine. She leaned over the railing and waved at Callie and raised her glass and took a drink. Then she turned and spoke to the young man, who said something back. She turned back to Callie and said, "Come on up, sweetheart, it's okay. Are you hungry?"

It took fifteen minutes of cajoling and eventually the woman coming down to the street before Callie agreed to go inside the Tower West. The woman came outside, (no wine glass, but still in a silk bathrobe) and introduced herself as Diane. She seemed nice, but she was jittery, and her head kept darting from side to side like a bird's. Like being outside made her nervous. She was older than Callie's mom, so maybe in her fifties, but it was hard to tell because she wore so much makeup, along with huge diamond earrings and a matching necklace.

"We haven't seen anyone else...alive, in days," she told Callie, looking at Jake and losing her smile for just a bit. She took a step back. "Is he okay?" she asked. "Is he... autistic or something?"

"No," Callie said. Her voice was flat. *Autistic? What was she talking about?* She had been putting the gun away in the backpack but continued to hold onto it as she watched Diane. "He was, um... affected, I guess, by whatever happened. He's, my brother."

"Oh," Diane said, and still seemed uncomfortable, not sure what to say. Her eyes widened and she went to the stroller and leaned in for a look. "Who's this little sweet-heart?" She knelt to have a better look.

"I haven't named him yet," Callie said and realized how silly that sounded. Why hadn't she named him? It's not like his mom was going to come back and say, "Oh, hey, thanks for taking care of Cody or Sam," or whatever his name had been. What was she waiting for?

I guess to see if this is all real. That was all she could come up with.

"Oh, he's a cutie-pie," Diane said. "Yes, you are, aren't you, little cutie-pie?" she added in a baby voice poking a finger into the baby's tummy.

Diane carried the baby and his diaper bag while Callie helped Jake up the stairs. Callie wore her backpack, in which she had stuffed a change of clothes for Jake along with the gun, wrapped inside a tee shirt. She wheeled the stroller across the elegant lobby to the stairway door.

"Leave it. Marcus will come down for it," Diane said. She carried the baby one-handed, against her chest (she's an old pro at this, Callie thought), and used the flashlight app on her cell phone to light their way up the stairs. There was some light coming from above, but without the flashlight, it would have been too dark to see her feet.

Jake stumbled into the steps at first. He was used to walking in a straight line on level ground. Stairs were some-thing new. Callie, a step above him. turned and pulled on his arm to get him to step up. It wasn't easy, but after a while, they got into a rhythm. Pull and step. Pull and step.

At the same time, she kept an eye on Diane and the baby, hoping she wasn't so focused on the baby she would leave them in the dust. In the dark. Callie cast a look behind her at the dim light from the street lobby door, from safety.

Is this a good idea?

balcony railing and looked down at Callie. Callie felt a surge of relief. *An adult. A woman.* A normal adult. Someone who could give her advice and help her decide what to do.

The woman, swaying slightly, wore a bathrobe and held a glass of wine. She leaned over the railing and waved at Callie and raised her glass and took a drink. Then she turned and spoke to the young man, who said something back. She turned back to Callie and said, "Come on up, sweetheart, it's okay. Are you hungry?"

It took fifteen minutes of cajoling and eventually the woman coming down to the street before Callie agreed to go inside the Tower West. The woman came outside, (no wine glass, but still in a silk bathrobe) and introduced herself as Diane. She seemed nice, but she was jittery, and her head kept darting from side to side like a bird's. Like being outside made her nervous. She was older than Callie's mom, so maybe in her fifties, but it was hard to tell because she wore so much makeup, along with huge diamond earrings and a matching necklace.

"We haven't seen anyone else...alive, in days," she told Callie, looking at Jake and losing her smile for just a bit. She took a step back. "Is he okay?" she asked. "Is he... autistic or something?"

"No," Callie said. Her voice was flat. *Autistic? What was she talking about?* She had been putting the gun away in the backpack but continued to hold onto it as she watched Diane. "He was, um... affected, I guess, by whatever happened. He's, my brother."

"Oh," Diane said, and still seemed uncomfortable, not sure what to say. Her eyes widened and she went to the stroller and leaned in for a look. "Who's this little sweetheart?" She knelt to have a better look.

"I haven't named him yet," Callie said and realized how silly that sounded. Why hadn't she named him? It's not like his mom was going to come back and say, "Oh, hey, thanks for taking care of Cody or Sam," or whatever his name had been. What was she waiting for?

I guess to see if this is all real. That was all she could come up with.

"Oh, he's a cutie-pie," Diane said. "Yes, you are, aren't you, little cutie-pie?" she added in a baby voice poking a finger into the baby's tummy.

Diane carried the baby and his diaper bag while Callie helped Jake up the stairs. Callie wore her backpack, in which she had stuffed a change of clothes for Jake along with the gun, wrapped inside a tee shirt. She wheeled the stroller across the elegant lobby to the stairway door.

"Leave it. Marcus will come down for it," Diane said. She carried the baby one-handed, against her chest (she's an old pro at this, Callie thought), and used the flashlight app on her cell phone to light their way up the stairs. There was some light coming from above, but without the flashlight, it would have been too dark to see her feet.

Jake stumbled into the steps at first. He was used to walking in a straight line on level ground. Stairs were something new. Callie, a step above him. turned and pulled on his arm to get him to step up. It wasn't easy, but after a while, they got into a rhythm. Pull and step. Pull and step.

At the same time, she kept an eye on Diane and the baby, hoping she wasn't so focused on the baby she would leave them in the dust. In the dark. Callie cast a look behind her at the dim light from the street lobby door, from safety.

Is this a good idea?

But Diane stayed with her, pausing on each landing, using the time Callie required to help Jake to coo to the baby. She really seemed enamored with him. And to be honest, it was nice to only have to worry about Jake for a while. It felt so freeing having *both* hands available.

As they went upward, the soft glow of light grew brighter. Diane turned off her flashlight. The door to the fifth-floor landing was propped open with a plastic camping cooler. The hallway was wide, and long, with huge windows at either end. Diane turned right and Callie and Jake followed. Diane stopped at the first door, which was open, spun, and said, "Ta da! Here we are."

Callie followed her inside and stopped. *Wow.*

The apartment was impressive. Wide and open, with dark brown hardwood floors, white walls, and floor-to-ceiling windows. The furniture was modern and sparse, just a couple of big chairs, a couch and a coffee table topped with camping lanterns that looked very out of place.

Marcus came in from the balcony, wearing an oven mitt, and holding a metal spatula. He beamed when he saw them.

"Hey! Welcome to our pad, man! Make yourself at home."

"Marcus!" said Diane in what Callie thought was supposed to be a whisper. "Put a shirt on. There are... children here."

Marcus blinked stupidly, then looked down at himself. "Oh yeah," he said. "Sure." He turned and disappeared down the hall and returned in a minute wearing a Hawaiian shirt, unbuttoned.

"That won't do," said Diane, turning and handing the baby to Callie. Callie stood Jake against the wall beside the door and stepped inside to take the baby.

Diane slid over to Marcus. "I didn't mean to yell at you,"

she murmured, buttoning up his shirt, and staring into his eyes. When she finished, they kissed. The kiss went on a little too long, so Callie looked away and moved to the balcony, suddenly interested in the view. But what was that smell? Was that...

"Are you cooking hamburgers?" Callie asked, hardly believing it.

Marcus broke away from Diane. "Oh, yeah, man." His smile faltered and he looked worried. "Is that cool? Are you vegan or something?"

Callie shook her head. "Oh, no. It just smells so good. And we've...we've been eating canned food and it smells so good..." The next thing she knew, she was sitting on the couch, holding the baby to her chest, and sobbing.

Sorrow, loss, exhaustion, fear, relief; so many emotions and feelings coming out at once. And the smell was magnificent.

"I'm sorry," she said, wiping her eyes on her sleeve. "I don't even know you and I'm crying like a baby."

Diane sat beside her and put a comforting arm around her shoulders. "Oh, sweetheart, it's fine. You don't need to apologize."

"I'm just really tired and scared and I didn't think I was ever going to see anyone again," she said, turning away in shame.

"Marcus," Diane said, her voice quiet, but in charge. "Don't let the burgers burn."

He had been staring at Callie, eyes wide, but he snapped out of it, nodded, and headed back to the balcony.

They sat like that for several minutes. Callie holding the baby, and Diane holding Callie. It was nice. Nice to be held. Nice to be comforted by someone else, even a stranger.

Mom.

Callie lifted her head and sat up straight. Diane removed her arm and stood up. She looked down at Callie and smiled.

"Can I get you something to drink, sweetheart? And your brother?"

Callie nodded. "Some water would be nice. Thank you."

Diane nodded. "Of course." She crossed over to the kitchen.

Callie glanced at Jake, still standing by the front door. She looked around the apartment. She hadn't noticed all the boxes before. Cardboard cartons piled up against the wall behind the dining room table. Plastic bins are stacked beside them. Supplies? Food?

This end of the dining room table was covered with pill bottles. The clear plastic amber bottles you got from the pharmacist. Dozens of them, all shapes, and sizes. Stacks of paperback books, some piled ten high, covered the far end.

Diane returned and handed Callie a plastic bottle of water. It was cold and wet, and flecks of ice sparkled on the label. Callie looked up at her. "It's cold. How?"

Diane waved a hand dismissively in the direction of the balcony. "Ask him. He's always going out and bringing stuff back. Every day it's a discovery of some kind. He's like a little kid."

But she was smiling when she said it. *She's proud of him*, Callie thought.

Diane said, "Now if you'll excuse me, I'm going to get dressed for dinner." Wine glass in hand, she turned down the hall and disappeared. A door closed.

Callie went to the front door and brought Jake in and sat him on the couch.

The enticing smell from the balcony was more than she could handle. Callie carried the baby out to the balcony.

Marcus sat on a deck chair, beer in one hand, the other in a bag of corn chips, beside a massive stainless-steel barbeque. The grill looked large enough to cook for a family of ten. Six hamburgers sizzled enticingly. Callie's stomach rumbled.

"Excuse me," she said. "Marcus?"

He turned. "That's me."

She smiled. "I'm Callie."

"'Callie'," he repeated, trying it out. He nodded. "Hey, Callie. Are you feeling better? Want some chips?" He pointed behind her to a colorful box filled with a variety of snack-size chips. The kind she used to take to school.

Callie shook her head, even though she was starving. "No, I'm good. Thanks." She sat down and straightened the baby's collar. "I'm sorry about making a scene like that."

"Dude," he said and held up his hands, one still encased in the chip bag. "Completely understandable. This whole thing so is fucked up—" He clapped a hand over his mouth. "Sorry."

He looked so mortified that Callie couldn't help laughing. "It's okay, "she said. "Hey, I need to change the baby and take my brother to the bathroom. Is that okay?"

Marcus looked puzzled, looking from her to the baby and then inside at Jake. Then he got it. "Oh, your brother. Sure." He pointed inside and made a curving motion with his hand. "First door on the left."

Callie almost bumped into Jake when she stepped back into the apartment. She had left him on the couch, but here he was, standing just inside the sliding door. So, he had walked a little on his own. Why? The smell of the hamburgers? Their voices? Whatever, it was a good sign, she reckoned. She sat Jake down on a chair and took the baby and her backpack into the bathroom.

The bathroom was huge and well-lit by several candles,

one of which had an overly sweet-smelling scent that reminded Callie of her middle school English teacher, who liked to light scented candles during tests. It didn't seem to help her test scores, but Callie realized it was more about the fact that many of her classmates had English after PE. A pine forest-scented candle beat the smell of thirty sweaty, hormonal thirteen-year-olds.

There was another door in the bathroom which opened into a walk-in closet, which in turn led into a bedroom. Curious, Callie walked through the walk-in closet, marveling at all the clothing and boxes of shoes. *Who has this many shoes?*

The bedroom had just a bed and a dark dresser. A dark bookshelf was set against the far wall. Small amber bottles with white caps. Dozens of them.

More supplies on the bed. Boxes of matches, candles, plastic-wrapped batteries, lanterns, cartons of protein bars, and packages of beef jerky. Several cases of bottled water were stacked in the corner. Marcus had been busy.

Several large jars on the floor beneath a window caught her eye. Callie bent down and looked more closely. The jars held pieces of some type of dried green plant, and it wasn't until five minutes later that she had the baby's diaper off that she realized what it was.

Pot. Those jars are all filled with pot.

Big deal. Lots of people smoked pot.

But still. Her eyes drifted back to the shelves of small bottles. *Those are medicine bottles,* she thought. *But why so many?*

18

They ate dinner on the balcony, at a rectangular glass patio table. Marcus and Diane sat in the middle, across from each other, and Callie sat at one end, with Jake close to her on her right. The baby had been fed and slept peacefully beside the couch in his stroller which Marcus had brought up while Callie was in the bathroom. Diane was wearing skinny jeans and a sparkly tee shirt that proclaimed her the "Coffee Queen."

Dinner was hamburgers, with buns, and salad, grown from a rooftop garden a few streets over, he told her. A Bluetooth speaker played "Hotel California."

"How did you get all this food?" Callie asked through a mouthful of hamburger. It was, without a doubt, the best hamburger she had ever had. Juice ran down her chin and she wiped it with a paper napkin. She drank from her ice-cold can of Coke. It had been forever since she'd had a cold drink.

Marcus leaned over and helped himself to another beer from a nearby cooler. "Well, after the shit hit the fan, a couple of days passed and I figured nobody was coming to save us, you know. No army, no cops. It was before the power shut off, right? Nothing on TV, and the internet was pretty much down. No news or anything. I figured we were on our own." He took a swig from his beer. "Like just two blocks from here, I found a delivery truck, the refrigerated kind, right? Frozen food and stuff in the back like for restaurants? The engine was still running. It was parked behind a hotel, just sitting there."

Diane, who hadn't even touched her hamburger, was either uninterested or had heard this story before, because she stood up, swayed slightly, balanced herself with one hand on the back of her chair, and went inside, her wine glass in hand.

Marcus continued his story, leaning forward. "And I opened up the back of the truck, and it's like 'Woah!'" His smile widened. "Totally filled with meat, steaks, burgers, chicken. Even ice cream. Everything's still frozen! I got in and drove it into the garage here. I let it run twenty-four-seven. I gas it up every day. Threw some ice cube trays in there too."

"Where do you get the gas?" Callie asked.

"Oh, that's easy," Marcus said. "I got a few gas cans. I siphon gas out of a different car every day."

"Did you guys live here before...it happened?" Callie asked.

Marcus laughed. "Here? Hell no! I shared a room with some buddies in a little shit hole. After I met Diane, and we moved in here. Why not, right?"

"So, you guys didn't know each other...before?"

Marcus shook his head. "Nah, we met up about three days after it happened. We dug each other, found this place, and here we are."

Callie stood at the railing, looking over the dark city. Nothing moved, despite all the vehicles on the street. So strange. Behind her, was the deep throb of the gas generator. On the boombox, Foreigner sang about how long they had been waiting for a girl like you. A pigeon cooed from somewhere close by. Other than that, silence. Callie felt pleasantly full and even better, she felt safe.

She turned to Marcus, who was packing some pot into a large glass bong.

"Do you ever see any other people?" she asked.

"People like you?" he asked, feeling around in his pockets for a lighter, then spying it on the table right in front of him. "Or people like your brother?"

"People like me," Callie said. "Like you and Diane."

His response was a sharp intake of breath, a bubbling, a long pause, then a slow exhale. His voice was rough. "A few. They don't want anything to do with us, though. Seems like everybody's scared of each other. You're the first one we've talked to."

Callie nodded.

"What about you?" Diane asked from behind Callie's shoulder. She was holding the baby, who blinked his sleepy eyes at Callie. "Have you seen any people?"

Diane saw Callie looking at the baby. "He was crying, so I picked him up. I can't get enough of him, can I? No, I can't." She buried her face in the baby's belly and he giggled.

Callie smiled, but it felt forced. She hadn't heard him crying. But it was nice to have someone else watch him, give him the attention she sometimes couldn't because Jake needed so much. She shook her head and glanced at Diane. "I'm sorry, what did you ask?"

"Have *you* seen any other people? People like us?"

Callie thought back to the old man who shut his garage door.

"Not really. Mostly the...other ones."

"Yeah. We used to see a lot of them around," Marcus said. "First couple days, we'd see like ten a day. But not so much anymore."

Marcus took another long hit, put his head back, and slowly exhaled. He offered the bong to Diane, who shifted the baby to her hip and sat on Marcus's knee to take a hit. She wasn't quite as good at it as him, because she began coughing as soon as she started.

Callie watched, helpless, as Diane hacked and coughed and jostled the baby.

Marcus laughed. "Lightweight." He held out the bong to Callie and raised his eyebrows. *Do you want a hit?*

"No, thanks," she said, holding up a can of Coke. "I'm good."

Thankfully, he didn't press her. Diane pulled a chair closer to Marcus and she took another hit. She didn't cough so much this time, and Marcus congratulated her. The smoke, redolent (another vocabulary word) of burnt leaves and a freshly washed skunk, wafted around her. Callie slid down the balcony, away from the smoke. "Come sit with us, sweetheart," Diane said. She held the baby close, and gently rocked him.

Callie sat back at the table, besides Jake.

"Do you need anything?" Diane asked. "Are you still hungry? A glass of wine?"

"No," Callie shook her head. "I'm good." She leaned forward. "Did you really see a lot of the...other ones? The ones who don't talk?" She added quietly, and probably unnecessarily, "Like my brother?"

Diana and Marcus exchanged a look, and Marcus nodded. "Especially the first couple of days. We thought they were zombies at first, you know, but then...," he spread his arms out, shrugging, trying to explain, "But they're not dead, are they?"

Callie shook her head. "No. I think it's like their brains are just...shut down."

Marcus nodded. "Shut down," he repeated. "Yeah, that works. They walk around and stuff, but it's like they don't even know we're there."

"What were they doing?" Callie's voice was hushed like she didn't want Jake to hear. Didn't want him to know what he was *supposed* to be doing. "The ones you saw?"

"Just walking," Diane said. "And that weird talking thing they do, where they open and close their mouths." She shivered at the memory. "It was really disturbing."

"They were just walking?"

Diane took a sip of wine. "They were all headed in the same direction. For three or four days. There always seemed to be one of them out there." She looked at Marcus for confirmation.

He nodded, held up a hand, and pointed up the street. "They were all headed that way. Not sure why."

Great, Callie thought. *The same way I'm going.*

Callie told them about the woman she had seen in the backyard of that house, digging. She thought of Jake, bouncing off the glass door in the middle of the night. *No way I'm going to tell them about that.*

"Do you think they're going somewhere? Like the same place?" Callie asked.

Marcus shrugged. "I guess." He looked over at Callie. "Hey, have you noticed that some of them...are different?"

Callie shook her head. "What do you mean? The way they act?"

Marcus shook his head. "No. They...look different. Like their legs are longer than they used to be, or their heads are, like...wrong. You haven't seen anything like that?"

The question hung in the air.

"I don't think so," said Callie. But this put a whole new fear in her. 'Different?' What did that mean for Jake?

Diane murmured something too quiet for Callie to hear, and Marcus nodded.

"What do they eat? How are they still alive?" Callie asked. "It's been over a week, right?" It was a relief to finally talk to someone about this. So many questions. She put a hand on Jake's arm. "I have to feed him. I don't know if he could eat on his own."

Marcus glanced over at Diane. "We've seen them eat."

Callie waited, but Marcus said nothing more. Diane was focused on the baby.

"So, what do they eat?" Callie asked, her voice quiet. "Is it—is it bad?"

Marcus said, "Sometimes. They eat whatever they can find. We've seen them eating garbage, food from stores, or even animals. I saw one carrying a loaf of bread and just chowing down, right through the plastic bag."

Callie thought back to the police officer in the street below who looked as though something had been eating him. She swallowed; her mouth suddenly dry. She had to force herself to keep from looking at Jake.

"Do they eat... dead bodies?" she said.

Marcus nodded. "But not like zombies or anything. These, the Quiet Ones," He smiled at this. "Whatever you want to call them, they are still alive, right? And they pretty much ignore us. Like, they don't even care about us."

"And they just eat whatever they can find?" Callie asked. Marcus nodded.

"What if they can't find anything?" Callie asked.

"I'm going to put this little guy to bed," Diane said, her voice loud, almost panicky. She stood up, a little wobbly. She took a few steps, stumbled, and collided with the door frame.

Callie rose and moved toward her, worried about the baby, but Diane steadied herself and entered the apartment.

She turned to Marcus for help, but he was standing at the balcony railing, gazing up at the stars. Callie followed Diane and peered into the apartment. Diane had the baby on the floor beside the couch and was changing him. Her movements were efficient and unhurried. Not like Callie, who sometimes felt like she needed a third arm to change a wriggling baby. And she still had trouble with the adhesive tabs that kept the diaper snug.

Feeling a twinge of guilt about leaving the baby in Diane's caring but unsteady hands, Callie joined Marcus at the railing, she leaned her head back and stared at the stars. So many more stars now that they weren't competing with the electric lights of the city. Tiny pinpricks of light in the black velvet night sky. But looking at the stars brought up memories of the meteor shower her family was supposed to see the night It happened.

Marcus was completely engrossed with the stars, his head tilted back, staring upward, hands on the railing, swaying slightly.

Callie wanted to break the silence. It was so nice talking to people again. She had not realized how much she missed it.

"She's really good with him," Callie said, nodding her head inside, toward Diane.

"Huh?" Marcus looked at her, blinked, looked where Callie was motioning, then back at her. His eyes were red-rimmed, half closed. "Oh, yeah. Diane. She likes kids. She had two grandkids, I think. One was a baby."

Callie nodded. That explained it.

"His name was Daniel," said Diane, stepping out of the apartment. There was a noticeable slur in her voice now, and her eyes, also red-rimmed and glassy, had trouble meeting Callie's. Diane smiled. She had lipstick on her teeth. "He was so sweet. He was only two." Her smile faded with the memory.

Was, Callie thought.

Marcus went around to the cooler and pulled out another beer.

Callie said, "Do you know what happened to him?"

Diane sighed, reached across the table for the wine bottle, and pulled the cork out. She filled her glass and put the bottle back. It wobbled and she steadied it, keeping it from toppling over. She picked up her glass and drank. She stared off into the night. She shook her head. "No. I called them over and over, but there was no answer. I—my daughter. Daniel. They..." Her voice trailed off.

She covered her face and wept.

Callie stared, mortified. *Did I do that? I just met these people, and I made them cry?* Why had she asked that stupid question?

Marcus moved to Diane's side and put an arm around her. "It's okay, babe," he said. "It's okay."

They sat like that, Diane weeping, shoulders heaving, Marcus beside her, leaning in and whispering, Callie on the opposite side of the table, afraid to say anything else. Jake at the other end...being Jake.

Diane said, through her tears, "I just miss him so much.

He was—" She let out a sound that was a combination of a sob and a snort, which was enough to make Marcus break out in laughter. Then after a moment, Diane began to laugh, mascara streaked, snot running from her nose. She and Marcus cackled with mad, desperate laughter, holding onto each other. Callie watched, bewildered and to be honest, a little frightened. These people were nice. But there was something... dangerous about them. Something wild and unrestrained.

"Babe," Marcus said, tears streaming from his eyes. "What the hell *was* that?" He kissed the top of her head and grabbed a napkin and wiped his eyes.

Callie watched them, saying nothing. Is this all they did? Hang out and drink and smoke pot?

Callie grabbed a couple of napkins and reached across the table and handed them to Diane.

"Thanks, sweetie," Diane said, wiping her eyes and lowering her head to blow her nose.

"I'm sorry," Callie said," I didn't mean to—"

Diane held up a hand and picked up her wine glass with the other. "Let's not talk about it. You didn't do anything wrong. Sometimes it hits me hard, that's all." She drank. And leaned forward and refilled her glass.

Marcus plopped down in his chair. He began repacking the bong with more pot. Then he stopped and stared at Jake, his eyes roaming over the blank face.

Pink Floyd's "Comfortably Numb" played in the background.

"Does he ever say anything?" Marcus asked, leaning forward, elbows on the table.

"Not really," Callie said. "He like, coughs and stuff, but he doesn't ever talk."

"What's going on in there?" Marcus said eyes narrowed, tapping his head, still gazing at Jake like a specimen at a zoo.

Diane giggled.

It made Callie a little uncomfortable. "I think I'm going to put him to bed. Is it okay if we sleep on the couch?"

"The couch?" Marcus asked. "Why would you sleep on the couch?"

19

It turned out that she had her own bedroom. A third (maybe a fourth; this place seemed to go on forever) with a queen bed. Big enough for her and Jake.

Diane offered to take the baby to her room, but Callie had insisted.

"Really, "she said. "You guys have done so much for us. If he gets fussy, I can settle him down easily." By the light of a camping lantern, she set up a bed for the baby on the floor and boxed him in with some cartons.

Diane stood at the door, one hand open against her chest, gazing down at the baby. "So sweet," she said. She looked at Callie. "Well, good night. If you need anything, we're right next door." She hugged Callie and kissed the baby on the head.

"Night," Callie said. She got Jake ready for bed in the attached bathroom (*How many bathrooms does this place have?*) and laid him down and pulled a sheet over him up to his chin. It was pretty warm, even with the windows open, but she remembered Jake had said once that he couldn't sleep unless he was covered with at least a sheet. Something about being scared of monsters, but if you were covered, they couldn't get you.

Callie stripped down to shorts and a tee shirt, used the bathroom herself, and slid into the bed. She heard muffled voices from the other side of the wall. Reminiscent of Mom and Dad talking in bed. She rolled over and sighed. Maybe these two weren't so bad.

Ahh. The mattress was perfect. Not too firm, not too soft. *Even Goldilocks couldn't complain,* she thought. She sighed, tired and content, and relatively safe.

Callie woke up having to pee. She glanced at her phone. She'd only been asleep for an hour. She drank too many Cokes, she guessed. She checked on both Jake and the baby before heading to the bathroom.

As she sat on the toilet, she heard voices through the wall. She leaned forward and listened.

"...take him." That sounded like Marcus.

"Why not?" Diane responded. "She already has that freak to take care of. She can't..." Her voice trailed off.

Callie swallowed. They were talking about taking the baby. She leaned closer to the wall.

Marcus said, "...can stay with us too. She shouldn't be out there..."

"I don't really care if she stays or goes. But that baby needs to stay...." Diane's voice trailed off, impossible to understand. Maybe they moved to a different room? Callie pressed her ear against the wall.

They went back and forth, and Callie only made out a few words. They were talking about her and the baby. And Jake. Jake the "freak."

She finished up in the bathroom without flushing (she didn't want them to know she was awake) and went back to her room, closed the door, and slipped into bed. She lay still, listening to Jake's rhythmic breathing. Should they leave now? Before Marcus and Diane got up?

She raised herself on her elbows just as the door clicked open. Callie dropped her head to her pillow and closed her eyes. She heard quiet footsteps crossing the room to the baby. Callie opened her eyes just enough to see Diane standing over the sleeping infant.

"My sweet little boy," she murmured. "My sweet little Tommy." She kissed her fingertips, then reached down and touched the baby. Diane glided across the room and into the hall, closing the door behind her.

It took Callie a long time to get back to sleep.

Callie walked out to the balcony with the baby on her hip, leading Jake with the other hand. Breakfast was bacon and eggs, which Marcus fried in a skillet on the grill. She could smell it from the living room. There was even cold orange juice. Incredible. Callie could get used to this. But she had to go. She had places to go, and people to see. Her dad used to say that.

Diane shuffled onto the balcony after she and Marcus had eaten, wearing her bathrobe, and carrying a cup of coffee with both hands, like it weighed fifty pounds. She looked terrible. Hair in tangles, her face haggard, bloodshot eyes, wrinkles that Callie hadn't noticed yesterday exposed around her eyes and mouth. She nodded at Callie, gave a half-hearted smile that barely reached her eyes, and kissed Marcus on the cheek.

Diane half sat/half fell into a chair and with a practiced motion, took a pill bottle out of a pocket, twisted the top off, shook out two pills, and popped them in her mouth. She swallowed a mouthful of coffee, leaned back, and closed her eyes.

Callie stood up. She cleared her throat, not sure what to say. Goodbyes were always tough for her. But she knew she had to head out.

She cleared her dishes and walked them to the kitchen. Beer bottles and dirty plates and bowls, most crusted with food, covered the counter. A fat fly sat atop a dirty coffee mug; one-third full of a mysterious gray liquid. Callie moved the mug and set her plate on the counter. She came back out to the balcony.

"Um, I can't thank you enough for letting us stay here, and the food." She smiled at Marcus. "It was really good. But we have to get going."

Diane opened her eyes and blinked several times before turning toward her. "'Going?' Going where?"

"California, "said Callie. "To find my grandmother."

"What are you talking about?" Diane sat up straight in her chair, brushing the hair out of her face. She reached into another pocket and came out with a pair of oversized sunglasses, which she put on.

Callie told them. About the phone message. Then the call.

"So what, you're just going to walk to California? By yourself?" Diane stared at her. She was angry, but it was hard to read her face behind the sunglasses. Callie looked for her eyes behind the smoked lenses but just saw a distorted reflection of herself.

Diane laughed a harsh bark that held no humor. She looked up at Callie. "Sweetheart, this is crazy. You're too young. It's too dangerous, especially for the baby." She gazed down at the baby, who was sitting in his stroller playing with a plastic doughnut.

Callie stood up. "I know it's dangerous. But I have to do it." She looked over at Jake. "We have to do it."

Marcus shook his head. "I don't know, man. Why not stay here with us? Or get your apartment next door? I could help you pimp it out. Generator, lights, maybe a DVD player."

Her own apartment. That was a thought. No more walking all day or sleeping in a different house every night. No more uncertainty of what's to come tomorrow. And the day after that.

Diane stood, with some difficulty. "He's right, sweetie. Stay here. It's safe, and we have everything we need."

Callie looked around at the empty wine glass on the table, the bong, the pill bottles, the empty beer bottles. Was this really the best place for her? And the baby?

Callie shook her head. "I'm sorry. But we have to go."

"Then leave the baby here," Diane said. "We can take care of him better than you."

"No," said Callie. "He needs to stay with me."

Diane slammed her coffee mug on the table, the impact knocking over a beer bottle, which rolled off the table and broke on the tile floor.

Nobody spoke.

"Then go!" Diane said. "Goodbye and good luck! You're going to get him killed!" She stormed off inside, only slowing to grab a wine bottle and glass from a credenza, before heading off down the hall. A door slammed, the force of it causing the glass sliders on the balcony to shudder in their tracks.

Callie carried the baby inside and put him in his stroller

and began loading up the shelf beneath his seat. Then she packed the backpacks, glancing down the hallway all the while. She didn't want a confrontation with Diane, especially if she was drunk.

Callie checked for the gun in the bottom of her backpack. Still there.

A quick trip back to the bedroom for Jake's backpack, and in a couple minutes, he was ready, standing by the front door in his oversized backpack, looking like a giant kindergartner on the first day of school.

Marcus came out of the kitchen with a plastic shopping bag filled with cold plastic bottles of water and soda.

"It's hot out there," he said. He looked sad, his face dark and tired.

"Thank you," Callie said. She was touched, and now it felt harder than ever to leave. On impulse, she stepped forward and hugged Marcus. He hugged her back, but his touch was gentle and cautious. He smelled like sweat and smoke, both cigarette and pot. He needed a shower.

Marcus carried the stroller down the stairs while she held the baby. Then she went back up and got Jake. Helping Jake down the stairs was more nerve-wracking than the way up because he was leaning forward, and she was afraid he would fall face-first onto the landing. She held his arm with an iron grip and led him, one step at a time, following the light from the open lobby door at the bottom of the stairway.

Marcus loaded the bag of cold drinks into the stroller and stood in the street and gave her rough directions to get to the freeway she wanted. She thanked him again and was off.

Callie stopped a few blocks away and looked back once before she turned a corner. Diane had joined him, and they both watched from the balcony. Marcus raised a hand in farewell. He held the bong in his other hand.

Diane was still wearing the sunglasses. She called out something, but Callie couldn't hear what she said.

"Come on, buddy," she said to Jake, giving his leash a gentle tug.

Callie and her boys turned the corner.

20

The sun was getting low before they walked down a freeway ramp and crossed a road into a suburban area. It was quiet. The only sounds were their footsteps, the hiss of the stroller tires on the pavement, and an occasional murmur from the baby. She really needed to name him. He couldn't be *the baby* forever. What next, *the boy?* Then *the teenager?* She smiled to herself.

She was contemplating Sam, or maybe Ryan. That was —*had been*—her father's name. The thought of her father pressed down on her like a weight. Another cinder block thrown into her backpack. Remembering was like that. Thinking about her mom, her dad, their house. Their life together. Life in general. Life before. Cinder blocks. Cinder blocks that weighed her down. Kept her from moving on. But you couldn't forget. You couldn't just pretend like nothing had existed before. Not like Marcus and Diane, with their drinking and drugs. That was no solution. At least not for her.

A loud squawk from the stroller broke her out of her thoughts. She stopped and reached down and pulled back the blanket so she could look at the baby. He was holding a jar of baby food (sweet potato and peas, it looked like) with two chubby hands and trying to bite the lid, his baby logic telling him this was the best way to get the contents of the jar into his mouth. His eyes widened and he smiled wetly up at her when he saw her.

"Hungry?" she smiled back at him. Callie turned to Jake, who was slowly shuffling forward, his eyes vacant and staring. "How about you?" she asked, expecting (and getting) no response. "You ready for some dinner?"

She took a swig of water from one of the bottles Marcus had given her, then helped Jake drink some. He was getting a lot better. He swallowed more than he spilled.

She yawned and stretched, twisting from side to side, glanced around at the houses, glad to be out of the city. It was nice to be able to see the sky in all directions, not just straight up. She felt trapped in the city. All those empty buildings, and all that death.

The nights had been getting chillier, and dark clouds spread out across the sky. It was probably going to rain again, so they needed to find shelter for the night. She looked for houses with no cars in the driveways. That generally meant no one had been home when it happened, so there were no bodies inside. Not always, but usually.

She decided on a one-story house, yellow, with white trim. The driveway was empty, and the front door was undamaged. It was very rare that she found a house where there had been obvious damage and/or looting. So rare, in fact that she rarely even thought about it anymore. There had to be people left who could loot, but since there were hardly any people...

Some part of her wished there were more signs of other people. A busted-in front door, or a campfire burning at night in the distance. But nothing. Besides Jake and the baby— *Ryan,* she reminded herself, other than Diane and Marcus, she hadn't seen anyone all day

Anyone alive, she thought glumly.

She wheeled the stroller up the driveway around the side of the house to a wooden gate, taller than her by a good two feet. She tried the metal latch. It opened, and she carefully pushed the gate open and led her brother inside and pulled the stroller behind her. She turned and latched the gate, bent down and picked up a twig and stuck it in the hole where the padlock would go. It wouldn't keep out a determined trespasser, but Jake wouldn't be able to get out, even if he wanted to. And it would keep dogs out.

She slipped the leash off her wrist and reached over and unsnapped the metal clip from his belt. "Okay, buddy. You're free." She stood and watched him. No reaction. No smile, no walking forward, no nothing. She sighed and checked on the baby. He was fussing a little, but he'd be okay for a few more minutes.

Callie tried a side door and it opened easily. She glanced once more at Jake and the baby. They weren't going anywhere. She pulled out a flashlight from a pocket in her backpack and slipped inside. She scanned the room. A kitchen. Neat and orderly. Tile floors and counters now covered with a fine film of dust. She sniffed deeply. The sickly-sweet smell of rotting fruit, and beneath that, a fouler smell emanating from the refrigerator. No way was she opening that. She'd learned the hard way not to open refrigerators. The smell was ungodly.

She knelt, and using her flashlight, carefully scanned the counter and corners for rat droppings. She hated rats, and since... IT... they seemed to be almost everywhere. She crossed to a doorway and checked out the rest of the house.

A small family/living area with a couch and a TV mounted to the wall, two bedrooms, one with a king-size bed and an attached bathroom, and the other smaller, with posters on the wall. Another room with a desk and a computer, and a bathroom.

In the kitchen, there was an unopened pack of bottled water. A hall closet supplied some blankets that she spread on the floor of the living room. She went to a door that led to the backyard and unlocked it.

She levered the stroller up over the threshold and wheeled it into the living room, then lifted the baby out and laid him in the middle of the blanket. He squinted up at her, his mouth pulled down in a grimace. He was getting fussy. "Don't worry, buddy," Callie whispered. "Give me five minutes."

She went outside to get her brother. Then she would clean and feed them both before putting them to bed.

She stepped around the corner of the house to get Jake and her heart stopped.

He was gone. She went to the gate, but it was still closed. She turned and saw him. He was *behind* the house, standing in knee-high weeds. He was... staring down at his feet.

Is he looking *at something?*

"Jake?" Callie approached him warily. He didn't acknowledge her. He had walked off one time before. Just a few feet. Like now. But it was always disconcerting. And yet, it was also a good thing. If he could walk off on his own, without being led or pushed, it meant he was thinking, didn't it?

Callie walked up and put a hand on his shoulder. She thought he trembled a bit, but it was hard to tell. "What's up, buddy?" she asked, glancing down to see what he might be looking at. At his feet sat a faded, half-deflated soccer ball. Her heart began to race. He knew what it was.

She stepped forward and nudged the soccer ball with her foot. It rolled a foot and stopped. She watched him carefully. Had his eyes widened slightly? He seemed to be focusing on the ball, but it was hard to tell. She kicked the ball a bit further. He took a step towards it. *On his own!*

Apparently, that was all he had in him. No amount of cajoling or nudging could get him to move towards the ball again. But it was something.

It was hope.

Later that night, Callie sat in a canvas deck chair on the back porch. The door behind her was open. Empty baby food jars sat side by side on the floor. One for the baby, and three for Jake. She'd clean up later. She'd had a protein bar and some applesauce she had found in the pantry. And a warm can of Coke.

The baby (*Ryan*, she reminded herself) lay on the floor on top of a folded blanket, a makeshift crib of propped-up throw pillows around him. He had eaten, was clean, and fast asleep in a pair of light blue sweatpants Callie had taken from Chuck's.

Callie liked to keep everyone together in one room. She would sleep on the couch. Like the baby, Jake had been fed and cleaned as well. She had gotten used to it now. Just something she did but didn't necessarily like. Like homework or cleaning the bathroom every Saturday.

Jake was asleep on a mattress she had pulled to the floor and dragged into the family room. He had rolled off a bed on more than one occasion and once had received a nasty bruise on his forehead. She had been really worried, as any bad injury could be a real problem these days. But he had shown no ill effects, and the bruise healed in a couple of days.

He did seem to dream some nights. He moved around a lot in his sleep. Did that mean his brain wasn't completely dead? Maybe there might be hope for him?

She sank back in the chair and gazed up at the stars. So many more than ever before. Without the pollution and the city lights, the stars blazed at night. Callie's eyes blurred. She blinked, and realized she was crying. She hadn't cried in days. It was a luxury she couldn't afford. She leaned forward and put her head in her hands and wept. She cried for Jake, and for the baby, who would never know his mother and father. She cried for her own mother and father. But mostly, she cried for herself.

21

Callie opened up a pocket on her backpack and took out her road atlas. She opened it up to a folded-back page and spread it across the kitchen table. She had found the atlas behind the counter at a gas station just after she started out.

She had a pretty good idea of where she was heading. Straight down Highway 101 along the coast was the best route. Not on the freeway, but parallel to it. Through neighborhoods where she could find shelter and food... and maybe people. She went into the kitchen and rooted around until she found a bill with an address on it. She was in Silver Beach. She thought she might have heard of it before but had never been there. She found it on her map and circled it with a red felt pen. She looked at the scale guide and estimated how far she had to go. On the map, San Diego was only inches. But in reality, she was looking at weeks, especially with the baby. *Maybe months.*

Callie took the atlas, tore out the pages for California and Oregon, folded them carefully, and placed them, along with the red pen, in the big pocket of her backpack. She snapped the pocket shut. She looked at her two charges.

The baby—*Ryan!* —was rolling back and forth, holding onto a stuffed zebra. Jake was sitting on the couch, staring straight ahead.

"Give me a couple minutes, guys, and then we'll be ready to go."

A quick rummage through the kitchen counters and pantries resulted in two cans of fruit cocktail, a plastic bottle of water, and some crackers. Finding food wasn't really an issue, because of cans and bottles. Once in a while she would find a fruit tree, and fresh fruit was always nice. She did miss meat, though. She'd tried some Vienna sausages she'd found, but they were gross. She hadn't finished them. Canned chicken and tuna were okay, but they weren't really *meat.*

A cheeseburger, though. She smiled at the thought. *NO. A double cheeseburger. French fries. And a vanilla shake.*

Now none of those things exist.

Callie backed the stroller out to the driveway, carefully led Jake down the steps, went back inside and shouldered her pack. She took a last look around.

"Thank you," she whispered before closing the door. She pulled the twig out of the lock on the gate, and then had a thought. She closed the gate, ran to the back yard, and picked up the soccer ball. She held it up before Jake.

"Remember this, buddy? I think we should keep it."

Did his eyes focus? It was so hard to tell. She forced the soccer ball in Jake's backpack, opened the gate, and they were off.

∾

They made good time today, which was good, because even though it still looked like rain, none fell, and that put Callie in a relatively good mood.

Until she saw the dolls.

She spotted the first doll, and not sure what it was, moved onto the sidewalk to take a closer look. She made a face. *Uggh!*

Someone had nailed a baby doll to a tree. A big nail, right through the center of its pink cloth torso.

She moved on and saw another one. This one was nailed upside down to a wooden mailbox post. Then another. And another. Some were not nailed, but hanging, twine tied to an arm or leg. There were dozens of them, and they hung from the trees like malformed, exotic fruit. It was unsettling, and she stopped.

Who would do this? she asked herself. And, perhaps more importantly, *Why?*

They stood at the center of an intersection in a neighborhood beside two cars. A silver SUV had smashed into the left side of a smaller car. She couldn't see the driver of the second car. Or the SUV, for that matter. Had they survived and escaped?

She approached the SUV and peered through the open back door. An empty infant seat. She glanced down at Ryan. He had been so lucky she had heard him crying. How many other babies had wasted away in empty houses, their parents lying beside them, dying themselves?

She noticed something on the hood of the small car. She walked over. *Ohh gross.* A dead cat, spread out, legs and tail pointing in five different directions.

She shook her head and stepped away. *Okay. This is getting weird.* The dolls. The cat. Was it a warning? Maybe someone wanted this street to himself?

The neighborhood looked safe enough. The houses were smaller and older, and there was one that was boarded up, but not too bad. No smoke, no broken windows or smashed-in doors. A dried-up corpse lay on a driveway, but that was nothing new.

Callie dropped Jake's leash and knelt. She took off her backpack. She pulled out her cell phone and turned it on. As it was booting up, she scanned the area again. She really didn't want to have to detour. She knew the freeway was only a mile or so to her left, and she wanted to stay close. But something felt *off* about this neighborhood.

The sky was dark and foreboding, the clouds heavy with rain. She wanted to get inside soon. A nice safe house. *She* could walk through the rain, but it was really too hard with both the baby and Jake.

She pulled out the creased map and unfolded it enough to figure out where they were. Her forehead scrunched in concentration. It was like her GPS map, but so much bigger.

She didn't want to backtrack, and going to the left would take her to what looked like a business park or a parking lot. She would feel too exposed. If she went about half a block ahead, she could make a right, and then that would lead her to another street that ran parallel to the freeway. She looked up and could see the green street sign about a quarter mile up the road. That's where they'd turn right. Then just skirt past this area. No problem, she thought as she turned off her phone. Easy Peasy.

Ten minutes tops.

A raindrop fell on her arm.

She looked at the baby again, and then at Jake. The windows of the houses seemed even darker. The rain began to patter on the roofs and the sidewalk. She turned Jake around and pulled a poncho out of his backpack and pulled it over him.

"What do you think, guys? You ready for a little jog?" She shouldered her backpack and tightened the straps. She even fastened the waist strap, just in case. *Just in case what?* she asked herself.

"Nothing," she muttered. "It's fine. Everything is going to be fine." Callie picked up Jake's leash and put her hand through the loop. She swallowed. "Let's do this."

She started at a fast walk. Another doll nailed to a garage door. The rain wasn't too bad. They'd soon be past this neighborhood, and if the rain stayed like this, they'd make another hour or so before it got too dark.

Her footsteps echoed hollowly on the pavement. *Am I always so loud?* There were old, towering trees in front of most of the houses, which both sheltered her from the rain but also increased the darkness. Some leaves skittered along the street, picked up by the wind. The hanging dolls slowly turned in the breeze.

The corpse of a teenage girl lay beside a soccer ball in the gutter. One of her legs was missing from just above the knee. It looked like... it was cut off? Callie moved away and went around a red VW Bug in the middle of the road. There was a definite cattish shape on the windshield. She didn't want to see if it was dead or alive. She kept her eyes on the street, occasionally glancing up to check her bearings. The intersection where she would turn right was getting closer.

A screen door slammed open and bounced off the house nearest her. Callie's stomach sank. *Don't look, don't look.*

She turned to look, and horror took her so tightly that she stumbled and fell to her knees. The stroller rolled away from her.

A clown stood on the front porch of the house directly to

her right. His face was painted white, his mouth a red gash. His eyes were circled in black. An orange halo of frizzy hair circled his balding scalp.

He stared at her, unmoving. It was impossible to read his small, dark eyes. A long, pointed nose over red lips open to display large, sharp teeth. A red, forked tongue. Two stubby horns on either side of his forehead. His hair beneath the mask was thin and stringy. He wore light blue coveralls, stained and dirty. They were halfway open in the front, revealing a filthy sleeveless white undershirt—wife beaters, Jake had called them. Back when things made sense.

He staggered down the steps to his front walk and stared at her. He was tall. And broad. And horrifying. She watched in paralyzed fascination.

The rain continued to fall.

Callie came to her senses and scrambled to her feet. She realized she wasn't holding Jake's leash. She whirled around and nearly screamed in frustration and terror. He was about twenty feet behind, beside the soccer ball that lay next to the dead girl.

"Jake!" Of course, he didn't react. She glanced over at the clown. He was striding towards her, and it was then she realized he was holding a hammer.

She turned towards the stroller, which was about five feet in front of her, out of reach, and then back at Jake.

The clown man was getting closer. His eyes were wider now, eager. Hungry. She could hear his heavy breathing.

"Please," she whimpered. "Please don't do this." The masked man glanced over at Jake and moved in that direction. He raised the hammer.

Callie looked again at the stroller. One of Ryan's hands grasped the blanket she used to cover him and was tugging at it. Those little fingers...

Callie darted toward Jake and grabbed the leash and wrapped it several times around her wrist. She tugged and he followed. She ran with her brother stumbling behind her, his poncho flapping madly. She ran and left the baby —*Ryan*—behind.

Tears coursed down her cheeks, mixing with the rain. Callie ran and sobbed, her throat raw with pain and guilt.

She ran and staggered and slipped and stumbled and got up and ran until her legs began to throb and her chest heaved. She slammed into the rear bumper of a car and spun and tumbled into the street. Tugging on the leash, getting to her feet, she sprinted up the nearest driveway, past a blue minivan and ran behind the house.

Callie was soaked to the bone, her clothes plastered to her back and shoulders. She took her backpack off and tucked it beneath the wooden porch.

Tugging Jake closer, taking up the slack in the leash, she leaned against the back of the house gasping, sobbing, hating herself. She wanted to vomit but nothing came out; just thick strands of saliva. She spat and wiped her mouth.

Jake stood passively beside her, his chest rising and falling. *Jake.* This was his fault. Her eyes narrowed as she stood up.

"Why did you have to walk away!" Callie sobbed, pushing Jake back a foot or so. She shoved him again, and he stumbled, teetered, and fell on his butt. He didn't try to break his fall.

Callie looked down at him, sitting on the cold, wet concrete. Her older brother, who had taught her how to do a layup, and helped her with her pre-algebra homework. He had even introduced her to Star Wars.

He was just sitting, not even trying to stand up or shield himself from the rain. She thought of a lyric from an old song her dad had played on Christmas last year. He had gotten an original vinyl album by the Who and was so excited.

"...*and Tommy doesn't know what day it is,*
he doesn't know who Jesus was
Or what praying is how can he be saved,
From his eternal grave?"

An eternal grave. That's what this was for him. And all those others. Only Jake was still alive. Because of her.

Callie's heart cracked.

She knelt and wrapped her arms around Jake.

"I'm sorry," she whispered into his sodden hair. "It's not your fault." She reached around him and half-hugged, half-lifted him.

Jake allowed himself to be pulled up to standing. He didn't really help, but he didn't resist, either. He was just... compliant. Was that the word?

She led him to a relatively dry spot against the back of the house. They were sheltered by a tattered awning.

"Now, you stay here," she said unnecessarily and headed back along the rear of the house, peering into windows, but it was too dark to make out anything of substance.

She tried the back door, but it was locked. She turned her body and shoved the door with her shoulder. It rattled in its frame but wouldn't open. Rubbing her shoulder, she glanced around and spied a cinder block supporting a drain spout coming down the corner of the house. She looked at the window.

In all the weeks she had been traveling, she had managed to avoid breaking into any houses. Open doors, unlocked windows. That was the way to go. Something didn't feel right about breaking into a house. It didn't make sense; it wasn't like there were laws any more... no one cared if she broke a window or two, but she could always find an unlocked house.

This is different. He could be after us.

She looked over at the minivan. There was someone in there. Behind the wheel. Which meant they probably had the keys. She swallowed. She didn't want to do this, but she didn't want to do a lot of things these days. She approached the driver's door. Between the clouds and the rain, it was extremely dark and hard to see, although there was clearly an adult-sized shape behind the wheel.

Callie went around to the passenger side and pulled the handle. The door was locked.

Resolutely, she went around to the driver's side and opened the door. The smell hit her with the force of a punch. A hot, foul, rotting fruit stench forced her away from the door. She gagged, coughed, and nearly vomited. She stepped away and forced herself to breathe deeply of the clean, moist air until she was able to compose herself. Breathing through her mouth to lessen the stench, she leaned into the car.

The rotting, jellied corpse of a woman wearing a burgundy warm up suit sat in the seat, her hands on her lap. In the seat opposite sat a gym bag and a cell phone.

Callie leaned farther in, aware of how close she was to the dead woman's shriveled, breathless mouth, her teeth lengthened by drawn-back gums. Her eyes were sunken, glistening holes. Callie reached around the wheel for the keys but wasn't able to quite reach them. She couldn't see over the steering console, so she had to operate solely by touch. Her face was inches from the foul face of the corpse.

Callie had a mad thought that the mouth would open and from her dark, dead throat, the voice screaming above the sound of the pounding rain.

"Get out of my car! What are you doing? Get out! Get out!"

Callie felt blindly for the keys. Her fingers touched something leather, which could only be a key chain of some sort. She followed it up and found the ignition key. And twisted and pulled. The lights on the dashboard lit up.

Callie cried out in frustration. She took a step away from the car, took a deep breath, leaned in and twisted the key the other way. It clicked off and she tugged it out of the ignition.

She jerked out of the car as quickly as possible and slammed the door.

It took her a few minutes to figure out the right key in the dark and rain, and she had to hold her flashlight in her armpit, but finally one slid in smoothly and the door opened.

Callie moved along slowly through the dark, unfamiliar house, the shadows thrown by her flashlight constantly moving and changing shape.

She opened the back door and grabbed Jake and pulled him in.

Then she fetched her backpack from under the porch. She looked around, thinking she had forgotten something, that *something* was off... and remembered. Ryan.

But she hadn't *forgotten* him; she had left him behind. And no matter how she twisted it, rationalized it, it all came out the same. She had abandoned him to be – what? Killed? Eaten?

***

Callie changed out of her wet clothes and was wearing a bathrobe she found in a closet. She sat on the bedroom carpet, cross-legged, staring at the light of the camping lantern. No way she could sleep. Ryan's face swam through her mind. And his little hand, those perfect tiny fingers, the last true memory she had of him. She didn't even have any pictures of him.

Somewhere outside a dog barked.

Callie crawled over to Jake, stretched out on a mattress. He was out. Fast asleep. The sleeping pill she'd ground up and put in his cold beef stew would make sure he stayed out.

Callie stood up, stretched, and took off the bathrobe. She got dressed quickly and efficiently. She had found a black nylon windbreaker in a hall closet and pulled that on over her sweatshirt. She debated tying a line around Jake's leg, and attaching the other end to the bed frame, but decided not to. If she didn't come back, she wanted him to have a chance at survival, slim as it might be.

She knelt beside him and kissed his cheek. He was getting stubbly. She'd have to shave him again. She put her lips close to his ear. "I'll be back in a little while."

She left the door open and made her way to the kitchen. She placed her backpack on the table, reached inside, and pulled out the gun, still wrapped in a tee-shirt. She took it and placed it in her jacket pocket.

Then she went to get her baby back.

22

The rain had let up; it was now a steady drizzle. She could make out dim shapes: the shape of a tree here, a car there.

Piles of clothing and half-eaten corpses she would see at the last moment and step over. She held her flashlight low, covering the lens with her hand, just allowing herself enough light to see a couple feet in front of her.

She remembered running—a*nd leaving Ryan behind*—from the Clown Man's house. She remembered she had made one left turn, so at the first intersection, she made a right. She found the sidewalk, and carefully made her way, house by house. Traveling slowly, step by step, eyes on the light just ahead of her feet. No sense looking too far ahead. She wouldn't be able to see anything anyway.

Is this it? kept running through her mind. She'd stop and look, try to recall what the house had looked like. A front door, a porch, okay, that was a start.

Then she stopped. Her— no, *Ryan's* jogging stroller lay on its side on a front lawn. She ducked behind a tree, shut her light off and scoped out the house.

No lights, but that doesn't mean anything.

She glanced at the baby stroller. Why would he just leave it there? Maybe he didn't need the stroller.

Just what was in it.

Then another, darker thought.

Could it be bait?

He had seen both Callie and Jake. Did he want them, too? Her thoughts flashed back to Jake, alone, helpless. *This is stupid. I should just go back. Jake needs me.* But another glance at the stroller silenced those ideas. Ryan had needed her too.

He *might* still need her, a dark part of her reasoned. Callie shook it off.

She stayed low and made her way around the side of the house. There was no fence, so she was able to keep close to the house, moving beneath the dark windows. She rounded the corner and found herself in a small backyard. The plants were overgrown, and she had to push away some sodden branches as she made her way closer.

A small concrete patio, three steps up to the back door. The house was small, maybe two bedrooms. She would have to be so quiet.

A few lonely stars peeked through a hole in the clouds. It was getting lighter.

Several cardboard boxes sat on the ground beside the steps. The contents glinted in the cast of her light. Bottles. Lots and lots of empty bottles. Beer bottles, larger wine bottles, and more. All shapes and sizes.

As she reached a shaky hand for the handle— *what are you doing?* — a slight hesitation, but she had to be sure. For Ryan. *For Ryan.* The door was unlocked, and the knob turned easily. She pushed the door open an inch and waited. Another inch. Still nothing. She pushed it open a bit more and slid in, still staying low. She gently closed the door behind her, but not all the way.

The smell was foul. The smell of spoiled meat. Of sweat. Of stale cigarette smoke. Of madness. But after the stench in the car, this wasn't so bad.

She took a chance and turned her flashlight on, again masking the glow with her fingers.

Something twisted beneath her foot, and she heard a faint jingle. She shone the light at the floor. A small collar. Pink, with a bell on it. And another one, beside it, this one bigger, with a metal name tag shaped like a bone. A green collar, larger. And a red one, the tags gleaming in the light.

What is all this? she asked herself.

She peered over the top of the counter and choked on a scream. The counter was littered with bones. Tiny bones from cats, birds, larger leg bones and ribs from dogs and who knew what else.

You know what it is.

Three small animal skulls placed in a row on a plate, their empty eye sockets regarding her solemnly. On the other counter, a key chain. Beside it, his hammer. A large carving knife, its edge mottled, caught her eye. She grabbed it and stuffed it into a jacket pocket. You never know.

The skin of a dog hung from the back of a chair. And on the kitchen table—*oh no*—tiny clothes. A little pair of shorts. A onesie. A boy's tee shirt. And the shoes. So many, it seemed.

Callie had never wanted anything so badly as to leave that house right then and there, and in many ways, it would have been better if she had. But she couldn't. She had to find

Ryan. Keeping low, she looked over the clothing again. Nothing looked familiar.

She gazed around at her surroundings in the glow of the flashlight. Sheets covering the windows. A couch. Cardboard cartons of liquor bottles—these ones full, unopened — stacked along the wall behind the couch. Dead rats, many crushed, littered the floor. A pile of clothes beside the couch. Empty cans of food, soda, beer, piles of cigarette cartons. And what were those? She moved the beam.

Magazines, DVDs. So many. Stacks of them against the wall. She swung the light closer.

Oh my God.

Japanese cartoons. Anime. And what were those? Sex movies. Porno magazines. Callie turned away and covered the light with her hand. She hadn't seen much in the brief glare of her light, but it was enough.

I shouldn't be here.

The dark hallway beckoned. She reached into her pocket and grasped the handle of the knife. A quick flash of her light showed three doors. One, on the right, was partially open. One further down on the left had a padlock on it. At the end of the hall, another closed door. She reached down, her fingers touching the handle of the gun.

Her heart pounded so loudly she thought it would give her away. She walked quietly, carefully. Staying close to the wall. Three doors. If Ryan was here, where would he be?

What's that?

A noise. A growl? *Is there a dog in here?* She pulled the gun out of her pocket and unwrapped it. She dropped the tee-shirt on the floor. She waited. The sound repeated and she relaxed. A little.

Snoring. Someone snoring. Someone *big* snoring.

Not someone. *The Clown Man.*

Walking so quietly, so carefully, practically levitating, it felt like she passed by the doorway without incident. A sidelong glance revealed only darkness and a foul odor. The snoring, at least, was a good thing, she told herself.

As long as he's snoring, he's asleep, and I know where he is.

She glanced at the door on the left, the one with a padlock, but kept going. She wouldn't be able to get in there. The furthest room first.

She took a few more steps and she reached the door. It was unlocked. The handle was stiff, and it turned with an audible click that made Callie wince. She gently pushed the wooden door open, and keeping the flashlight low, swept it across the room. A bathroom. Filthy. Dark stains all over the floor. The toilet seat up. The smell was worse here, dank and sour. With her gun hand, she pulled her shirt up over her mouth and nose and stepped in a little farther.

A window over the bathtub, allowing what little light there was to weakly penetrate this foul space. Boxes stacked along one wall. More alcohol. And soda. Once water stopped flowing through pipes, the bathroom became just another storage room.

A sound. A squeak. *Rats?* She swung the light left to right, at the same time bringing her feet closer together, trying to take up as little space as possible.

The bathtub. Something in the bathtub.

The tub was full of... what...blankets, dead animals...? No, something alive. Something that squeaked. Not a squeak. A coo. A baby's coo.

Not believing, but hoping against hope, Callie knelt beside the tub. The shower curtain was long gone, and the plastic shower curtain rings hung like rib bones picked clean.

The tub was filled with towels and blankets, but in the

center a boxy shape covered by a towel. She pulled off a corner, revealing a plastic laundry tub—and stared into the beautiful blue eyes of Ryan, pooled in the beam of the flashlight.

He squinted and turned his head, so she quickly shut the light off and put it in her pocket and stashed the gun in another pocket and reached down and scooped him up. He was wearing only a diaper, which looked incredibly full and about to fall off. Other than that, he seemed fine.

She resisted the urge to hug him and kiss him over and over. That could wait.

"We're getting out of here," she whispered, holding him tightly. The gun was in the waistband of her jeans, the flashlight tucked beneath her arm so she could hold the baby. This was going to be difficult. And to top it off, Ryan began squirming.

"Shh," she whispered, kissing the top of his head. "It's okay. Shh."

But he continued to squirm and now began to cry. Callie crouched in the hall and set Ryan down and pulled out her flashlight, checked out the floor in front of her. All clear. A faint light was beginning to filter in through the living room. She could make shapes of the furniture. She picked up Ryan, tucking the flashlight beneath her arm. She used one foot to pull the bathroom door closed.

Ryan cried out and wrenched away from her. She grasped him even more tightly, struggling to keep him from falling. The flashlight fell and clattered on the floor.

A loud groan from the bedroom. "Shut th' fuck up!" followed by a hollow thud. A bottle hitting the floor. She froze. Ryan squirmed even more and let out a loud squawk.

More noise from the bedroom; rattling of things falling

over, thumping of a big man— *a really big man*—getting up on unsteady feet.

One month ago, Callie would have been too frightened to make a rational decision. But now her choice was clear.

No hiding.

She moved toward the bluish cast of light emanating from the kitchen, towards the door, and escape.

The hallway grew suddenly dark as something immense moved in front of her, blocking the light from the kitchen.

The Clown.

He was huge, and gross, and up close, the most frightening thing she had ever seen. His makeup was mostly wiped off, revealing a face shiny and pale, a scruff of beard on his chin and neck. His piggy dark eyes glaring at her, full of madness. One of his eyes was bloodshot and half-closed, the skin around it shiny and yellowed. His pendulous, hairy belly hung over his stained, baggy sweatpants. She could smell his stench; sweat, urine, and who knew what else.

"What are you doing!" he roared. "That's mine!"

Ryan was screaming. Without realizing what she was doing, Callie backed away. Away from escape.

The Clown Man strode forward. He was carrying a large black flashlight in one hand, and he turned it on, shone it at her face. She turned her head, and a big, meaty hand snatched at Ryan, grabbing him by an arm. He cried out in alarm and — *pain*— and Callie instinctively tugged back.

"Let go, you little bitch!" His spittle spraying her face. The Clown twisted Ryan's arm and the infant yelped, his face contorted with terror and pain. Callie let go of him, holding her hands up in supplication.

"Please, don't hurt him. Please, just let us go."

"Shut up!" A massive hand slapped her across the face, rocking her head to the side, bringing her to her knees. "It's mine now." He reached down and grabbed her coat. "And so are you."

White spots in Callie's vision. Her ears rang. Her jaw stung. But he had Ryan.

He had *Ryan.*

She was being dragged down the hallway, back toward the bathroom. *Or the room with a padlock on the door.*

She struggled to slide herself out of the oversized jacket, but he had her left elbow in a painfully firm grip. She was stuck. She reached down with shaky hands, grasping for the gun, her fingers fumbling, and dropped it.

"No!" she cried, grasping for it in vain as she was pulled farther down the hall.

He mumbled to himself. "Goddamn bitch, try to steal my baby. I'll show you, yes, I will. Show you. Gonna eat you up. Eat you *all* up."

Callie stared back at the gun, growing harder to see in the dim light, and then her hand slid into her jacket pocket and clutched the carving knife. She moved in one motion, not allowing time to second-guess herself, twisting her body around, and stuck the knife into his calf.

The Clown Man hollered, took a lumbering step, and fell to one knee. His flashlight thudded on the carpet, and the shadows danced crazily in the narrow space.

Before he could turn on her, Callie, crying out in fear and anger, yanked the knife from his calf with a wet, sucking sound, and stabbed him in the lower back. The knife went in, caught on something, but she leaned on it and it slid into the hilt. The blade struck something solid, so she tried to pull it out, but it was stuck fast. She moved it back and forth, struggling to loosen it, and he howled. Blood leaked from the wound, covering her hands, making her grip slippery.

Still on his knees, he dropped forward, supporting

himself on one hand. He clutched Ryan to his chest with the other. Ryan was no longer screaming. Callie stood up and moved away. The knife stuck out of his back.

The Clown Man's breath came in quick, short gasps. He coughed once, dropped Ryan on the floor, and shakily stood up and faced her. He leaned on his uninjured leg. She was disgusted to see that the front of his sweatpants was stained with blood. He reached behind him, struggling to reach the knife, but he was too bulky. Too much fat. He couldn't get his arms around. He roared like a maddened bull and slammed against the wall as he lurched toward her.

"You... little... shit!" he wheezed, coming closer. Callie inched away, looking around desperately for another weapon. She looked back down the dark hallway behind him, caught the glint of the gun.

In the living room, hazy with the morning light, she had more space to maneuver, but was no closer to helping Ryan. She picked up an empty beer bottle and hurled it at the Clown Man. It bounced off his massive chest. He didn't even seem to notice. His face was a mask of hatred and pain, his big red mouth turned down in a grimace. Blood leaked from one corner of his mouth. He put one arm out and leaned against the wall, panting. Then he started forward again.

She picked up another bottle, this one larger and squared at the bottom, and flung it at him. It caught him in the forehead, knocking his head back with an audible *thunk*.

He groaned and stepped back, putting a hand up to his head. Another bottle crashed into the wall beside him, and he ducked. A clear glass bottle caught him in the knee, and he grunted in pain.

"Goddammit!" He straightened, and still wheezing, lurched for her. The back of her legs hit the couch. She had nowhere to go.

He was five steps away. Three.

Callie looked around her for something, anything. She grabbed a wine bottle, holding it like a club. She side-stepped, stepping closer to the kitchen. She knew she could outrun him if she made a move now. But what about Ryan, squirming in the hallway?

I can't leave him... again.

The Clown Man was leaning over, one hand on a knee while the other reached around behind him, vainly grasping for the knife. She went to move around him, but he looked up and was on her.

"Goddam... bitch! You... stabbed... me!" He was gasping, weakened, but still dangerous, still a monster. She swung the bottle, but he blocked it with a big meaty hand, closing his fist over hers. He bared his rotten teeth at her. Up close, his bad eye looked infected. *I hope it hurts*, she thought.

He clamped a warm, sticky hand around her throat and lifted her up. She felt her feet leave the floor, completely helpless.

No. Not fair. Jake. What about...

She had a quick glimpse of Ryan lying on the floor in the hallway just before everything went black.

23

She gasped. Her throat burned, and it was difficult to breathe. So much pressure on her chest. She could barely exhale. Her wrist hurt. It was dark. And that smell. She struggled to move, but it was hard, like something was pressing down on her. Something spongy... flabby... cold. She gagged.

It's him. He's lying on top of me.

A wave of claustrophobia swept through her. She squirmed, and pushed and twisted, and slowly wormed her way out from beneath the lifeless body of the Clown Man. She got to her feet. Her legs were wet with blood.

Not mine. His.

Callie rubbed her wrist. It really hurt, but she flexed her hand and rotated it back and forth. It moved okay, and it didn't look swollen.

She heard faint crying.

Ryan!

She raced down the hallway and knelt beside him. He was alive and moving, still a bit fussy. She lifted him and cradled him and let the tears come.

"I'm so sorry, so sorry." She held him at arm's length and inspected him. He looked fine. Probably traumatized—*you and me both,* she thought, and heard the cry again. Muffled, nearby.

Her eyes went to the padlocked door.

She approached the door and listened. Definitely crying. A child. She reached up and tugged at the lock. The crying stopped.

"Hey," she said, leaning in. "I'm going to get you out of there. I'm going to help."

She walked back to the kitchen counter, giving the stinking corpse on the floor a wide berth, and found the key ring. She took a moment and tore down the sheets covering the windows. It made a difference. The room brightened considerably.

She used one of the sheets to cover the Man.

She placed Ryan on the floor beside the locked door and tried a key. Then another. Finally, she found the right one. She removed the padlock and turned the handle and opened the door. The room was another bedroom, but bare, the only furniture was a stained mattress. Against the far wall were three large dog crates. Two were empty, but the third held something. Callie moved closer. Wary. Afraid of what she'd see.

It was a little girl.

She squatted on a filthy blanket as far back in the crate as she could get. Her hair was ratty, and her face was dirty. With her was an old teddy bear, a plastic water bottle and an empty bag of pretzels. There was a tiny padlock, the kind Callie's mom used for her suitcase, keeping the crate locked.

Callie dropped to her knees in front of the crate.

"Hey. Don't worry. I won't hurt you."

The girl shuffled forward.

"My name is Callie. What's your name?"

"S-Samantha." Her voice, a whisper. She looked like a fourth or fifth grader, so that would make her—Callie did the math—ten or eleven.

"Okay, Samantha." She nodded at the baby in her arms. "This is Ryan. We're going to get you out of here, okay?"

Samantha nodded.

Callie set Samantha on the front step, the baby in her lap. She hurried back inside, found the gun and then paused and looked around. Anything else? There was food, a lantern, and water bottles.

No. She didn't want anything from this house. *What about the woman in the bed?* Callie shook her head. No. She couldn't help her.

On the way out of that nightmare house, she took one last look at the sheet-covered Clown Man, the knife still sticking out of his back standing up like an accusing finger.

You killed someone.

She had. But he deserved to die. And she thought she could live with that.

Callie gave Samantha her coat and they made their way from that dark house as fast as they could.

She found the new house with no problem. Jake was where she had left him (of course—where else would he be?) and when she saw him, Callie burst into tears, and despite her wet, bloodied clothes, even though he was still asleep, went and hugged him. And held him. Jake blinked awake and stared.

Samantha stared at Jake. "Is he like the...the other ones? Who don't talk?"

Callie nodded. "Yeah. But I'm taking care of him. We're going to find my grandma. She'll know what to do." *I hope so.*

Samantha said nothing, just sat on the far edge of the couch and pulled her knees up to her chest.

Callie rummaged around in the kitchen, and they ate canned soup for dinner. The power was out, but there was running water and the gas was still on. The soup was warm, at least. After dinner, Callie and Samantha carried the dirty dishes into the kitchen. As Callie rinsed them off, she turned and saw that Samantha was about to open the refrigerator. Callie slid over and held it shut.

"If there's no power, then the food's gone bad. And it stinks." She wrinkled her nose, waved a hand in front of her face, "Pheee yoo!"

Samantha nodded; her dirty face solemn. "Sorry," she said, her voice barely audible, and turned away.

Callie went to her, knelt in front of her. "It's okay, sweetie. I'm not mad. I just didn't want you to have to smell that. It's so gross." She stuck her tongue out and mimed throwing up.

Samantha didn't meet her eyes. Then she moved to a window and stared into the darkness.

Ryan went down easily; after all, he had been through an ordeal and his sleep schedule was way off. *Sleep schedule,* she thought. *What's that?* She couldn't remember the last time she had a good night's sleep.

Callie knelt on the floor, with baby Ryan kicking and giggling. He was twisting and turning, trying to roll onto his stomach, and just when she thought she'd got the diaper fastened, he rolled over or kicked his chubby thigh and then it would come unfastened.

"Come on, Ryan," she said, keeping her voice light but very close to losing her temper. She was tired and it had been a long, terrible day. She held Ryan down with one hand while she worked on attaching the diaper with the other. He strained mightily against her hand, his little round face a mask of concentration and exertion. She let go and sat back on her heels. She wiped a stray hair out of her eyes.

"I can do it," said a soft voice in her ear. Callie jerked around. She hadn't realized Samantha was standing beside her.

"What?" Callie said.

Samantha moved around and sat down on the other side of Ryan. She held out a finger, which he reached for and grabbed immediately. Samantha smiled a soft, sad smile as she looked down at him. She looked up and met Callie's eyes. "I can change him. I have—had a baby sister. I can do it." She looked back down at the baby.

Callie nodded and stood up. "Thanks."

She went to Jake, who was standing against a wall. She took his hand and led him to a recliner, and sat him down, then tilted him back. He started for an instant when she pulled the lever and leaned the chair back, his hands reaching out grasping at the air, his eyes widening and head jerking forward in a moment of off-balance awareness.

There is something there, she thought. *He wouldn't have reacted like that a week ago.*

The family room couch was a pull-out bed, so they unfolded it and Callie found some clean linens and pillows and made the bed. When she was done, she saw Samantha on the floor, still wearing Callie's coat, her arms wrapped around Ryan. Callie put a blanket over the two of them and lay down on the sofa bed.

Sleep eluded her. The man she had killed appeared in her mind each time she closed her eyes. She told herself over and over it wasn't her fault, she didn't have a choice... but it didn't help. *Is it ever going to get easier?* she wondered, before finally drifting off to an unsettling sleep.

It was still pouring outside when Callie woke up. Samantha was already awake, sitting in a chair, head down. Callie glanced at her but said nothing. Ryan was still sleeping. She checked the time, almost midnight. She looked at Samantha.

"Can't sleep either, huh?"

Samantha shrugged.

"You want some tea?"

Samantha shrugged again and nodded. She stared at her hands, which were twisted together in her lap.

"Be right back," Callie said.

Callie opened a kitchen cabinet, flashlight in one hand, looking for some herbal tea she had seen earlier, and found something even better. Hot chocolate mix. She prepared two mugs and she and Samantha moved to the darkened living room. The two girls moved around the dark room, lighting candles, and placing them on shelves and tables. Callie picked up a framed picture of a family; the parents smiling and happy, two daughters and a son, laughing. She placed it face down on the table. She sat on the couch and motioned for Samantha to sit beside her.

Callie watched her as she spoke. Her black hair was matted and filthy. Soft brown eyes that looked old in her young face. Eyes that had seen things no ten-year-old should have to see.

Samantha's voice was soft, and her syntax was hesitant. Her voice was steady, with very little inflection. Sometimes she would trail off in the middle of a sentence and go into deep thought.

Her story was the same as Callie's. The main difference was that her parents and infant sister had been home when It happened. She said they were like Jake. Still alive, but... not there. Samantha had tried to help them. Had sat them up, even fed her little sister. But she hadn't been able to take care of them.

She was quiet for a long time after admitting that. Callie went in and checked on Jake and Ryan. Both still sleeping.

Samantha continued. Nowhere to go. No one to help. She had been scavenging farther from home than usual (her house was a couple blocks away) when the Clown Man had snatched her up. She didn't know how long she had been in his house. He kept her in the cage in a dark room. Most of the time. Callie didn't ask her for any details.

She looked Samantha over, this thin, frightened girl who had been through unspeakable horror.

"Do you want to take a shower?" she said. "And get some clean clothes? There are probably some clothes upstairs you can wear." One of the rooms upstairs looked like it belonged to a girl about Samantha's age.

Samantha didn't answer right away. She ran her fingers through her hair until they got stuck. She looked up at Callie.

"Stay with me?" she said, her voice so faint.

Callie nodded. "Sure."

They walked up the stairs, both carrying candles, which cast long, distorted shadows on the walls.

Callie stood just outside the door as Samantha got into the shower, pulled the curtain, and as soon as the water started, Callie hurried in, scooped up the filthy rags Samantha had been wearing and shoved them into a trash can. She marched the trash can down the hall and put it inside one of the bedrooms and closed the door.

She sat on the bathroom floor with her back against the wall as Samantha showered. Callie did all the talking. She told a story about a time about five years ago, she was close to Samantha's age, when she and her dad were coming home from Portland and the car broke down on the freeway. And it had been snowing for the first time in forever. It didn't just snow. It snowed *a lot*. So they played in the snow while waiting for the tow truck. They even built a grayish, dirty-looking snowman.

"After the tow truck had dropped us off, we went to Denny's to wait for Mom to come and Dad had let her order anything. I got pancakes with whipped cream and strawberry topping. And a chocolate milkshake. Dad just ordered coffee and watched me eat."

She drifted off, remembering how he had laughed when she eventually slid down in the vinyl booth, moaning and holding her belly.

Callie smiled at the memory. She opened the photo app on her phone and looked at some pictures of her parents. Like always, a sharp pain in her chest. But it wasn't as bad now. She thought about what that might mean. Was she getting used to the idea of never seeing her parents again? And what about—.

"He looks nice," Samantha said. She was standing beside Callie, wrapped in a towel, her eyes on the too-small screen. Callie was so lost in thought she hadn't even noticed her.

"Oh. Yeah," She turned off her phone and turned to Samantha. "Let's find something for you to wear."

They walked down the hall to the bedroom, each lost in her own thoughts. Memories. Good and bad. Thoughts and hopes for the future. Good and bad as well.

There were two beds in the girl bedroom. Sisters?

Samantha walked around the room, her eyes scanning the posters, picking up the stuffed animals and dolls, looking at them and putting them back.

Callie set a candle carefully on the dresser and went through the drawers, one by one, pulling out several changes of clothes. She tossed them on the bed. "These should fit. We can go to a store tomorrow. We need some more stuff, anyway." She turned. Samantha wasn't looking at the clothes. She was gazing out the window, holding the curtains back with one hand.

"What are you doing?" asked Callie.

"There's something out there," Samantha said. "It might be a monster."

24

Did you say, 'a monster?'" Callie said, moving to the window, but carefully, to not draw any attention from whoever(whatever) was outside.

"It's right across the street." Samantha's voice was calm. She said it the way someone might say, "It looks like it might rain."

Someone out there? Who?

Callie moved beside her and looked down. *Something* was moving up the sidewalk across the street. It was dark, all the streetlights were out in this neighborhood, and it was hard to see, but there was definitely something there. A shape lurched out of the shadows in front of a house. A man, moving unsteadily, the way drunks in movies walk, off balance. He was tall, almost...almost too tall to be a man... and his legs were so long. Callie gasped, put her hand to her mouth. The man's legs bent backwards, like a bird's legs... He stepped from beneath the tree into the light and Callie saw he was holding something in its hands. Something that was moving.

"Is that a cat?" Callie asked.

The man bent his head down toward whatever he held and moved into the shadows.

"What was that?" Callie said. Her voice was quiet as though she thought the man might hear her from all this way. "What was wrong with him?"

"He used to be a person. But now he's not."

Callie stayed at the window, both hoping for and fearing another glance at the man-thing. She turned to Samantha. "But what is it?"

"I told you," Samantha said. "Monsters. They come out at night."

"You've seen them before?"

Samantha looked up at Callie, her eyes honest and confused. "And other things. Haven't you?"

Callie's mind flashed back; the shape in the sky, blotting out the stars. And what about that woman in the backyard of that house? She had never really had a moment to process that, she was so preoccupied with Jake and the baby. She looked out the window, scanning the street and sidewalks below. But if there was anything else out there, she couldn't see it.

"They talk, but they don't say anything? Those people?" Callie asked.

Samantha said, "Uh huh. They're alive, and awake and everything, but they don't make any noise. That's how my...my parents were."

"And Jake," Callie said. "Quiet Ones."

A crash from downstairs. Then a thump.

Callie grabbed Samantha's hand, and they hurried down the stairway.

They slowed at the foot of the stairs. Callie put her hands on Samantha's shoulders. "You stay here," she whispered. She left the candle with Samantha and slowly rounded the corner where they had left the boys.

Baby Ryan was crying, apparently startled awake. Jake, though... Jake was trying to get out of the chair. He flailed around, struggling to get out of the recliner.

Beside the chair, a lamp lay shattered on the floor Jake was sunk so far back in the recliner it was difficult for him to get out, and he was rocking back and forth with such force that the feet of the chair were coming off the floor and landing with a rhythmic bang. Callie went to him and put a hand on his shoulder, spoke softly. His chest was heaving, and his eyes were darting around the room.

"Jake, Jake, it's okay. Shhh. Shhh." She pushed down on him and moved her hand to his chest until eventually he stilled. His gaze landed on her for a moment and lingered...Callie leaned forward. "Jake? It's me. It's Callie."

His eyes were still on her, but no he wasn't seeing her.

She heard Samantha behind her, soothing the baby. Callie turned.

"How's he doing?"

Samantha nodded. "He'll be asleep soon. He's tired." She looked up at Callie. Her voice was quiet. "You know why he was acting like that, right?"

Callie shook her head, ever so slightly. "Why?" she asked. Barely a whisper.

"The monster was calling him."

Callie turned. "What do you mean?"

Samantha's eyes were rimmed with tears. "It's calling them. Sometimes they want them to dig."

"I saw that," Callie said. "There were a bunch of...people, digging. Did you see it too?"

Samantha looked even more miserable and nodded. Callie got it.

"Your parents?"

"My mom." She wiped her eyes. "One day she got up and went outside. I followed her. I thought she was better. But she wasn't. I kept calling her, but...but she didn't answer." She wiped her eyes. "I left her there..."

"Do you know why they're digging?"

Samantha shook her head. "But when the monsters come out, that's when they call them." She nodded to indicate Jake. He was a *them*.

Callie digested this. Monsters. Getting the Quiet People to dig for them?

Samantha had been through so much. She had met a monster. She was dealing with some major trauma. Callie let it go for now.

Samantha was standing by Jake, looking down at him. "Why do you... keep him, when he's like that? Do you think he's going to get better?"

Callie nodded. "I know he will."

They slept late the next day. It was still raining in the morning, and Callie felt a little run down, so monster or no monster, she decided to stay an extra day. She told Samantha, who nodded but seemed to have no opinion on it. They ate oatmeal for breakfast, with brown sugar, the way her mom made it. Of course, Ryan made a mess of it, as he usually did. But all in all, it was a good breakfast. All four of them at the table. Callie hadn't realized how much she missed having something to talk to...who could talk back.

Samantha volunteered to wash the dishes. If they were staying, it made sense to keep things clean. A girl after Callie's own heart.

When Samantha finished in the kitchen, Callie rummaged through a downstairs closet for more blankets, and she found a trove of puzzles and board games. She turned to call Samantha to come take a look when she heard her cry out. Callie dropped a jigsaw puzzle of an orange kitten and headed for the kitchen.

"Samantha! What is it!"

She swung into the kitchen and her socks slid on the linoleum and she nearly fell. She caught herself on the island. Samantha was sitting on the floor, in front of the refrigerator. At first Callie thought she was crying. But she wasn't. She was laughing. "Samantha?" Callie knelt beside her. "What is it?"

"You were right," Samantha said through her giggles, tears streaming from her eyes.

"What?" Callie asked, trying hard to understand.

"I wanted to see if it was as bad as you said. So, I opened it." She pointed at the refrigerator.

Understanding swept through Callie. She began to laugh. "Was it?" she said.

"It smelled so bad." Samantha began giggling again. Callie sat beside her and joined in.

They sat on the kitchen floor together, laughing.

It turned out to be a nice day, after all. Callie had a headache and took some aspirin she found in the kitchen pantry.

They sat Jake at the dining room table with them and played Monopoly, taking turns moving for Jake. Ryan was bursting with energy, and they took turns getting up to extricate him behind a table or under a chair as he half squirmed/half crawled around the family room. They piled up couch cushions and created a kind of pen for him. Samantha ran upstairs and returned; arms loaded with stuffed animals. She dumped them into Ryan's "pen" and that kept him busy the rest of the afternoon.

Callie cut the game short and went to take a nap. She lifted the blinds and checked the weather. The rain had stopped, and there were even some blue patches interspersed here and there among the dark gray sky. As she sank into the bed and pulled the covers over her, she decided they should get going tomorrow morning. Time was getting away from them.

25

Callie slept the entire afternoon and on through the night. Samantha checked on her, but Callie had been sleeping so deeply that she left her alone.

When she woke up, Callie felt better. Her throat was still sore, and her back was stiff, but overall, she felt better. She checked her phone, as she did most mornings. Out of habit, she supposed. The battery was half full. She waited impatiently for the apps to load and update. She still had two bars. That was something. And then, Ding! Her message notification showed she had a new voicemail. Her heart practically leaped out of her chest.

Callie switched to the voicemail screen. It had to be Grandma. Who else would call her? *Could* call her? But it wasn't her number. She hit the play icon. Grandma's sweet, familiar, comforting voice filled her, bringing tears to her eyes.

Grandma's voice was hushed and urgent. "...Callie, sweetie, this is Grandma. I'm using this number because... they took away our cell phones. I need you to be careful, Callie. Really careful. You've probably noticed strange things happening. Stay safe. Stay indoors as much as you can. I'm not sure—I have to go. I love you..."

Callie sat on the edge of the bed, the light slanting in through the cracks in the blinds. Callie looked at the number. A 619-area code. She pushed the "call" icon and held the phone up to her ear. Clicks and buzzing, then a dull ringing. It rang and rang. Callie was almost ready to end the call when a female voice answered: "Research division. This is Munoz."

Callie swallowed. Why didn't Grandma answer? Who was Munoz?

"Yes? Hello?" said the voice. Sharp and direct.

"Can—can I speak to, um, Kathleen Austin, I mean Dr. Austin, please?" Callie said.

There was a pause. More buzzing and crackling.

"Who is this? How did you get this number?"

"Dr. Austin called me. Yesterday. She's my grandmother."

Another pause. Longer. Muffled voices in the background. Munoz, whoever she was, talking to somebody.

"One moment," said the voice.

Another pause. Longer.

A thud as the phone was put down.

Thank God, thought Callie. They were going to get her grandmother.

Then somebody picked up. A throat cleared.

"This is Commander Roberts. Who am I speaking to?" A male voice. Not Grandma.

Callie sputtered, "This is Callie Hawthorne. Dr. Austin is my grandmother. Can I please speak to her? Please?"

"How did you get this number?"

"Dr. Austin is my grandmother." Was he even listening? Why were they asking her all these questions?

"Can I please speak to my grandmother?" Her voice was soft and husky, close to breaking. Her throat felt closed, and she willed herself to keep from crying.

His voice was quick and clipped. He was used to giving orders, not answering questions.

"Young lady, where are you right now?"

"I'm in Oregon."

"Oregon?" He said something she couldn't hear, holding the phone away from his mouth. Then he was back. "Listen to me. Are you in a safe location?"

Callie looked around her. The white walls. The family portraits of strangers. But was anywhere really safe?

"Yes. I think so. Can I please talk to—"

"We've lost contact with Oregon," Commander Roberts said. "What you need to do is stay inside. Do not go outside for any reason. We have no idea of the situation there. Do you understand?"

Callie hesitated. There was no way she was staying put.

"Little girl, do you understand?"

"Yes," she said automatically. *Little girl?* She was almost fifteen. "Now can I please talk to my grandmother?"

Another one of those maddening pauses. "I can't allow that. We're shorthanded here and we need her. She should not have called you." Then, with a softer tone, "I will tell her you called."

"But—" Callie protested.

"I'm going to hang up now," Commander Roberts said. "Do not call this number again. It's our only working line and we need to leave it open. Remember, stay inside. We will get this situation under control soon."

Click. He hung up.

Callie stared at her phone. The unknown number stared back. She hit the phone icon and waited. The phone rang three times and then an automated recording came on, explaining that the line she was calling was no longer in service.

She put her head down.

"Are you okay?"

Callie looked up. Samantha stood in the doorway. She was wearing yellow flannel pajamas and had a kitchen knife in one hand.

Callie nodded. "Yeah. My...my grandmother called. She left a message. Then I called back and this guy told me to stay inside and not to leave."

"What guy?"

"Some navy guy, I guess." Callie shook her head. "He said the 'situation' would be 'under control.'"

"Well, that's good, right?" Samantha asked.

"He told me not to call back." She looked up at Samantha, her face streaked with tears. "I just wanted to talk to my grandma. She's all I have."

Samantha crossed the room and placed the knife gently on the nightstand, sat beside Callie.

Callie sniffed, wiped her eyes, and said, "He also told me they've lost contact with Oregon."

By noon the following day, they crossed underneath Highway 101 and started the (according to what Callie remembered) eighty-plus mile trek toward the coast. The houses were spaced much farther apart now, many with long gravel driveways and converted barns in the rear. Weather-beaten cars in various states of repair were planted in the driveways. They heard a dog bark once, and Callie reached for the pistol, which they now kept in the upper pouch of the baby stroller, just below the handle.

Neither one was talking much, and Callie hadn't been sleeping well. She was always tired, but when it did come time to sleep, usually in a strange house, all of them together in one room, she couldn't. Doubts and fears ran through her head, keeping her from relaxing. What if they couldn't get to Grandma? What if Jake never got better? What if they met someone else like the Clown man...only worse?

They encountered many stalled cars or pickup trucks, either tangled together or alone, off to the side of the road, some up against the trees that had stopped their final, fatal rides.

They avoided looking too closely in the cars.

By late afternoon, when the sun had just sunk below the tree line to the west, the shadows lengthened and became dusk and the air turned chilly, Callie was feeling just awful. Her head ached and her throat really felt sore. And she was cold. So cold. She was straggling far behind Samantha, who had the baby stroller and had been moving at a good pace all day. Callie had forced them to stop to rest at least five times and was now at the point where she felt like she couldn't go on anymore.

"Samantha," she called. "Can we stop? I don't think I can go much—" And she stumbled to her knees. dropping Jake's leash. He continued to walk past her until he reached Samantha, who simply reached down and picked up the leash, gave a gentle tug, put a hand on his shoulder, and he stopped.

Callie leaned forward on her hands and closed her eyes. She was still cold but could feel the perspiration on her face.

Her skull felt like it was full of thick wet cement that sloshed around every time she nodded or turned her head.

Samantha knelt in front of her. "Can you stand up?"

Callie nodded and balancing carefully, stood up. She wobbled a bit, hands held out, but she was up.

"I can't go anymore," she said. "I'm sorry. I think I'm sick."

Samantha nodded. She glanced around, then pointed up the road.

"Can you make it around this curve? I think there's a house up there. I can see a roof."

It wasn't a house. It was an auto parts store. But it was open. Two trucks in the parking lot. The front door stood open, a car battery keeping it from closing. The interior was dark; not the usual overly bright fluorescent tube lighting one expected in a place like this.

"Stay out here for a minute," Samantha said, sitting Callie down on the concrete steps. *No problem.* Callie hung her head. It weighed a ton. And hurt.

Samantha placed Jake's leash in Callie's limp hand, thought better of it, then tied it around the handrail.

Samantha was in and out in five minutes with plastic bottles of water and Gatorade. Once they finished drinking, Samantha led them inside. First, the stroller, bump, bump bump up the steps, then Jake, and finally the last trip for Callie. Callie was so weak she could barely stand, and, one arm over Samantha's shoulder and the other on the handrail, she made her way up the steps and into the store.

Samantha had been busy. There were two tarp-covered forms on the floor down one aisle, and another up against the back wall. Samantha led Callie behind the counter, where she had created a makeshift bed out of more tarps, bags of cleaning rags, and tee shirts.

"I'm sorry," Callie said, head lowered. She felt as though her legs were about to collapse, like they were made of spaghetti. "I should be helping you."

"You're fine," Samantha said. "Just get some sleep." She helped Callie lay down and went back around the front of the counter.

Hours or minutes later, Samantha squatted down and nudged Callie. "Callie." Callie blinked her eyes open.

Samantha held Callie's backpack.

"Do you have any medicine or anything in here?" she asked.

Callie, with a supreme effort, propped herself on her elbows and shook her head. Mistake. A wave of dizziness swept over her and she collapsed onto her side, moaning softly.

Samantha stood up. "I'll see if they have anything in the back."

Callie didn't respond. It seemed the safest choice.

Samantha returned with a small plastic bottle. She shook it. A few pills rattled inside. "All I could find was this. Ibu-something."

"Ibuprofen," Callie whispered. "That should be good." She sat up with some help from Samantha and took two of the pills with a swig of water... Then she sank back down. "I'll be better in the morning," she said.

But she wasn't. Her head throbbed with every beat of her heart, and her joints were stiff and painful. The light was so bright she kept her eyes covered with a Pennzoil tee-shirt.

Samantha looked worried. "Are you going to be okay?"

Callie's lack of response was response enough.

Samantha sat beside her through the night, giving her water and speaking to her in a quiet voice. "You're going to be alright. You're going to be alright."

"I need medicine," Callie said, blinking and rubbing her face in the morning when she felt fairly awake and aware of how sick she was. "Real medicine."

So, it was decided. By Callie, mostly, despite being sick and delirious. Samantha needed to get medicine.

Samantha would venture back along the road to one of the houses they passed to find medicine for Callie. But only as far as she felt comfortable.

"There has to be something that can help," was all Callie would say when Samantha asked her exactly what she was looking for. "Just grab everything you can find." And, then, more ominously, she added, "We're running low on food."

When Samantha announced that she would also be taking Ryan, another near argument occurred, but Samantha rightfully said that Callie couldn't even take care of herself, so how could she look after Ryan. Samantha added that Jake could stay with Callie. Jake was easier than Ryan. Callie didn't necessarily agree with that but didn't protest for two reasons. The first was that she couldn't bear to be parted from both Jake and Ryan. And the second was that she didn't have the energy to fight.

Samantha took Jake for a quick walk around the parking lot, just to let him stretch his legs, then brought him back inside, fed him, changed him, and sat him down behind the counter near Callie. She set a flashlight and three water bottles against the nearby wall and went around the front of the counter. When she returned, she placed the gun on the floor beside Callie and then the box of bullets beside it. Callie looked at the gun, then up at her.

"You take it," she said, her voice raspy.

"I'll be back before it gets dark," Samantha said. "Just get some rest. I'll close the front door. I'll be fine."

Callie forced a grin she didn't feel and gave a weak thumbs up.

26

Callie was in and out of consciousness all day. Mostly, her thoughts were clear when she woke up but other times, she was groggy and couldn't even remember where she was.

And then the doubt crept in. Where was Samantha? Where was Ryan? And then, the worst thought of all: What if they didn't come back? *What if she just decides to leave with Ryan?* ran through her aching head. So many doubts and questions, and no answers. Just her belief in Samantha.

Once, she awoke shivering with fever and fear, certain that she was back in the Clown's house, feverish and helpless. Her heart pounded, her breath coming in short, painful gasps. Fortunately, that passed quickly, and she fell back into a dream.

She was at the shore. The sand was cold and gritty beneath her bare feet. The surf was black in the darkness, with flecks of gray foam rolling in. Clouds overhead, blotting out the stars. At the horizon, the sun sinking, sinking, then gone. In its place rose an immense shape, a darkness, like it was swallowing light, filled the sky. The red eyes opened, each as large as the moon, full of fire and knowledge, and gazed into her heart.

Callie sat up, breathing hard, her face soaked with perspiration. It was getting dark. Hadn't Samantha said she'd be back by dark? Was it still the same day? How long had she slept?

She looked over to make sure Jake was there (he was sitting up, facing the door) and drank a bottle of water. Her throat was dry and sore, and the water felt so cool and soothing. She opened another bottle and swallowed two more ibuprofen. She finished the second bottle of water.

Half an hour later, she really had to pee. She sat up slowly, crouched, waited for a wave of dizziness to pass, and then pulled herself up to the counter. Her legs were shaky, but she felt stronger. This wasn't so bad. She looked around and took in her surroundings for the first time. A small country auto supply store, three aisles of shelves stocked with car parts and accessories, and merchandise. Advertisements, some probably older than she was, covered the walls, but she couldn't even tell what most of them were for. She put her hand behind her neck and rubbed it. Stiff from sleeping on the floor. She leaned her head forward, and in the corner of her eye—

Somebody was standing by the front window!

Callie ducked down behind the counter. Her head swam, and she knelt and toppled onto her butt. She had caught a glimpse of a figure standing up next to the front door. Just a glimpse. It definitely wasn't Samantha. *Too tall.* Callie breathed in, then out, and cleared her head. She reached for the gun.

This time she remembered to take the safety off. She kept low, ignoring her protesting knees and back until she was at the end of the counter. It was so quiet. She peeked out and jerked back. He (it) was still there. In the same place. Like, the same place. Callie thought for a second, then peeked out again.

The figure was silhouetted in the front window, resplendent in his silver and red NASCAR team uniform, a brilliant smile on his clean-cut, square-jawed face. Callie let out her breath, slid the safety on. *A cardboard cutout. I almost murdered a cardboard cutout.* She didn't know whether to laugh or cry. The world was crazy, and she was going along for the ride.

The rest of her trip to the cramped, filthy bathroom was uneventful. She brought Jake with her and turned him toward the wall. She didn't want to leave him on his own.

Once she was back on her makeshift bed, she drank another bottle of water. She remembered her mom had always told her to drink lots of water when she was sick. Something about "flushing out your system." She smiled. Mom and her theories. She gave Jake some water. He was getting much better at drinking; hardly any water went down his chin, and he even reached one hand up, as if to take the bottle. *Baby steps*, she thought and lay back down.

Callie jerked awake. A thud from the front of the store.

It was pitch dark. Not even moonlight to light the store.

Her fingers scrabbled for the flashlight. She held it for an instant, dropped it, then searched for the gun.

A metallic scraping as the front door was forced open. *Someone's coming in.*

Callie leaned her back against the counter, holding the gun two-handed. She breathed evenly and quietly as her eyes slowly adjusted to the dark. Dim shapes began to materialize from the blackness. A person. Maybe two? She reached up with her left hand to brush the hair out of her eyes. She was feverish and having a hard time focusing. A beam of white light from the front of the store. A grunt, then a thud.

Callie pushed her back against the counter and slid up, ready to turn and fire.

And then: a chirp, a gurgle. *A baby?* Her mind muddled, she tried to piece it together. *Why is there a baby here?*

Callie reached down and picked up the flashlight with one hand, and holding the gun in the other, stood and spun around, pointing both at the front of the store.

Samantha froze, her eyes wide open, her mouth an "O" and held her hands up, palms out. "Woah! Woah, Callie, it's me!"

Samantha had found all kinds of medicine, including some prescription bottles, but Callie stuck to the tried-and-true combination of ibuprofen, water, Nyquil, and sleep. Samantha had loaded the stroller with cans of soup, stew, cookies, and some candy bars.

They spent two days in the auto parts store. Callie slept while Samantha kept the boys occupied. She spent most of her time with Ryan, playing with him, holding him, and walking him around outside. She interacted with Jake, but to Callie, it looked more like an obligation. Samantha never spoke to him, and rarely looked him in the eye. She didn't treat him like a person.

Callie realized that Samantha didn't really like Jake.

They set out after three nights in the auto parts store. It was a bright, sunny day, although it was breezy. The chill of autumn was definitely in the air. Callie was feeling much better, although she tired easily, and they still needed to stop and rest every couple of miles.

But they made great time, all things considered. Now that Samantha was pushing Ryan's stroller, Callie was able to walk faster, which was completely fine with her. She was hoping to make it to the coast highway in about six days, which would mean they'd have to walk almost fifteen miles a day. It sounded like a lot when you said it out loud, but it was about six hours a day. She had done the math while she was lying on the floor of the auto parts store, going stir-crazy.

Samantha had taken over all the Ryan duties; not only pushing the stroller, but feeding him, changing him as well, and putting him down at night. At first, Callie had been a little jealous, but she recalled the look in Samantha's eyes that first rainy morning, when she talked about her baby sister. Samantha needed this. And truth be told, so did Callie. It was hard enough caring for Jake. And she had convinced herself that he was improving, he was more receptive to food, chewing now instead of simply sitting, open-mouthed like some giant baby bird.

But the road was easy, and actually quite beautiful, the leaves all greens and oranges and yellows, with an occasional red thrown in for good measure. They passed cars that had veered off the road, some smashed into each other, one after another. A metal train of death.

It was chilly, but they were well prepared for the cold.

Even Ryan was wearing a red one-piece snowsuit. He had put up a major fight, squawking and arching his back, locking his knees, fighting for all he was worth, but in the end, Callie and Samantha had won. They stood above him, triumphant, as he gazed back, his eyes sparkling with angry tears, lower lip jutting out. But Samantha poked his belly and he giggled. And just like that, it was over.

And he looked so cute.

The worst part about this highway, though, was the lack of houses. That seemed crazy after the horrors she had faced in the Clown Man's house, but in many ways, it was true. Houses provided shelter, food, and clothing.

They passed the burnt-out skeleton of a small church, the black block letters on the sign out front proclaiming "THE RAPTOR IS HERE."

Occasionally, they passed by broad green fields, sometimes stretching off for miles. Barns and farmhouses dotted the landscape. One afternoon a cow walked across the road.

Callie stopped. She saw where the cow had broken through a wooden fence. She pointed across a field.

"It'll be easier just to go straight across," she said. "We can cut through over there." The road they were traveling on wound around the farm, around the fields, and they could see the dark curve of asphalt in the distance where the highway continued.

The fence had broken when a car, now burned and blackened, plowed through it, so it was a simple matter of lifting the stroller over a strand of barbed wire and guiding Jake. His pants caught on the wire, and he glanced down, a reaction that pleased Callie. She bent down and helped him lift his feet over, one at a time.

It felt good to walk on grass and soil, soft and alive under their feet, after so many days of pavement. A goat standing atop a hay bale stared as they passed by but seemed neither impressed nor bothered by their presence.

Samantha stopped, put a hand up to shield her eyes, and looked at the farmhouse.

"You think we should stop here tonight?"

The farmhouse, two-story and well kept, looked warm and roomy, and inviting. They would have their pick of bedrooms, most likely. A nice fireplace. Big windows, so they could see in all directions. They might even have some guns in there, too.

But it was too early to stop for the night. And truth be told, Callie felt guilty for delaying them while she was sick.

"I think we should keep going," Callie said.

Samantha nodded, and Callie caught her looking back at the farmhouse several times until it was out of sight. She put an amiable hand on Samantha's shoulder. "Don't worry. We'll find something just as nice up ahead."

In that she was wrong.

27

Something unsettling occurred mid-afternoon after they had reached the road again. As they made their way along the empty highway, they heard an unfamiliar sound: a car engine. The girls exchanged a glance, then stopped, trying to figure out where the sound was coming from.

Callie said, "Get off the road," and started for the bushes that now grew over the edges of the road. Samantha followed, the stroller skipping and bumping over twigs and the uneven ground.

Branches slapped at Callie as she moved farther into the underbrush, struggling to lead them as far from the road as possible. The engine was closer now. It sounded big. And like it was moving fast.

"Get down!" Callie hissed, kneeling and pulling Jake down by his shoulder. Samantha crouched beside her, watching intently. She had one hand on Ryan, still in the stroller.

A bright red pickup truck came barreling past, heading the same direction they were walking. They could hear the thumping bass of the stereo as it rocketed past, impossibly loud in the primeval silence.

They waited several minutes until the sound of the engine was long gone before they made their way back to the road.

"We should find a place to stop for the night," Callie said.

They slept in a roadside honey and jam stand. So much for electricity and a warm shower. The stand was really just a wooden shack: four walls, a dirt floor, and a roof. There hadn't been any honey or jam left, Callie discovered to her dismay, after breaking the padlock off with a large rock. But shelter was shelter.

They decided not to light a fire. It was too dangerous inside the wooden stand, and they would be too exposed outside. Who might see their fire? Or what? The red pickup truck disturbed her. There were other people out there, sure, but could any of them be trusted?

Dinner was cold stewed beef and rice for Ryan, apple-sauce and crackers for Jake (he even held a cracker, his fingers stiff and awkward, but after one bite, he seemed to forget about it and zoned out, still holding the cracker until Callie took it from him and pushed his arm down to his side).

Callie and Samantha had granola bars and split a can of grape soda. Sleeping was difficult. There wasn't much space, the ground was hard, and occasional gusts of wind shook the honey stand and poked its fingers through the gaps between the boards. Their sleeping bags kept out the worst of it, but nobody slept much. Not even Jake.

At one point, Jake sat up, rousing Callie from her half-sleep. "What is it, buddy?" she whispered, putting a firm hand on his arm. He struggled to get to his feet, but she held him tight. If he were to run off in these woods at night...she wasn't sure she could find him.

A sound from outside. A branch snapping. Then nothing. Even the wind seemed to die down.

Callie listened intently, one hand on Jake, the other now holding her pistol.

A shuffling sound, outside, leaves crunching. Something was out there. And was that...breathing? A heavy snuffling sound, something breathing...or sniffing. *For us?* Callie thought. Sweat, cold as ice in the chilly night, made its way down the back of her neck. Her throat felt tight, and it was hard to breathe. She counted to fifty. Then 100, willing herself to breathe in and out.

They sat like that until Jake eventually fell back asleep, still sitting up. She lowered him to the ground, then before going back to sleep herself, looped the leash around his leg and then hers.

When they awoke, everything was damp with dew. Cold and wet. No way to start a day.

Before they set out, Callie wrapped the gun in a t-shirt and placed it gently in one of the pockets on the back of the stroller. Waist level, easy access.

Samantha exited the shelter first, pushing the stroller, but she stopped so suddenly, Callie bumped into her back.

"What?" Callie said, a little annoyed.

"Look," Samantha breathed, staring at the soft, wet ground.

Callie moved beside her. Footprints littered the ground around the stand. But not human. Large, four-toed prints circled the stand. They were nearly twice as long as her footprints.

"What do you think made those?" Callie whispered. "A bear?"

Samantha shrugged. "Probably a monster."

Callie glanced at her to see if she was joking. She wasn't.

"Okay, let's get going," Callie said. She was determined to find a house tonight. One with electricity and running water. Warm water. The works. *Good luck with that*, the negative Callie said. She hadn't had cell service in two days and her data was spotty at best.

But so far, nothing. Just highway and lots of trees. A deer crossed their path, a few hundred feet ahead. A male, a buck, with antlers. He stopped, looked their way, and leaped off into the undergrowth. As he disappeared, Callie glanced back and saw Jake staring at the spot where the buck had disappeared into the woods.

Listening to the deer crash through the forest, Callie thought of the gun. She hadn't had meat, fresh meat, in weeks. Beef stew, tuna fish, and some canned chicken. That was about it.

But she knew herself well enough to know that she couldn't kill a deer. Unless it was attacking. Did deer attack people? And if she did kill one, who would cut it up? Not her. No way.

It was overcast, getting hard to tell where the sun was. It had to be a little after noon. And no shelter for the night.

As if she was reading her mind, Samantha said, "Where are we going to stay tonight?"

"I don't know," said Callie. "Hopefully, we'll find a house."

They walked on.

"Do you think it's much farther?" Samantha asked.

"Are you getting tired? Do you want me to take the stroller for a while?"

"No. I'm okay," Samantha said.

"Are you hungry?" Callie asked.

"Uh uh," Samantha shook her head.

They walked on. The trees, the highway, the birds twittering madly in the trees. But no houses. No shelter.

"Do you think it's much farther?" Samantha said.

"I don't know!" Callie snapped, stopping and whirling around. "I don't know where we are, and I don't even know where we're going. So, no, Samantha, I don't know when we will find a house. Or *if*."

Samantha nodded and lowered her head and picked up her pace a little.

Good, Callie thought, petulant, annoyed at Samantha. How was she supposed to know where a house was? But she looked at Samantha, a ten-year-old girl, her entire family dead, pushing a baby in a stroller, and a wave of guilt washed over her and she sped up, tugging gently on Jake's leash.

"Hey," she said, putting a hand on Samantha's shoulder. Samantha shrugged it off and kept walking, moving even faster.

"Samantha, stop. I'm sorry."

Samantha stopped but didn't turn around.

"I didn't mean to yell at you. I want to find a house, too. I'm cold and I'm tired and I want to sleep in a bed and…"

She trailed off. She had heard something.

"It's okay—" Samantha started, but Callie held up a hand to quiet her. "Shhh."

She stood still, listening. Not the birds, not the wind through the trees. Something else...something familiar...

Somewhere, it was hard to tell exactly where, but close.

"Is that... music?" Callie asked.

Samantha, wide-eyed, nodded. "Yeah. I can hear it too."

Then a child's high, excited shout burst through the trees and bushes.

Callie and Samantha looked at each other.

They skirted along the highway, close to the trees that crowded alongside it, stopping every few feet to listen. They heard the music, louder now, and laughing again, and a faint shout. A second child's voice replied.

They rounded a bend. More highway, trees, silent sentinels on both sides of the road. A blue SUV lay on its side in a ditch beside the highway. They had gotten to the point of avoiding getting too close to the cars. Not looking inside. So instinctively, Callie averted her eyes from the SUV.

And she almost missed it.

There was something odd about the SUV, where it was lying. It hadn't crashed into a tree, like many of the other cars. It had crashed into a wooden post, which was now slanted at forty-five degrees. A dented mailbox hung loosely from the post. Below it, half buried in the dead leaves, was a hand-lettered sign reading "FAMILY WORSHIP CHURCH."

Callie looked closely. The SUV lay beside the entrance to a driveway.

The driveway was gravel, very narrow, and covered with leaves. If the truck hadn't been there, they probably would have walked right by it.

And as if to confirm that this was, indeed, the source of the shouting, they heard it again, closer, now. A dog barked. But it didn't sound like an angry bark. A happy bark.

Callie took a couple of steps down the drive, then stopped. Children laughing. That's got to be a good sign, right? She looked at Samantha and nodded, held tight to Jake's leash, and pulled him a little closer.

Side by side they followed the narrow drive. The trees were much closer together, the foliage thicker here, and the scant light that managed to find its way through was hazy and gray.

The voices were clearer now. Two, maybe three children. No adult voices. Callie had mixed feelings about that. If there were adults, that meant grown-ups would be in charge, and she could go back to being a kid. She might not have to be in charge, to make decisions no fifteen-year-old should have to make. But then again, if there *were* adults— her mind drifted back to the Clown Man's living room— it could be bad.

A narrow road led off to the left, but they stayed on the main driveway which widened a bit and came around a bend into a clearing surrounding a large, white house. The house was big and broad, with two stories and lots of windows. It had once been white, but now the paint was peeling in many spots, and the roof had bare, dark patches where shingles were missing. One of the upstairs windows was broken and patched with a piece of plywood. All of the other windows were covered with sheets of clear plastic, stapled or nailed in place.

A dilapidated barn, the red fading to dull orange, sat farther back. Beside it, a metal shed leaned drunkenly. Directly in front of the garage was a large fire pit, now extinguished.

Across the driveway a garage stood open, packed with old furniture, boxes, plastic milk crates, what looked like car parts and garden tools, and an old rust-covered pickup truck.

An ancient tractor, tires long gone, supported by railroad ties sat, forlorn and forgotten, in a patch of long grass.

Samantha nudged Callie and nodded to the right. A mud-spattered red pickup truck was parked off to the side, in front of the garage.

"Is that the one we saw yesterday?" Callie asked, looking ahead, trying to speak without moving her mouth, the way prisoners in old prison movies sometimes did.

"I'm not sure," Samantha whispered.

There were three children standing off to the side of the house. The older boy was tall and lanky with fine blonde hair that hung to his shoulders, and he looked to be about Callie's age. He held a green Nerf football against his chest. The other two were younger still, maybe five or six. Two ragged little boys. They had matching buzz cuts, their clothes baggy and soiled. Twins, maybe? It was hard to tell because all three of them were wearing white hospital masks across their noses and mouths. The older boy had drawn a bloody mouth filled with sharp, jagged teeth on his mask.

A black and white terrier-mix barked at newcomers, but his tail was wagging. A little brown dog cowered behind the three kids, growling. To add to the surreal scene, a white goat wandered behind them, nosing around the grass.

The older boy, without taking his eyes off Callie and Samantha, shouted, "Simon! Simon, come out here! Hurry!" He continued staring at them. The little boys moved closer to him, their eyes never leaving the newcomers.

"Hey there," Callie said, giving what she hoped was a reassuring wave.

No response from the three kids, except the two little boys, who moved closer together. The black and white dog gave up its barking and approached them, tail wagging ferociously. Callie took a step back while Samantha bent down and let it sniff her hand.

The front door opened, and another boy pushed through a sheet of plastic hanging from the frame and stepped out onto the porch. He was tall, older, and looked like a high school senior, maybe seventeen or eighteen, with unruly dark hair. He was clad in jeans and a black tee shirt. He was also wearing a hospital mask.

And he held a rifle, pointed right at them.

28

Callie, of course, had never had someone point a gun at her before. She felt helpless, sick to her stomach. *Is he going to kill us?* The cold dark eye of the rifle barrel stared, unblinking.

One of the little boys shouted, "Strangers, Simon! Strangers!"

The blonde kid turned and shoved the younger boy. "Quiet, idiot!"

"Put your hands up," Simon said, looking from Callie to Samantha and then Jake. His voice was soft, with no real threat in it, but he was pointing a rifle at them. How much more threat did he need?

She slid the loop of the leash over her wrist, and she put her hands in front of her, open, empty, and raised them. Her mind flashed back to her seventh-grade history teacher, who had told her class one day that the reason we (people) wave hello is basically to show strangers that we have no weapons, and that our hands are empty. Callie didn't know if this was true, but she sure hoped so. *Hello,* she thought crazily. *My hands are empty. Please don't kill me.*

She lifted her hands higher and said to Samantha, without looking at her, "Put your hands up. Show him your hands."

Simon stepped down to the driveway, the rifle never wavering. The other kids moved closer and clustered behind him.

"Who are you?" he demanded. "What do you want?"

"Yeah, what do you want?" the blond boy asked. He was almost strutting behind Simon now. His voice was mocking all confidence.

"We don't want anything," Callie said. Her heart was pounding, and her throat was so dry. "We were just walking on the road... and...and we heard your music."

Blondie turned to Simon. "They were spying on us!"

Simon shook his head. "Shut up for a minute, will ya?" He turned back to Callie. "'Walking?' Walking where?"

Callie didn't answer.

His gaze shifted from Callie to Samantha to Jake. He motioned at Jake with a nod. "What's his deal? Is he... like one of them? Can he talk?"

Callie paused. "He's fine. He's with us."

"I can see he's with you. And I can see he's not 'fine.' What are you doing with him? What's with the leash?"

"He's my brother," was all she said. What else was there to add?

That seemed to strike a chord with Simon. His gaze softened a bit and he nodded. And then, thankfully, he lowered the rifle. It was pointed *toward* them, but not *at* them. "You got any food?" Before Callie could respond, he turned and nodded to the others. "Cody, go see what they have."

The blonde boy, Cody, approached them. The little ones remained on the porch, whispering to each other.

Cody looked back at them. "Come on," he said.

The two young boys scrambled down the steps.

The black and white dog began to bark again.

"Max!" Simon said, eyes still on Callie, an edge to his voice. The dog stopped yapping and sat down at Simon's feet. Callie gave a silent thanks.

Callie felt a sharp tug on her backpack, and she lowered her arms enough to let one of the little ones pull it off her shoulders. He took it and dragged it back to Simon. The other one followed, lugging Samantha's backpack across the gravel driveway.

Cody tugged at Jake's backpack, but the chest straps were still connected, and all that he accomplished was yanking Jake backward, almost toppling him. The little brown dog ran around them both, yapping.

"Wait!" Callie said, moving toward him, lowering her arms.

"Stay where you are!" Simon said, raising the rifle again. Callie froze, helpless, watching as the kid tugged on the backpack until Jake fell backward onto the ground. The dog continued to bark but didn't look like it was going to attack. The blond boy knelt, and using his feet and lower legs, like he didn't want to touch Jake with his hands, rolled Jake over onto his stomach and began unsnapping and unzipping various compartments and pockets of the backpack. One of Jake's arms was pinned under him at an awkward angle.

"Stop! You're hurting him!" Callie cried.

The two little boys moved toward the stroller. Samantha moved in front of the baby. She bared her teeth at the nearer of the little kids, who faltered and backed off.

"Hey!" Cody stood up from ransacking Jake's backpack and advanced on Samantha, one of his hands balled into a fist. Callie watched with mounting terror as his other hand reached down toward a large knife in a leather sheath on his belt.

"Knock it off!" Simon said. "Cody!"

Cody froze. He turned to say something to Simon and Samantha seized the opportunity and grasped the handles of the stroller and rolled it away from him. The little ones looked at Simon, waiting.

Simon glared at Cody. He pointed at Jake. "Just take his backpack off, idiot." To Callie: "Don't worry. He wouldn't have hurt her. He just likes to show off. He's sorry. I'm sure."

Callie looked over at Cody, who didn't seem sorry in the least. He stared back at her, eyes narrowed over his monstrous mouth.

Simon motioned with the rifle barrel. "You take off his backpack. Don't do anything stupid."

Callie nodded, one eye on his gun. She thought about *her* gun in the stroller, and wondered what it would take to get to it before they found it. Because they would find it. And what then?

Callie squatted beside Jake and sat him up. She took his arm that had been twisted beneath him and gently stretched it out, watching to see if he grimaced or showed any discomfort. He seemed fine. But it was hard to tell. She unsnapped the clasps on the chest straps and looked up at Cody. "I told you to just unsnap them. You could have hurt him!"

Cody picked up the backpack, and scooped up the odds and ends he had already taken out: matches, ChapStick, a pocket knife, a granola bar, a water bottle. "What's it matter?" he sneered. His voice was low, so only she could hear. "It's not like he can feel anything. He's one of those retards."

"You shut up!" Callie said, rising to her feet. She looked down at him. "You just shut the hell up!"

She glared at Cody, who put on the classic "Who me?" look that teenagers have been using since Cain was asked if he knew where his brother was.

"Hey," Simon said from right behind her.

Callie whirled around.

Simon held up one hand as if to say, "Woah, slow down, missy," and smiled at her. At least his eyes smiled, kind of crinkling in the corners. And she could see the shape of his mouth smiling beneath his mask. She really saw him for the first time. His eyes were a clear, light blue. "I'm sorry about this," he said. "We just want to protect ourselves. We're not trying to hurt anyone."

Callie looked away and bent down to help Jake to his feet. "No, you're just trying to take our food."

"Look, we don't even know who you are," Simon said. "How do we know you aren't going to rob us or kill us?"

Callie looked at him. "Right. Because that's just what we look like; a bunch of people who will rob you and kill you!"

Simon smiled again. "Can't be too sure. The Lord works in mysterious ways."

Behind him, the two little ones were rummaging through Callie's backpack. A squeal of excitement and triumph. They raced over to Simon, a Snickers bar held in one grimy fist.

Simon looked down at them. "I'm in the middle of a conversation." His voice was cold.

The boys looked at the ground. "Sorry," one of them said.

"What is it?" Simon said.

A grubby hand held out a Snickers bar. A quiet voice, their eyes still looking at the ground. "Can we have it?"

Simon took the candy bar and held it out to Callie. "How about it? Can my sisters have this?"

Sisters? Callie gazed down at the two filthy children. *Those are girls?* She said, "Does it matter? You're going to take it, no matter what I say."

"You don't know that," Simon said. "But it would be awfully nice of you to offer."

Callie looked away.

Simon said, "They haven't had candy in weeks."

Callie shrugged. "Take it."

He tore the wrapper and opened the Snickers, took a small bite and held it up over the grasping hands of the two little girls. They jumped and stretched their arms out but couldn't quite reach it.

Simon laughed and lowered the candy, but a quick hand reached in and snatched it away. Cody ran up the steps and to the side of the house, his prize held high. "It's mine now, suckers!"

The two dogs ran after him, barking. The girls followed, crying out in indignation.

Callie continued probing Jake's arm, watching his face carefully for any sign of discomfort or pain. She looked up at Simon. "Can we go now?"

Simon put his hands on his hips and cocked his head. "What, you don't like us?"

"We don't like having guns pointed at us and people stealing our backpacks." Callie stood up and faced him. "Can we please just leave?" She tried to sound strong. She wanted to sound strong. She didn't feel strong. She was terrified. These kids, especially Cody, were wild. And wild was dangerous, especially these days.

Simon nodded agreeably and hoisted the rifle up onto his shoulder. "You're right. I'm sorry. But we can't take any chances. I got the kids to look after. You know what's out there, right?"

Callie nodded. She knew.

Simon picked her backpack and handed it to her. Callie took it warily. He asked. "Where are you headed? There's not much around here."

Callie wasn't about to tell him anything. "Portland," she lied. She shot a look at Samantha, who nodded once, then looked away.

The three kids came back around the side of the house. They were walking now, masks beneath their chins, much quieter, Cody leading the way. The little girls looked molli-fied, licking their fingers. *Their gross, dirty fingers, Callie* couldn't help thinking. They climbed onto the porch behind Simon. Cody sat on the railing, watching Callie. He pulled his mask back up, his narrowed eyes above the red, fanged cartoon mouth. She didn't like him. He made her nervous. His eyes were so pale and... dead looking.

Simon glanced at the girls, pointed at his mask, and they both fumbled theirs back on. He turned his attention back to Callie. "Portland. Are you walking the whole way?"

Callie nodded.

"How old are you?"

"Old enough," Callie said.

Simon laughed. "Okay, if you say so."

"So is that *your* baby?" Cody asked. Callie was beginning to hate him.

She glared at him. "I found him."

Cody walked over to the stroller, poked a finger in at the baby. Samantha flinched but didn't say anything. A tiny hand reached up and grasped Cody's finger. He jerked it away and returned to the porch.

"Good thing he's not one of those retards," Cody said. "Like him." He pointed at Jake.

Yes. Callie hated him.

Simon shushed Cody with a raised palm. "Did you know his parents?" But gently this time, not hostile.

Callie still didn't say anything. Just shook her head.

Simon looked into the distance, rubbing his chin. "Well, that was good of you to take him in. You'd think after something like...this happens, more people would work together. But humankind is flawed. It's in our nature." He looked at Samantha and Ryan, then Callie. He pushed his hair back and looked around at the sky, the farmhouse, all of them. "You know, there's a reason for all of this."

"There is?" Callie said.

"Sure is," Simon said. "It's all part of a plan. His plan."

She looked around. Who was he talking about? She pointed at Cody. "*His* plan?" What the heck were they talking about?

Simon, smiling patiently, said, "The Lord has a plan for all of us. You think it was an accident you found your way here?"

"All part of His plan," Cody nodded.

Callie didn't know quite what to say at this, so she kept her mouth shut.

Holding the rifle under one arm, Simon clapped his hands together, like he had come to a decision. "Why don't you guys get your stuff and come on up to the house," he said." I was just about to serve dinner."

Dinner. As in a meal. When was the last time they had a real meal, not just scrounging out of cans or plastic bags? Have some dinner, and then be on their way. Maybe these guys weren't so bad.

But she didn't really believe that.

29

Simon led the way into the house. The little girls carried Samantha's backpack, each one holding a strap, as she and Callie maneuvered the stroller up the porch steps. Cody stayed at the railing, watching, not even offering to help.

Callie saw one of the little girls filching a granola bar from Samantha's backpack. The girl caught her looking and froze. Callie put her fingers to her lips, *shh,* and smiled and winked. The dirty little girl grinned back, her cheeks rising beneath her mask, and the granola bar disappeared into a pocket.

Callie longed for a chance to get the gun out of the stroller, but not with Cody there. She didn't want to leave him with the stroller out here, afraid he would go poking around and find it. But what could she do?

Samantha lifted Ryan out. The little girls approached her, reaching tentative hands to touch him. The girls seemed alright, Callie thought. And Simon, too. But not Cody.

As if to further prove her point, when she walked Jake

up the steps to the front door, Cody swung off the railing and blocked her path.

"No way," he said. "The retard's not coming inside." He puffed out his chest, as if daring her to do something. "No way."

Callie fought the urge to smack him right across his smug jerk face but realized that wouldn't help matters. "He's not retarded," she said, enunciating carefully as if talking to someone who was, in fact, mentally challenged." I will take care of him. You won't even notice he's there."

Cody shook his head. "No way. He has to stay outside. He might be... um..." he struggled for the word. "You know, um...where we could get sick from him?"

"Contagious?" Callie asked.

Cody nodded. "Yeah. How do we know we can't catch it?"

"It?" Callie asked. She knew what he wanted, but he was acting like a jerk, and she wasn't going to make it easy for him. "'It' what?"

He motioned with his hands, trying to express physically what he couldn't verbally. "This whole thing. With ... with that weird noise, and the people changing. How do we know we won't catch it from him?"

"Because it's not a disease, you doofus!" Callie said and stepped around him. "It was caused by that noise, or whatever that was."

Cody shrugged. "Maybe, maybe not." He slid smoothly back so he stood between her and the front door. "But he's not coming in."

"Fine," Callie said. "Then we'll just leave." She looked over at Samantha, one step behind her. "Okay?"

Samantha looked miserable but nodded.

Simon pushed aside the plastic sheet and poked his

head through the doorway. He was wiping his hands on a kitchen towel.

Simon looked at Callie, then at Cody. "Everything okay? We're just about ready to sit down."

Callie and Cody both started speaking at once. Simon listened as best he could, his eyes shifting back and forth between them, and held up his hands.

"Stop," he said. He turned and pointed at Cody. "You don't make the decisions around here. Now get inside and keep an eye on the stew. Don't let it burn."

"But she—" he threw a hand out, pointing at Callie.

"Now," Simon said. He rose up to his full height, standing over Cody, who, even though he was also standing tall, stood several inches shorter.

Cody muttered, "She's gonna get it," under his breath, scowled at Callie, and stomped inside. One of the little girls stood in the doorway and Cody shoved her roughly out of the way.

Simon waited until Cody was completely inside. Then he turned to her. "He gets a little full of himself sometimes."

Callie didn't respond. She wanted to say, "He's *full of something*, but wisely, she held her tongue.

Simon cleared his throat. "The thing is, we would really prefer it if he stayed outside."

Callie shook her head to make sure she had heard correctly. "What? Why? There's nothing wrong with—"

"He's been corrupted," Simon said. "His soul is not his own."

This was unbelievable. Callie closed her eyes and lowered her head. Why was everything so hard?

She opened her eyes, glared at Simon, took Jake's arm, and gently turned him around. "Okay. That's it. We're leaving. Samantha, can you get the stroller?"

Samantha nodded, her face downcast, and placed Ryan in the stroller. Ryan began fighting and crying. He was hungry. They were all hungry.

This sucks, Callie thought. *This really, really sucks.*

"Wait! Wait!" Simon moved down the steps, and then he too, stood in her way. "You don't want to go out there at night."

"Well, we aren't going to stay here," Callie said. "Not unless you let him come inside. If you want to shoot us, then I guess that's what you'll have to do."

Simon held a hand, finger raised. *Just hold on one second.* He looked at Jake, then at Callie. "What if he stays on the porch? Just right outside the front door. We can even leave it open. The dining room is just inside."

"There's nothing wrong with him!" Callie said. "I've been with him every second since It started, and I'm fine."

Simon nodded. "I know," he said. "I get it. I really do. He's your brother. And nothing is more important than family. But, he's not really your brother anymore." He pointed to his chest. "Not on the inside. Not where it counts. Only the Lord knows what really happened to him. I sure don't. Do you?"

Callie shook her head. Her eyes burned with angry tears.

Simon said, "We don't know where they go or why. We just know they aren't the people they once were. They change into something else."

He knelt down in front of her and reattached a piece of the plastic sheet to the door frame.

"Just right outside the door," he said. "You'll be able to see him the whole time. It would make Cody—all of us, more comfortable."

Callie looked at Samantha, who was kneeling beside

Ryan, talking softly to him. Her face was wan, and she had dark circles under her eyes. She was worn out. Samantha caught Callie's eye and nodded. "Please," she mouthed.

Simon pushed the plastic sheet aside and Callie leaned in and glanced around the front room. It was dark and cluttered, and the smell was stronger. She wrinkled her nose and turned her head.

"Oh, yeah," said Simon. "It kind of stinks. We still haven't cleaned out the refrigerator. I guess we're so used to it we don't smell it." He snapped his fingers. "I'll tell you what. I'll open the windows in the dining room so we can air it out. How's that sound?"

Callie nodded, and holding a hand over her nose, ducked back in for another look. She couldn't see anything through the darkened interior, just the dim shapes of furniture and boxes, but she could make out the end of a big wooden table in the next room. She pointed to the chair at the end of the table and turned to Simon. "Can I sit there? So I can keep an eye on him?"

Simon nodded. "Absolutely."

"Okay," Callie said. "Just for dinner."

"Great," Simon said, clapping his hands. He went back inside, turned, and said, "Dinner will be ready in a few minutes. Hope you're hungry." He winked and was gone, the plastic sheet covering the doorway waving after him.

30

Callie held Jake's hand as they walked around the front yard. "Remember that one time when it rained so much the school got flooded? Even the front office? And they had to give us a week off?" Jake, if he remembered, gave no response. "And you let me help build that dam in the gutter? I mostly just stood and watched, but it was so cool helping my big brother." She smiled at the vague memory of standing on the sidewalk in the pouring rain wearing her pink raincoat, the hood up, holding a stick as Jake and his friend Sam clogged the sewer with branches and mud. "You and Sam plugged up the sewer and the whole street flooded. Dad was so mad." She couldn't help but smile at the memory. But a glance over at the porch and the smile disappeared. At some point, Cody had come back out and returned to his seat on the porch railing. She wondered if he had been sent out to keep an eye on them. He didn't say anything when she looked at him, but she could feel his eyes following her as she strode back up the steps. She wanted to show him he didn't intimidate her.

Callie slid a wicker chair in front of the door. She tied the leash to the arm of the chair.

"Gotta make sure the retard don't get away, right?" Cody asked.

Callie ignored him. She made sure the chair was in view of the table in the dining room and sat him down in it.

"Does he ever try to just walk off? Like those other ones?"

Callie thought about Jake at the sliding door at home, and then again at the empty house the other night. She shook her head.

"Then why is he tied up?"

She tugged on the leash, making sure it was fastened securely. She wrapped it around the arm of the chair.

Cody jumped off the railing and stared down the driveway. He turned to Callie. "Where do you think they're going?" His voice had lost some of its edge. A genuine question.

Callie paused before responding. She could be hostile and give him a smartass answer, or she could engage him, maybe get to know him. "Probably to get away from you," she said and moved over beside Samantha as Cody muttered to himself and stomped his way down the porch steps. Callie couldn't help but notice that Samantha, who was busily changing Ryan's diaper, was smiling.

"Are we staying here tonight?" Samantha asked as she buttoned up Ryan's pajamas and tickled his fat tummy. He giggled and pushed her hands away, smiling his toothless smile.

"I'm not sure," Callie said. "I think so. That okay with you?"

Samantha nodded. "I'm so tired, and I would love to sleep in a bed," she said. She looked around and spoke in a soft voice. "But they are kind of weird." She glanced over at Cody, who was standing in the driveway chucking rocks at the trees. "Especially him. He's a jerk."

Callie nodded. "And what's with the masks? How do they eat dinner?"

Samantha smiled again, which made Callie happy. The poor kid had been through so much. *We all have,* she thought.

One of the girls (it was still hard to believe there was a *girl* underneath all that grime and filth) pushed aside the plastic sheet and said in a quiet voice, eyes downcast, "Dinner's ready."

Callie put a hand on Jake's shoulder, feeling a twinge of guilt. "We'll just be right inside," she told him.

Samantha set Ryan in his stroller, and together, they pushed aside the plastic sheet and stepped into the dim house. It took a few seconds for her eyes to adjust, as the only light was provided by a half dozen candles placed around the entry and dining room. But the smell of food took center stage. The odor was overwhelming. The delicious, almost-forgotten smell of cooked meat. Callie and Samantha exchanged smiles. But beneath the enticing smell of cooking was something else. Something familiar.

I know that smell, Callie thought. She glanced back at the front door. Cody was leaning against the wall beside an open window. He was watching them. Her, probably.

Simon came in from the kitchen, a dish towel lying across one shoulder, holding a large metal pot, which he placed on the table. Steam wafted from the open top. Some kind of stew. It smelled even more fantastic up close. He wiped his hands off on the dish towel and motioned for Callie and Samantha to sit down.

"Please. Have a seat." He turned back to the kitchen. "Girls! Let's go!"

The little girls rushed in, one carrying a basket of rolls, the other with a two-liter bottle of Sprite. They put their burdens on the table and ran back to the kitchen and returned, one carrying a glass pitcher of (was that milk?) and the other with a stack of bowls.

Cody slunk in behind Callie and pulled out a chair and plopped himself down. Simon took the seat at the far head of the table. Callie, after exchanging a look with Samantha, took the opposite seat, closest to the front door where she could keep an eye on Jake. And make a run for it if it came to that. She took the cloth napkin off the plate and unfolded it and put it on her lap. Her mother would be proud, she thought and smiled a little. Samantha sat beside her, with Ryan's stroller right behind her. The girls took their seats.

Cody and the little girls looked at Simon. He nodded, pulled his hospital mask up over his head, and placed it on the table beside his plate. Cody slid his mask down to his neck, but the girls took theirs completely off.

"Let us join hands," Simon said. Callie took Samantha's hand in her left, gave it a reassuring squeeze (*I'm right here),* and with her right, took the hand of the little girl to her side. It was sticky. She made a mental note not to eat with that hand.

Simon began speaking, in a clear, steady voice. "Father, we have gathered to share a meal in Your honor. Thank You for putting us together as family, along with our new friends," At this, he looked at Callie and Samantha and smiled. "... and thank You for this food. Bless it to our bodies,

Lord. We thank you for all of the gifts you've given to those around this table. Help each member of our family use these gifts to your glory. Guide our hearts and minds through these trying times and steer us to Your purpose for our lives, until we are delivered unto You. In Jesus's Name, Amen."

"Amen," Cody said, his voice loud and steady.

The little girls mumbled something that might have been "Amen."

"Amen," Callie said, feeling, rather than seeing, Cody's eyes on her.

"Alrighty," Simon said with a broad grin. Mr. Charming was back. "Who's hungry?"

The two girls raised their hands. Samantha started to raise hers, but stopped and placed it back in her lap. Simon ladled some stew into a bowl and passed it to Cody, who made a big show of hawking up a big loogie then pretending to spit in the bowl, and looking up to see who else thought it was funny. No one did.

"That's yours," Simon said without missing a beat and passed the next bowl to one of the little girls.

For several minutes, the only sound was the clink of spoons on bowls, chewing, swallowing, and the occasional request for something to be passed. The stew was hearty; full of meat, onion, carrots, and peas. Callie couldn't remember anything tasting so good-- and the milk - the milk was so good, thick and creamy, almost like a milkshake.

"So where did you say you were from again?" Simon asked.

Callie swallowed and wiped away a milk mustache. "We didn't," she said.

Simon looked taken aback. "Okay. Sorry. Just trying to make conversation."

"Have you met any other people?" Callie asked, trying to take control of the conversation.

"A few," Simon said. "But mostly the... other ones. Corrupted, like your brother. They're always heading west, toward the coast."

Callie ignored the "your brother" remark. "Do you know where they're going? Or why?"

Simon shook his head. "We don't go too far from the house. We really have pretty much everything we need. We have a good-sized garden out back. We're self-sufficient. Especially since we got our cow. The Lord has truly blessed us."

"You have a cow?" Callie asked.

Simon grinned again. He was *very* handsome, she thought. "We do. She belonged to a neighbor, but when..." He gestured at the ceiling." ... All this went down, Cody brought her back here. We figured out how to milk her, and I plan on learning how to make cheese."

Simon pointed a spoon at Samantha." What about you? You're awfully quiet. What's your story?"

Samantha glanced up at Simon, then back at her plate, and shrugged. "Nothing much."

"So...is this your house?" Callie asked, her voice sounding a bit too loud.

Cody narrowed his eyes. "What's that supposed to mean? You think we stole it?"

Callie said," No, no, I was just wondering. Like how all four of you didn't get...get..."

"Turned into retards?" Cody asked.

"Enough," Simon said. He turned to Callie and leaned forward on his elbows. His voice was soft. "Who are we to question the Lord's plan? He spared the four of us for a reason. He sent you to us for a reason. Our place is to wait and do His bidding."

Callie glanced at Samantha, then Cody, and back to Simon. "His bidding?"

The little girl on Callie's right shifted in her chair.

Cody leaned forward. He was smiling, his voice shrill with excitement. "He wants us to create a new Eden."

"A new *what*?" Callie wasn't sure what she had heard.

"A new Eden," Simon repeated. He spread his arms. "What better place than here? We have everything we need." He looked back and forth from Callie to Samantha. "And now that you're here, it's so much more clear. We will be the new Adams and Eves."

Callie stood up suddenly, nearly toppling her chair. "I think we should leave," she said and threw her napkin on the table. "Thank you for dinner, but we need to get going."

Simon stood up so fast that his hip slammed into the table, rattling the bowls and glasses. "Wait!" he said to Callie. "You can't leave now. It's not safe."

"We'll take our chances," Callie said. "We've done it before."

"You're not going anywhere," Cody said. He slid in front of the doorway.

31

Simon shot a glance at Cody, and said, "Stop being so dramatic." He stood up and sighed. "He's right, though. We can't let you leave at night. It wouldn't be safe."

"Can't, or won't?" Callie asked.

Simon shook his head. "You're making a mistake. There are worse things than the corrupted people walking around at night. You'll be safe here."

"Not with him we won't," Callie said, scowling at Cody. "No way am I sleeping in the same house as him."

Cody smiled around his plastic cup of Sprite. "They don't know," he said.

"Know what?" Callie said. She looked from one to the other.

Simon glanced at Cody. "Is that thing still in the back of the truck?"

Cody nodded. "It's a real ugly one."

Simon turned toward Callie and Samantha. "Follow me. You need to see what's out there."

The girls glanced at each other but stood up and

followed Simon outside. Callie stopped on the porch beside Jake.

"You can bring him," Simon nodded.

Callie stood Jake up and they followed Simon's flashlight toward the red pickup. Cody trailed behind them. Simon unlatched the tailgate and let it fall open. A large oblong bundle, about six feet long, wrapped in a black tarp and duct tape lay in the truck bed.

"Hold this," he said, handing Callie his flashlight. Simon climbed into the bed of the truck and tugged at the bundle. He looked over at Cody. "Are you going to help or not?"

"I got it in there by myself," Cody said.

"Just help me, "Simon said.

Cody moved to the tailgate, and together they turned and tugged the shape off the bed of the truck. Cody stood back as it thudded on the ground. Simon jumped down and they dragged the object away from the truck, toward the fire pit.

"Stop here," said Simon. He knelt beside the bundle, which was now, to Callie's eyes, looking uncomfortably human-shaped. Simon looked up. "This is why you don't want to be walking around at night." He took out a knife and cut through the duct tape and reached down and pulled the tarp away and stood up.

Callie gasped and stepped back. Samantha grabbed her arm.

The figure was, or had been, human. Callie wasn't sure what it was now. It looked like a man, but the head was... wrong. It was too long, the forehead abnormally tall. The hair was patchy, long in some spots, but in other areas, the scalp was exposed. The blank, dead eyes were sunken and overlarge, almost too big for the face. The mouth was open, showing toothless gums and a thin, gray tongue.

There was a blood-stained hole in his chest.

"What is that?" said Callie, her voice a whisper.

Cody smiled. "That's nothing. Check this out." He tugged the rest of the tarp away, exposing a shoulder that led into a long, fleshy tentacle. No hand, no fingers, just dozens of tiny, mouth-like suckers.

Simon motioned at the darkness around them. "This is what's waiting out there. In the dark."

"But what is it?" Callie said. "What happened to him? Is it a man?"

"Used to be," Cody said. He glanced up at Callie. "He was like your brother. Then...this..."

Callie turned to Simon. "What does he mean?"

Simon nodded. "It's true. Something happens to them. We're not sure what, but some of them change. Turn into this." He nodded at the monstrous form.

"No," Callie said. "No, that's not true. You're lying." Her voice grew louder, and she realized, dimly, that she was shouting.

Simon shook his head. "No. We're not lying."

"But he's fine!" she said, motioning toward Jake. "Look at him."

"Closer to the ocean. That's where we find most of them," Simon said. "So it's a good thing you're heading inland."

Callie watched as Cody wrapped the misshapen figure back in the tarp and dragged it toward the fire pit.

Samantha moved close to her. "Don't listen to them. It's not true. Jake won't turn."

Callie said, "But what if it is true? What if--" She shook her head, disgusted with herself for even thinking about it.

They walked back to the house in silence. Callie sat Jake

in his chair on the porch and stood beside him until Samantha took her by the hand and led her back inside.

The dining table was clear. The girls had been busy. The sounds of dishes clinking, and childish laughter came from the kitchen.

"Be reasonable," Simon said, sitting back down. "Stay with us. We have plenty of room."

"And you'll let us leave in the morning?" Callie asked.

"If that's what you want, "Simon said. "We'd prefer that you stay here, but we're not going to hold you against your will."

Callie looked at Samantha, then over at the baby in his stroller, now awake and peering around the room with wondering eyes.

Then she caught a glimpse of Jake. Jake, all alone on the porch. A wave of guilt swept over her. Callie turned on Simon. "What about my brother?" She pointed at Jake. "Can he sleep in the house too?"

No response from Simon.

"Let 'em sleep in the barn," Cody said, walking in, accompanied by the smell of smoke.

Once they got used to the odor, the barn wasn't so bad. It was actually better than the smell in the house.

Simon, wearing his mask, held up a kerosene lantern, letting them get a good look at their accommodations. Cody stood just outside the barn entrance, holding the rifle. He ignored Callie when she asked him why he needed the rifle just to walk them to the barn.

The board walls appeared sturdy, although there were

some gaps and holes here and there, but the structure was still solid and safe.

The cow lay in one of the stalls. She looked up curiously when they came in but decided they weren't a threat and turned away.

The old rusted-out skeleton of a tractor rested against one wall and some ancient leather harnesses and farm tools hung from various nails and hooks. And cobwebs, lots of cobwebs. And she heard a bird fluttering around in the eaves.

But all in all, it wasn't too bad. It was relatively warm, and the walls would keep out the worst of the chill.

Callie shrugged. It was better than nothing. Definitely better than the jam stand.

"Is this really what you want?" Simon asked.

"We'll be okay," she said." We've slept in worse places."

He nodded at that, resigned now. "Okay. But it's going to be cold. Are you sure you have enough blankets?"

"We'll be fine," Callie said. She just wanted to get this over with. Get to sleep, wake up, and leave. First thing.

She put a hand on Jake's shoulder and gave him a gentle nudge forward. He shuffled into a stall. She helped him sit down.

From behind her, Simon said, "Are you sure you don't want to come back in for a bit? Just for dessert? The girls made chocolate pudding."

Callie looked past him, at Cody standing in the doorway, holding on to one of the big sliding doors.

Callie asked, her voice bright and innocent, "Can my brother come? He loves chocolate pudding."

Simon scowled, turned away, and exited the barn. The big door slid shut with a hollow boom.

"See you in the morning," Cody jeered from the other

side of the heavy door, then there was the sound of metal rasping over metal and the solid click of a padlock.

Callie and Samantha looked at each other and Callie jumped to her feet and ran to the door, stumbling over a bucket in the darkness. and tugged at the door handle. It moved only a few inches, then jerked to a stop. She was able to fit her arm through the gap and felt around, grabbed onto a chain, and tugged. It was solid, with no give at all. She pulled her arm back in and pounded on the big wooden door. The blows boomed around the empty barn but had no impact other than disturbing the bird in the rafters.

"Hey!" she called. "Hey, let us out!"

"Sweet dreams," Cody's voice called out mockingly. It sounded fainter, farther away.

"You fucker!" Callie shouted. "You assholes! Let us out of here!"

If he heard, he didn't respond.

"Shit," Callie said, kicking the door.

32

Callie went over to Samantha. "I'm sorry. This is my fault. But I couldn't stay in that house any longer. I know they'd make us leave Jake outside, alone. I just couldn't."

Samantha nodded but didn't say anything. Just closed her eyes and nodded.

Callie reached out in the dark and clasped Samantha's hand. "Don't worry. I'm going to get us out of here."

Samantha allowed Callie to hold her hand.

At least she didn't pull away. That's something, Callie thought.

They made a kind of camp in one of the stalls. With her flashlight, Samantha found some old horse blankets that weren't too musty, and she and Callie shook them out and laid them down on the floor. Jake was already asleep, lying on his side against the wall. Callie was about to lay a blanket over him, but she stopped, clutching the blanket to her chest, and peered at him curiously. *Was he changing? Like*

that ... thing in the truck? He looked fine. She hadn't seen anything-

"What's wrong?" Samantha asked.

Callie shook her head. "Nothing. I was just thinking about what they said about how some of the people ... change." She turned to Samantha. "Does he look ... normal to you?"

Samantha peered down at Jake. She shrugged. "I guess. I haven't known him that long. But he looks fine."

Callie nodded and laid the blanket over Jake's shoulders.

"We can still have dessert," she said, reaching into her backpack and pulling out two cans of fruit cocktail. "I didn't want anything those two little girls made. Did you see how dirty they were?" She made a disgusted face and was pleased to see Samantha grin.

They sat down and by the light of her camping lantern, Callie opened one of the cans using a hand can opener.

A scrabbling sound from one side of the barn. A creak. The cow lowed softly. Callie stood up. *It better not be that little shit, Cody.*

A board swung to the side, just slightly, letting in pale yellow moonlight.

Callie approached the door, flashlight in hand. The gun was still in the stroller, and she thought about going back to get it.

She turned back to find the little girls standing there. The taller one was holding a lantern. They were each carrying a small plastic bowl with a spoon sticking out.

"This is for you," said one of the girls, holding out her bowl. Chocolate pudding.

Callie took the two bowls and said, "Thank you. Does Simon know you brought this to us?"

The taller girl shook her head. They both looked frightened.

"Are you going to be okay?" Callie asked. "Will you get in trouble?"

The taller girl shook her head again. "They're watching TV. Simon fell asleep. We're real quiet." She turned to her sister. "We have to go."

As the girls turned to go, Callie said "Hey, wait a second." She handed her bowl to Samantha and squatted down and rummaged through Jake's backpack. She pulled out a bag of M and M's. She held it out to the girls, and said, "You keep this quiet. Don't let Cody have any."

They nodded, and whispering excitedly to each other, made their way out of the barn, swinging the board back in place.

Callie and Samantha ate quickly, and scraped the bowls with their spoons, savoring every bit of the pudding, grinning at each other. Callie woke Jake up and served him a spoonful and Samantha gave some to Ryan, who strained against the belt in his stroller and fussed for more. Samantha spoke softly to him and smashed up a peach slice from the fruit cocktail and popped it into his mouth. Ryan smiled his goofy baby smile at Samantha, who kissed his cheek.

Callie watched, grinning herself, feeling a pang of ... what? Jealousy? If she was jealous, what was she jealous of, exactly? It was a relief to have someone else take care of Ryan. Wasn't it?

Callie couldn't sleep. She was too wound up from the events of the afternoon. That man-thing. Would that happen to Jake? Or were they trying to scare her?

She stood up and walked over to the loose board, swung it as far as she could. She squeezed and forced her way through, scraping her back in the process, and finally stood outside. She glanced back at the narrow opening.

Samantha could get through no problem, and Ryan, but not Jake. He was too big. She'd need to take him out through the door.

She would need the keys.

She shimmied back through, into the barn, twisting and turning her body, and walked over to their sleeping area. She looked around. Shadows and bars of light through the cracks in the boards gave her enough light to see.

"Samantha," she whispered. Nothing. Just the sound of breathing. Okay. She'd be back in five minutes. No reason to wake her up. She grabbed the two bowls, and then picked up her flashlight. You never knew.

As she approached the house, she saw that one of the windows was lit with a blue, flickering light. She remembered the girls saying something about watching TV. *Must be nice.*

She climbed the porch and knocked on the front door. No response. She knocked harder. She could hear faint, muffled music. She tried the knob. The door was unlocked, and she stepped inside, pushing past the plastic sheet.

She took a good look around. Overstuffed chairs and a coffee table covered with cardboard boxes and stacks of old magazines and paperback books. Empty Mason jars and milk bottles stacked on the floor. And was that—yes, a stuffed raccoon stood on the credenza. All this crap and none of it meant anything anymore.

Dim light and sound came from further back in the house, past the dining room. Callie kicked a chair, stumbled, and moved against the wall. She thought of Simon with the rifle. Or worse, Cody.

Nothing happened. No one came into the room, guns blazing. Just the music from the TV. Familiar music. She knew that song. A Disney movie, but she wasn't sure which one.

She stepped away from the wall and moved deeper into the house. The odor of cooked meat was disappearing beneath the smell of mold and rot and stale cigarette smoke. The dining room. A long table in the center. Several chairs surrounded it. They were all empty.

The smell worsened. How had she not noticed it before? How could they have eaten with that smell? She held her hand to her nose. She knew that smell. She moved through the dining room. Simon's rifle leaned against the wall beneath a painting of a horse.

Callie cut her light and peeked into the next room. The TV was small, the old-fashioned tube kind, not even a flat-screen. It was on a table against the far wall. The volume was cranked so high it was almost distorted, and the twins bounced on the couch and sang along with the misunderstood princess. Simon sat in an easy chair in the corner, staring at the TV. But it didn't look like he was watching. His eyes were glazed, unfocused and she jerked back.

"Hey!" a voice shouted in her ear.

Callie screamed and dropped the bowls, and her heart sank at the sound of the porcelain shattering on the hardwood floor. She whirled around.

Cody stood, facing her, grinning. His hospital mask hung around his neck.

The music and singing shut off, the sudden silence making her feel more exposed.

Simon rose from his chair, holding the remote in one hand. He tossed it on the couch. The twins were staring, open-mouthed. Simon turned to them. "Put your masks on." They complied, eyes wide and frightened.

Simon approached Callie. His shadow was long and distorted in the unhealthy blue light of the frozen image on the TV. "What's going on? What are you doing in our house?"

Cody put a hand on her shoulder and shoved her back against the wall. "She wants to get us sick. She wants to take our house."

Callie swallowed. "I—I just came in to bring back your bowls." A stupid excuse, but it was all she could think of. She looked at the shards on the floor. "I'm sorry, I didn't—"

Simon stared at her. No sign of the smile no; that charming young man from earlier was gone. "What are you doing in our house? How did you get out of the barn?"

"I wanted to say thank you. For the pudding. Nobody answered when I knocked."

"She broke in!" Cody said, and reached out and shoved her again. Harder. He was getting worked up, smiling a dangerous smile. "You know what we do to trespassers?"

Simon looked confused. "What pudding? I never—" He turned to the two girls, who were sitting together on the couch.

"Did you take food out to them?" His voice shook with anger. The two girls hugged each other and sank into the couch.

Oh shit, Callie thought.

Simon closed his eyes and took a deep breath. He looked down at the pieces of broken ceramic. "That's Mom's favorite bowl." He spun back around and faced the girls, taking a step toward them. "You used Mom's favorite bowls? You idiots! Why would you do that?"

The little girls clutched one another even more tightly.

Simon spun to face Callie. His blue eyes were clouded with anger. A darkness he hadn't shown until now.

Cody held Callie's collar in one sweaty fist and reached behind him with his other hand. He came out holding a brutal, long hunting knife. His smile widened. Triumphant. Malicious.

Callie thought of Samantha and Ryan. *Oh shit. What will happen to them?* And Jake. Who would take care of Jake?

Cody pressed the tip of the knife under her chin and ran it down her throat along the front of her shirt. "Not so tough now, are you?"

Callie stepped back, but there was nowhere to go. Her back was pressed up against the wall. She waited for Simon to tell Cody to stop, that that was enough. But he didn't. He folded his arms and watched.

"Wait," Callie said. "Just -- just wait a minute."

"Too late for that," Cody snarled. "You probably infected us all." He reached out and ran his fingers through her hair. He smiled, and for the first time, she was close enough to smell his meaty breath and saw that his teeth were yellowed, his gums brown and blue.

She gagged and turned her head. Cody slid his hand down the back of her head and along the back of her neck, tugging at her hair.

"You're kind of pretty," he said. His hand crawled down her back.

Images of her grandmother. Her parents, Ryan's mother, dead on the kitchen floor. The Clown Man, the monster in the back of the truck, and her parents, all flashed through

Callie's mind. She had been through so much. And she was going to let this little piece of shit stop her? Enough.

Callie lashed out, her right knee pistoning up, catching Cody right in the crotch. His eyes rolled up and he exhaled with a soft, "Oof," like they did in comic books. He stumbled back, dropping the knife, his hands going to his groin. She thought for a split second about picking it up, but Simon was moving toward her.

Callie turned and ran for the front door. She tore around a corner, her shoes sliding on the hardwood, and too late, realized she was headed the wrong way. The front door was behind her. Simon, his heavy footsteps thudding closer, was behind her. Ahead of her, a long, dark hallway straight ahead, and a staircase on the right, leading up to utter blackness. No way in hell was she going up there. She pounded down the hallway, Simon's footsteps right behind her.

Through the darkness and the narrow shafts of light that shone through the cracks in the sheet of plywood nailed to the window at the end of the hall, she could make out the dim shape of a door. If she could reach it, lock herself in, and go for a window... if it was unlocked ... she couldn't think of that.

Her left thigh crashed into something hard. A bright flash of pain ran up her leg. She spun around, nearly losing her balance. Clattering wood and breaking glass behind her. She kept running. Then a stumbling, from behind her, thumping, more wood banging on the floor, and Simon roared in pain and anger.

She put her head down and reached the door at a dead sprint, grabbed the handle, and turned. It opened and she threw herself inside, slammed the door and felt for the latch, and clicked it locked. She leaned her forehead against the door, breathing hard, fighting back tears. *I have to get out of here. Samantha and the others are alone. I have to get* us *out of here.*

The knob rattled, then a pounding on the door.

It was an old house, with old wooden doors. It was strong and solid. It would hold. But not forever.

The smell was bad here, and she resisted the urge to gag. Something sweet, flowers, maybe cut the edge of it, but there was something sour and old beneath the flowers.

The pounding at the door stopped.

Callie flicked her flashlight on and took in her surroundings. She was in a spare bedroom, cramped with cluttered bookshelves, chairs, and an old roll-top desk shoved against one wall. Cardboard boxes were piled up against the far wall, partially blocking the bottom of a window. She shut off her flashlight and shoved it in her back pocket.

She moved to the window and pushed apart the curtains. They wouldn't separate, so she just tore them down, the flimsy curtain rod bending and giving way before clattering on the floor. She turned her head as dust cascaded onto her face.

She rubbed her eyes and shook her head, then picked up one of the cartons covering the window. It was heavy, and she felt the contents shift and the bottom give. She slid it back onto the other boxes before it fell apart.

A solid kick at the door resounded through the room.

Several sheets of plywood covered the window. Yellow light shone through the spaces between the boards. It looked loose.

"Screw it," she said, and leaned in and tugged at one side of the plywood. It didn't budge. "Open this door!" Cody screamed, his voice now high-pitched and frantic. The pounding was harder and faster. They were going to get in. It was only a matter of when.

She put her foot up against the wall and pulled harder. There was a screech of nails, and the left side of the plywood pulled away from the window. She yanked harder and the whole sheet came down. She shoved it off to the side and attacked the pile of boxes.

Using both arms, she leaned it and swept aside the top box and it hit the floor with a heavy thud. She pushed another box onto the floor and another, then—there! Moonlight revealed the silver latch on the lower sill. She grasped it and twisted. It wouldn't budge.

"No!" she said, grabbing her flashlight. It was worse than being painted shut. Dark, metallic circles dotted the frame. The window was nailed shut.

33

A solid slam against the door, hard enough to rock it in its frame. A crack appeared above the knob. She had no time to waste.

Callie looked around for something to break the window. Something. Anything. *There.* A lamp on the nightstand, beside the bed, which held...a body. *Of course. Of course, these kids would have a corpse in a bed.* Her mind was fragmented, part of her horrified at the figure on the bed, another part desperate to escape this room.

A dead woman lay on top of the bed, her dark hair fanned over the pillow. Her gray, flabby arms lay folded over her chest. Her gnarled and twisted fingers held fresh flowers.

No time to freak out, Callie told herself, although she wanted to scream.

Another thud, and a louder crack. She risked a quick look. The frame was splitting on the right side of the door. She could see faint light shining through.

She grabbed the bedside lamp. It was almost torn from her hand as the cord refused to come out of the wall.

She yanked harder, and it pulled free. She turned her head away, shut her eyes, swung the lamp by the base, and shattered the window. She shoved the lamp into the window frame and scraped it around, knocking out all the shards of glass so she wouldn't cut herself. She threw the lamp on the floor and grabbed a handful of the comforter from the foot of the bed. One of the dead woman's shoes got caught up in it and Callie shoved the foot away. It moved, but barely.

Another thud as someone slammed up against the door, accompanied by a muffled shout.

Callie turned and tugged on the comforter with all her might, twisting her body, pushing with her legs. It came loose. But the body came along with it, tumbling to the floor, the flowers scattered beside it.

Callie threw the comforter over the bottom of the window frame and as quickly as she could, threw herself over and out. It was a bit of a drop to the ground, and she landed awkwardly, twisting her left knee, and falling onto her butt. She scrambled to her feet and yanked the comforter out of the window. Let them cut themselves.

The door crashed open in the room as she turned toward the barn. She started running, but her knee gave out and she stumbled forward. Callie stifled a scream as a figure rushed from around the front of the house and a strong hand grabbed her arm.

Simon. He snarled down at her. He wasn't wearing his mask and there was no sign of the charmer she had met earlier that day. There was only anger and madness in his eyes.

She tried to pull away and he shook her so hard her teeth rattled together.

A wail from inside the room. "She hurt Mama! She threw her on the floor!"

"You don't know what you've done," Simon said, his voice low and hoarse.

Cody clambered out the window and jumped to the ground. He stood beside Simon.

A gunshot rang out and reverberated through the trees. Callie and Simon instinctively lowered themselves and looked around, but he didn't release her arm. He still held her, his grip tightening.

"Let her go," said a quiet voice. "Let her go or I will kill you."

Samantha stood, eyes narrowed and focused, arms held out, pointing Callie's pistol at Simon. Callie squirmed out of his grip. He made no move to stop her. She moved beside Samantha.

She reached out to take the gun, but Samantha, without looking away from Simon, said, "I have this. You get the baby. And Jake."

Callie looked at her. Samantha's eyes were narrowed and unblinking. She stared down at Simon, who stood frozen, arms held out to his sides.

Callie held out a hand to Simon. "Give me the keys to the barn."

Simon just looked at her.

"Don't do it," Cody said.

Another shot rang out, and dirt jumped up from the earth just in front of Simon's feet. He cursed and reached into a pocket, he held out a keychain and tossed it at Callie's feet.

Callie ran to the barn, fumbled with the keyring, found the right key, unlocked the door, and slid it open.

She sprinted past the cow, who now seemed interested

by all the commotion, got to the stall and gathered up her and Samantha's sleeping bags and backpacks, and shoved as much as she could into the baby carriage. She shouldered her pack and knelt and woke up Jake and stood him up. He blinked and looked around, saw her, and opened his mouth but nothing came out. She stood him up and grabbed his sleeping bag.

Another gunshot from outside, a cry of pain, and excited voices shouting, strident and frightened.

Callie picked up Ryan, startling him, and he started wailing. She stuffed him in the stroller on top of the bundled-up sleeping bags. She took Jake's hand and pulled and with her other hand pushed the stroller out of the barn.

There were now two figures standing where before there had been three.

Cody stood beside Simon, his hands up. Simon was on his knees, holding the side of his neck. Blood, black and shiny in the moonlight, seeped through his fingers. Callie moved behind Samantha, and asked, "You alright?"

"Yeah," Samantha said, but she sounded less sure of herself.

"Can you give me two minutes?" Callie asked.

Samantha nodded. Callie said, "Hold them. I'll be right back."

She sprinted toward the front of the house and took the front stairs two at a time and burst through the front door into the dining room. Was it there? Where had she seen it? Her head whipped from left to right.

Yes, right where she had seen it. Callie grabbed the rifle and ran back outside.

She came around the corner of the house. Samantha was still wielding the pistol, straight-armed, at the two boys. Simon was bent over, head down, silently crying. But he was crying tears of anger and frustration, not pain. Blood seeped between his fingers, and his eyes were narrowed and hate-filled. He looked dangerous now. *And crazy, Callie* had time to think as she joined Samantha.

Cody stood beside him, his face looking weak, defeated. His smugness was gone.

"We're leaving," Callie said. "We're leaving and don't you even think about following us."

Simon looked away, muttering under his breath, but Cody glared, his teeth gritted in anger and frustration.

He's the one we have to worry about, Callie thought. *He's crazy.*

"Ready," Callie said. Samantha nodded and lowered her gun.

Callie kept the rifle trained on the two while Samantha repacked the stroller and strapped in a wailing Ryan with quick, panicked hands.

"Okay, "she said from behind Callie. "Let's go."

"Go," Callie said, her eyes never leaving Simon and Cody. "I'll catch up with you."

"You can't do this," Simon hissed. "They won't let you go." He smiled a grotesque, twisted smile that didn't quite reach his eyes still filled with fury and indignation. "They'll find you."

Callie dared a quick look behind her. Samantha and Jake were just at the start of the driveway, just past the red pickup truck.

"You could've been nice," she said, turning back around and speaking to Cody. "You could've just let us leave. But you had to lock us in the barn? What's the matter with you?"

No answer. Not that she expected one. Cody looked at her, started to say something, then stopped. What could he say? She wanted him to say something.

"Stand up," Callie said.

Cody leaned over and helped Simon to his feet.

"Get in the barn," Callie said.

"He needs help," Cody said. "Your stupid friend shot him."

Callie raised the rifle. "Get in the barn."

She followed, several steps behind, as Cody held Simon into the barn.

"All the way to the back," she said.

Simon limped to the far wall, leaned against it, and slid to the ground.

Cody knelt beside him and looked up at her. "We need to help him."

She backed up until she stood in the doorway. "You should have just let us leave, "she said. "You did this."

Simon, a blood-stained hand pressed to his neck, hung his head." Just go," he said.

Callie slid the door shut and quickly slid the lock through the hasp. She heard footsteps from the other side of the door and clicked it shut just as Cody slammed into it. There was a brief moment where she thought the lock wouldn't hold, but it did. Cody slammed into the door again.

Callie turned and ran. As she made her way down the driveway, she risked a glance back at the house. Those two little girls...

"Not my problem," she muttered through gritted teeth. She had enough to worry about.

Callie sprinted down the gravel drive, the rifle banging against her thighs until she caught up to Samantha and the boys. Without speaking, she took Jake's leash, gave Samantha the rifle, and they ran until they reached the main road.

Once on the asphalt, they slowed to a walk, but moved

steadily and quickly, occasionally glancing back, fearful of seeing headlights or hearing the fearsome roar of the truck engine. But there was nothing. The road twisted and turned, the trees blotting out most of the moonlight

At last, they spied a wooden post topped with several mailboxes gleaming white in a rare patch of moonlight. They looked sad, Callie thought. Waiting for mail that was never going to come. Beside it, a driveway, now overgrown, trailed off into the darkness.

The girls paused and looked at each other. Callie looked back the way they had come and shook her head.

"No. It's too close. Let's keep going."

Samantha nodded and they kept moving.

Eventually, when they couldn't go any farther, they did find a house. They walked for several hours until the sky in the east began to lighten. They were both exhausted and cold, their feet leaden. Callie couldn't remember the last time she had slept. Even Jake was dragging, which forced Callie to slow down. She was forced to tug at him every few feet, and he stumbled and fell to his knees twice.

A pole, which held six or seven small signs containing family names, stood behind some hanging branches. Calli grabbed the pole, pulled at it, then pushed. A sign reading "The Kincaids" fell off, landing in the mud. She pushed harder, and the pole leaned, so she put all her weight on it until it was nearly forty-five degrees, away from the road. That was better. Harder to find.

A crushed gravel road led into the woods. The houses were spaced further back along the twisting half-mile muddy, rutted driveway.

They chose the house at the end of the road. An older house that had once been green, but was now a yellowish puke color, stood in a clearing, surrounded by pine trees. Off to one side, beneath a clothesline that connected the house to a large tree, a body lay in the mud. An upended laundry basket, half full of molding clothes sat on the ground, forgotten. Shirts, towels, and various pieces of laundry were scattered about the yard.

The front door was unlocked. Callie went in first, flashlight in hand. The house was small, with two compact bedrooms, a kitchen, a bathroom, and a living room crowded with worn furniture and stacks of newspapers. She stepped into the bathroom and turned on the faucet. It worked! Running water.

But best of all; a wood-burning fireplace.

Callie lit a fire after some trial and error (and help from Samantha), and the four of them slept on the living room floor, warm and sheltered, and safe.

Callie woke up first. It was still daylight. The sky was steel gray, clouds tumbling over one another, rain threatening again. She had maybe slept for three hours. She stood and stretched, sore from sleeping on the floor, still exhausted. But someone had to stay awake. What if Simon and Cody followed them? She glanced out the front window. Nothing unusual. Just trees and bushes. Lots of hiding places.

The fire had burned itself to embers, so she added a couple of logs and crumpled up newspaper to get it going again.

There was a scratching at the front door. Callie froze, ducked down, and crawled to the stroller. She grabbed the handle and tilted it down to her so she could reach into the storage pocket. She pulled out the pistol, rolled over, and aimed it at the front door. And waited. The scratching again, and then a soft meow.

Callie, still on her hands and knees, moved to the door and reached up, and opened it just a bit. A cat leaped in through the narrow space. Before she closed the door, Callie carefully scanned the yard. Then she turned to look at the new arrival.

It was a big, tough-looking black and white cat. It wasn't wearing a collar. A fresh scar ran across its nose and one of its ears was clipped. He was nonplussed, as cats often are, by strangers, rubbing up against Callie's leg and purring a broken purr. She reached down and scratched him behind his ears.

"Is this your house, buddy?" Callie asked the cat.

The cat led her to the kitchen, where he stood outside the pantry, looked up at her, and meowed. Callie opened the pantry door and found several cans of cat food. A cat bowl sat on the kitchen floor. She fed it, and then set down a bowl of water.

She used the bathroom and discovered that not only was there running water but there was hot water. Maybe things were looking up.

She took the longest shower of her life. She shampooed her hair, and rinsed it out, leaning against the tile as she let the warm water wash over her. Maybe three more days to the coast. Then what? A fairly straight shot to California, keeping the ocean on their right side as much as possible.

But was the coast safe? Images from her dream came back to her. The enormous red eyes. The feeling of dread when she thought of the ocean. What did it mean? Was it connected to the Quiet Ones' silent exodus?

A knock on the bathroom door shook her from her reverie. Callie twisted the knob and shut the water off. She reached out and grabbed a towel and stuck her head out of the shower. Samantha stood in the doorway, holding Ryan.

"You need to come out here," she said.

"Is it the cat?" Callie asked, twisting a towel around her hair. "He came in a little while ago. I think he—"

"You need to get out here now," Samantha said.

What is it?" Callie asked, following Samantha into the short hallway that led into the living room.

Jake was sitting on the couch, alert and awake. The cat was fast asleep in his lap. But that wasn't what caught Callie's attention.

The front door of the house was open, and on the porch stood the two ragged girls.

34

Callie shouted, "No!" She crossed the room, picked up the handgun, and gave it to Samantha, who was saying something, but Callie couldn't hear. Her pulse raced in her ears, a white swooshing sound, her face felt flushed, and a million thoughts worked their way into her head. *Get out. Get dressed. Hide. Run.* She grabbed the rifle and went to the front window. Samantha was still talking. The little girls were still standing on the porch. Callie scanned the yard. No sign of anyone else, or the red truck. Samantha was still talking. Callie shut the door on them and turned to listen to what Samantha was saying.

"...okay. They ran away and followed us," she was saying. "They were behind us the whole time." She reached out and grabbed Callie's arm. "They said they're alone."

Callie shrugged. "And you believed them? How do you know they're telling the truth?"

"They brought this." Samantha held out a set of keys with a black plastic remote.

Callie looked at the truck keys and considered them. A peace offering? A trap? "Give me a second."

She raced into the bathroom and yanked on her jeans and a sweatshirt, then came out, still holding the rifle.

She opened the front door and looked at the girls, then with a quick jerk of her head ushered them inside. She watched the trees and underbrush surrounding the house carefully for any sign of movement. Nothing.

Locking the door, Callie strode over to the two girls, who were standing by the fire, warming their hands.

"What are you doing here? Why did you follow us?"

The little girls looked miserable. They took each other's hands and looked up at her with wide, haunted eyes.

"Can we come with you?" said the one on the right. The other girl —*the dirtier one*, Callie thought, nodded.

"The cleaner girl said, "We ran away."

"How did you find us?" Callie asked. Her heart rate had returned to its normal pace, but she was still worried, considering her options: *stay or run?*

"We saw your smoke," the girl added. The cleaner girl did all the talking.

Shit! Callie hadn't even thought of that. The smoke from the fire must be visible for miles.

"We have to put the fire out," she said to Samantha. "If they found us, then so can those psychos."

Samantha went into the kitchen. There was the clatter of pots and pans banging around.

Callie glared at the girls. "Where are your brothers? Did they follow you?"

Samantha swooped in behind her and poured a pot of water on the fire. Hissing and steam filled the room.

The little girls looked puzzled. "Brothers?" asked Clean Girl.

"Simon and Cody," Callie snapped. "Did they follow you?"

The girls exchanged glances and shrugged.

"They're not our brothers."

"*Did* they follow you?" Callie repeated. The stress was returning. *Stay or run?*

That shrug again. *Shit!*

"Simon got hurt," the dirtier girl chimed in. She pointed at Samantha. "That girl shooted him. He was on the floor when we left."

"How did they get out of the barn?" Callie said.

Clean Girl shrugged. She looked at Dirty Girl, who also shrugged.

"Where was Cody?" Callie said.

Clean Girl: "Looking for medicine."

Callie held out the keys. "These are the keys to the truck?"

Both girls nodded.

"The red truck?"

Nod. Nod.

"Are these the *only* keys to the truck?"

That infuriating shrug again.

Samantha was moving from window to window, looking out into the yard. "I can't see anybody." She turned to Callie. "What should we do?"

Callie took a breath, then let it out. "I have an idea to give us some time."

Callie went out front and made sure there was no more smoke coming from the chimney. The rain was coming down now, so that would help hide their tracks. She made her way back up the driveway to the road but saw nothing unusual.

She slipped through the front door into the house, where the little girls were helping Samantha tape newspaper to all the windows. From the outside, the house would look dark and empty. She'd miss the fire, though. It was beginning to get cold. There was a box of old toys in the back of one of the closets, and she found a stuffed tiger, which she gave to Jake. He took it, his fingers closing over it, and he slowly lowered his head.

"It's a tiger," Callie said. "Tiger." She stood up and patted his head and helped them finish covering up the windows. It looked like it would work but made the inside of the house dark. Samantha found some candles in a cabinet, and these helped.

The girls stood on either side of Jake, staring with open fascination. The tiger lay on the floor between his feet.

"Can he hear?" asked one, the taller one. Mia Samantha had told her when she'd come back in.

"What does he eat?"

Then, the tough one. The one Callie didn't like to think about. "Is he always going to be like this?"

Callie said, "No more questions. You two need showers."

The girls were herded into the shower, with lots of shampoo and vigorous hair washing; Callie took one head, and Samantha took the other, and within minutes they were elbow deep in suds, scrubbing and brushing. The girls' hair was a mess; even though it was cut short, it was dirty and uncombed. At one point Callie had to use a pair of scissors to cut out some major knots. When it was over, water and strands of hair covered the bathroom floor, Callie's shirt was soaked, and the younger of the two girls, Taylor, was in tears.

But dry towels and promises of hot chocolate changed the mood, and soon they were gathered in the tiny living room, steaming mugs in their hands, the comforting sound of rain on the rooftop.

It turned out they weren't twins. They weren't even sisters. Taylor was seven and Mia was six. They knew each other from school; in fact, had been at a friend's birthday party when It happened. They were the only two at the party unaffected and remained in the house for two or three days, but eventually had to leave. They didn't say why they *had* to leave but shared a knowing look. They wandered for a couple more days, sleeping in stores, until Simon, out foraging in a supermarket, found them and brought them back to their house.

They talked late into the night. Jake fell asleep in an easy chair, a handmade quilt on his legs, the cat curled up in his lap. Samantha took an exhausted Ryan into the back bedroom and changed him on the bed, then brought him back in and put him in his stroller and put the back down, so he was lying flat. She wheeled the stroller into the bedroom.

Mia fell asleep against Callie before she had even finished her hot chocolate. Callie handed the mug to Samantha and carried Mia into the small bedroom and laid her down on the bed and covered her with a blanket. Samantha led Taylor, yawning herself, into the room and helped her crawl into bed beside Mia. Callie stood in the doorway and Samantha put a hand on Taylor's head and said good night, but when she turned to go, Taylor grabbed her hand. She looked from Samantha to Callie.

"Please," she said. "Stay with me. With us."

Samantha agreed to sleep on the floor, so Callie brought in some spare blankets and a pillow. Callie made a bed for herself on the couch. She fell asleep to the sound of the rain, and Jake's rhythmic breathing beside her.

She had the dream again. Only now it seemed so much closer. The cold, the dark, immense presence, the red eyes.

Callie sat up in the dark. The dreams were getting more vivid. Were they connected to It? To that horrible man/thing? With these unsettling thoughts rattling around in her head, Callie fell back asleep.

A loud thud woke her. Callie jerked up and blinked in the dim light. Jake stood by the front door, pounding and clawing to get out.

"Jake!" Callie jumped up, stumbled over the blanket tangled around her legs, kicked it off, and ran to him. She wrapped her arms around his chest, clasping her hands, holding his arms down, but he continued to buck and shove himself at the door, shaking the small house, rattling the windows.

Callie's head slammed against the door frame and saw stars, but she didn't let go. She pleaded with him to stop, but he fought, and struggled and slammed her into the door for what seemed like hours.

Finally, he stopped. Callie dragged him down to the floor with her, both of them panting, completely drained. Within minutes, Jake was asleep, leaning on her shoulder. Callie touched her forehead, where she had banged it. Her fingers came away bloody, shiny black in the moonlight. She looked over at the others.

Taylor and Mia cowered in the bedroom doorway, holding each other. Samantha sat cross-legged on the floor in front of the couch, holding Ryan. Even the cat seemed upset, peering out from beneath the couch, his green eyes blazing.

"Why didn't anyone help me?" Callie asked.

No response.

"Why didn't you guys help me?"

Samantha stared at the floor and mumbled something.

"What?" Callie asked.

Samantha looked up. "I said, 'He's *your* brother'."

Callie laid Jake down on the floor. She stood up and marched across the room and ripped Jake's blanket and a pillow off an armchair. She knelt beside him and set the pillow under his head and laid the blanket over him. Then she whirled on Samantha. "Are you kidding me? After all we've been through?" Her face screwed up and she mimicked in a high voice, "'He's your brother.'" She glared at Samantha, who looked stunned, even hurt by the cruel mockery. "How the hell can you even say that?" Callie demanded, stepping toward her.

"He slows us down," said Samantha. "You know he does." She put her head down, considering something, then raised her head and asked. "Don't you ever think about leaving him? What if he changes into one of those things?"

"You sound just like Cody," Callie said. "You know that, right?"

"I just think he's too much trouble, sometimes," Samantha said. "We could move so much faster if—"

"How long have you felt like this?" Callie asked. In the back of her mind, she couldn't help remarking how like her mother she sounded. "Have you always hated him?"

"I don't *hate* him," Samantha replied, but she wouldn't meet Callie's eyes. "But he's so much work. And what if he gets out one night? What if he changes? What then?"

Callie shrugged and said, "Then we'll go find him."

"So you go to find him and then you don't come back? What then?"

Callie said nothing. Mia and Taylor, wrapped in blankets, watched in silence.

"If we left him, he wouldn't even know it," said Samantha. "He wouldn't feel anything. He's not Jake anymore. Why can't you see that?"

"He's my brother," Callie said, tears welling up in her eyes. Tears of anger, or loss. She wasn't sure, and what did it matter? "My family is gone. He's all I have left."

"What about us?" Samantha said, standing up, holding Ryan tight to her chest. "I kind of thought we were family. Is he more important than us?"

Callie opened her mouth, but nothing came out, so she shook her head. "You are," she finally said, her voice husky with emotion, moving closer, her anger gone, but new tears coming. "You are important to me." She embraced Samantha, who didn't resist, and kissed the top of Ryan's head. "Of course you are." Samantha wrapped one arm around Callie and moved a little closer.

Callie glanced over at Taylor and Mia, who were staring wide-eyed, and motioned them over.

They walked over, tentative, unsure, but then joined in as Samantha and Callie reached for them in a group hug. They held each other for some time, Samantha and Callie's crying eventually turning to sniffling. Callie thought how strange and wonderful it was, after all the death and pain, that they had found each other; four girls and a baby boy. Family now. Her eyes lifted to the window, and she caught the reflection of Jake, lying on the floor, fast asleep. Alone. She closed her eyes.

Callie got everyone settled, back in their makeshift beds, exchanging a good, strong hug with Samantha, who murmured, "I'm sorry," in Callie's ear.

"You don't need to be sorry," Callie said. "It's all right."

"No," Samantha replied. "It's not. I wish I could have helped my little brother. The way you help Jake. I wish—" she broke off and turned her head. Callie held her. She didn't say anything. There didn't seem to be anything to say.

Callie pulled her sleeping bag over to where Jake slept on the floor and lay it down beside him, in front of the door. She had a thought, and got up, found the stuffed tiger, and tucked it into Jake's chest. She watched him. One hand reached out, felt the tiger, and pulled it close. She lay down again. Samantha's words reverberated in her brain. The girls' question: "Will he always be like this?"

It was a long time before she fell asleep, and she didn't hear the footsteps pass by the front door.

35

The next morning, they set out early. Callie got them up, made a quick breakfast of stale cereal without milk, and began packing. Taylor and Mia were troopers, cleaning up, packing, and getting ready without a complaint. Mia actually smiled a few times.

Callie made a point of getting Jake ready as quickly as possible, made sure he was dressed, backpack strapped on, standing beside the front door even before she was set to go. After some internal debate, she left the rifle under the bed in the back bedroom. They had the pistol. That should be enough. Besides, the rifle scared her.

It was wet and cold, the dark clouds promising rain, but not just yet. Callie looked up at the dark sky without much hope. They had to move. They couldn't stay here again. Maybe they could get a couple of hours in before it started raining. And that was assuming they found a house. She looked around at her little group, and her family, and smiled at the little girls. "Ready?" she asked.

Mia smiled back, but Taylor looked worried. Callie couldn't blame her. There was so much to be worried about.

The least of which was if those two nutjobs were going to come looking for them.

"What about him?" Mia asked, holding the cat.

Callie shrugged. "I guess we leave him here. He looks pretty tough. He's probably used to being outside."

"I'm going to miss him, "Mia said.

Taylor reached out and petted the cat's head. He pushed his face into her hand and nuzzled her. Mia set him down and the cat, tail up, trotted around the side of the house.

"See?" said Callie. "He likes being outside. He'll be fine." She didn't like to think too much about animals, the pets that were trapped inside houses and apartments.

Jake wore his heavy rain jacket, the hood pulled up. Callie wrapped the loop of his leash around her wrist, but Samantha intercepted her, held out her hand, and said, "Let me take him."

Callie looked stunned, but Samantha grinned. "No, really," she said. "I'll walk with Jake today."

Samantha, still smiling at Callie's incredulous expression, took the leash, patted Jake on the back, and said, "Let's go, buddy." Jake, ever obedient (at least in the daytime, she reflected as she felt the bump on the back of her head), followed.

Taylor and Mia both had a hold of Ryan's stroller, tugging it back and forth, arguing about who would push it. Callie stepped between them.

"Hold on," she said. "You're upsetting the baby." But they weren't. He was enjoying both the shaking and the attention.

Callie decided they would take turns pushing the stroller. "I'll time you, "she said. "You each get thirty minutes. Then you switch. Okay?" The girls looked at each other, then at Callie, and nodded.

Mia would push first since she was older.

So, for the first time in weeks, Callie was walking with no burden other than her backpack. It felt odd, even unnatural, but liberating at the same time. As she looked ahead of her, at Samantha and Jake, and the girls with Ryan, she thought, I *could get used to this.*

They walked down the driveway to the main road and headed toward the coast, Samantha with Jake trailing right behind her, then Mia pushing Ryan, Taylor close by, and Callie bringing up the rear. They walked in silence, each one looking around carefully, checking the shadows, the dark places beneath the trees, half-expecting Cody to come roaring out of the underbrush. But there was no sign of him. There were plenty of corpses, though, lying where they fell. All of them appeared to be headed toward the coast. Once again, Callie thought of her dream, the dark shape coming out of the water. The red eyes. Was there a connection between the Quiet Ones and her dream? Or was that crazy?

They had been walking for about an hour when Taylor pointed back behind them and shouted, "Hey look!"

The cat was following them. As they stopped to look back at them, he took the opportunity to also stop and busied himself grooming one of his back legs. As soon as they began moving, he did as well.

He stayed within sight most of the day, occasionally loping off into the trees for his purposes, but he kept pace with them throughout the day, to the utter delight of Taylor.

They did see one living person, a female Quiet One, skeletal, her clothing shredded, crawling over the leaf-covered asphalt, struggling to get to wherever they were all going. *I guess we're going to find out,* Callie thought. *We're headed in the same direction.*

No one spoke about it, or the other dead bodies they passed. Just part of the scenery. Live people were rare, the dead more common in this new world.

It began raining, (thankfully, not until late afternoon), just as they were passing a roadside produce stand/restaurant/tourist shop. Samantha pointed to some wooden picnic tables beneath an awning along one side of the building. "Over there," she said, leading the way.

As the sprinkles increased to a downpour, they hurried across the gravel parking lot, avoiding the larger puddles, weaving their way through the deserted cars, to the picnic table.

Mia pushed the stroller up against the table. Samantha went into her backpack and came out with some crackers, which she gave to Mia to feed Ryan. Callie handed Jake's leash to Taylor, who looped it around her hand. Callie said, "You two wait here for a second. You're both in charge of the boys for right now, okay?"

The little girls nodded, all duty and seriousness. Samantha pulled the pistol out of the stroller pocket. She and Callie walked toward the front door of the market.

Callie pulled up her hood against the driving rain and strode up the wooden steps (FRESH PRODUCE AND SMOOTHY'S—COME ON IN! announced the bright, hand-painted sign mounted in the front window).

Callie stopped, causing Samantha to bump into her. Something was wrong. Something was off. The bottom part of the door was cracked, a big white spider web radiating over the lower half of the door, obscuring their view of the inside of the store. There was a dark mass, something piled on the other side of the door. She stepped closer. It looked like a big stack of old clothing...but it wasn't. *Those are people,* Callie realized.

"What is it?" Samantha asked. "Why'd you stop?"

Callie pointed to the front door. "That," she said.

Samantha stepped beside her for a better look. "Yuck," she said.

There were close to a dozen corpses piled up along the base of the front door. A face, impossible to tell if it was male or female, was pressed against the glass just below the "PUSH" sign. A sunken, yellowed eye stared at them.

"They couldn't get out," Samantha said. "They were pushing on the door. But it opens in."

Callie walked up to the door and pushed on it, and it opened several inches until the mass of bodies stopped it. The face stuck to the glass, peeled off and the head flopped sideways. The stench of death and shit and rotting food wafted out and she let go of the door and stepped back, waving a hand in front of her face.

"What do you think?" she asked, after taking a few breaths of clean air. She had to raise her voice to be heard above the sound of the rain. It was really coming down, pounding the roof of the store and the cars in the parking lot. "Keep going, or deal with this?" nodding her head at the pile of dead Quiet Ones.

Samantha motioned at the sky. "We can't keep walking in this." She put her face up the front door and placed her hands on either side to cut the glare. She moved to the front window, and walked along it as she scanned the inside of the store. "It looks like there's a door in the back. We should check it out."

They passed the girls and Jake at the table. "Everything okay?" Callie asked.

Taylor nodded at Jake. "He tried to follow you."

What do you mean?" Callie said.

"When you walked away, he got up and went after you. I had to push him back down. He's strong," she said.

"Wow," Callie said. She smiled. Another good sign. She put a hand on Jake's shoulder. "Hang tight buddy, we'll just be a little bit." She turned toward Taylor and Mia. "Come and get us if anything weird happens," she said and added, "Anything."

She tugged on the leash, making sure it was secure, and she and Samantha headed off toward the rear of the store.

The rear entrance had double doors for loading. A metal ramp led up to it, and the two girls found a wooden dolly, a flat wooden cart, probably used for hauling produce boxes.

"This will help," Samantha said, pushing it up the ramp.

Once inside the store, the stench was overpowering, and Callie bent over and dry heaved before rushing back outside. She stood, hands on her knees, and spit. She looked up at Samantha.

"This is going to be harder than I thought."

Across from a janitor's closet was an employee break room right. A row of square beige lockers mounted on the wall, a refrigerator, a microwave, and a table and folding chairs. Callie grabbed a box of tissues off the table and brought it back outside. They each took a tissue and tore off pieces and twisted and then stuffed it up their noses. They looked at each other and smiled, despite all the horror around them, as they both had white tissue sticking out of their noses and looked pretty silly.

They walked up the ramp, took big breaths, and strode into the store. They paused to get their bearings, turning their heads to take it all in. It was a combination country store/diner, with rows of souvenir t-shirts and hats, beef jerky, chips, cookies, and other grab-and-go type treats.

Glass cases containing soft drinks, juices, bottled water, and other drinks ran down one wall.

There were three tables at the far end of the store, beside a counter with a small grill. A menu advertising burgers, sandwiches, smoothies, and fries was tacked up on the wall. A wooden door led out to the picnic tables.

Five more bodies covered the floor of the restaurant area.

The smell was strong, even with the tissue in her nostrils.

Callie said, "Let's go," and the girls walked toward the pile of bodies, pushing the cart before them. The floor here was littered with scraps of bright cardboard boxes and plastic bags, which looked as if they had been torn open by animals. Bits of food and crumbs covered the tiled floor around the front of the store.

"What happened?" said Samantha, looking around. "Do you think raccoons got in?"

"It was them," Callie said, pointing at the mass of bodies at the glass door. "They were eating."

Callie looked down and grimaced. The corpses were all tangled up, arms and legs and heads intertwined. It was hard to tell which head went with which body. But there was no way they could stay here unless they got rid of the bodies.

She reached down and grabbed a blue jean-clad leg. Samantha grabbed the other leg and they tugged and pulled on the corpse and freed it from the pile. Getting it onto the cart was more difficult because Samantha had to hold the cart to prevent it from rolling away. So Callie had to get in close to the body, turning her head away and grabbing it under the arms, and lifting it across the cart.

She returned to the pile and reached down and lifted a

young boy. He was so little and weighed next to nothing, and she almost began to cry. One of his shoes fell off when she plucked him from the pile. She was gentle when she laid him on the cart. Samantha placed the shoe beside him.

Callie nodded and as she pulled, Samantha pushed, and they rolled the cart to the back of the store, through the double doors, and down the ramp.

There was a dumpster behind the store, and they went around it and dropped the bodies on the wet ground. Callie avoided looking down when they dumped the bodies off the cart. But she heard the solid thud as they hit the ground.

Callie pulled the cart back to the base of the ramp and stopped. She and Samantha looked at each other, their faces grim.

"You okay?" Callie asked. "Ready to go again?"

Samantha said, "No. But let's get this over with."

They stood around the pile, deciding who was next. Callie sighed and reached down and grabbed an arm wearing a heavy wristwatch and tugged. The pile shifted, and one body rolled onto the floor. Callie stepped back to avoid it. A girl about her age, with dyed pink hair, fell onto her back. Her head thumped against the floor with a crack. Callie grimaced at the sound, let go of the arm, and bent to lift the girl.

"Look at her hand," Samantha said.

Callie glanced down at the girl's outstretched hand. The fingers were fused with a thin fleshy webbing, only the tips above the last knuckle unconnected. "What the hell..."

That's when the girl opened her eyes.

36

Callie screamed and stumbled backward, colliding with a shelf, and sending several bags of chips to the floor. Samantha put her hands to her mouth and shuffled back a few steps.

The girl with pink hair blinked her eyes and stared up at nothing. Her mouth opened and closed, but she made no sound other than the clicking of her teeth.

"What do we do?" Samantha asked, her voice hushed. "What are we supposed to do?"

"I—I don't know," said Callie. She was close to tears, looking at the poor girl, the girl who hadn't wanted any of this, but there she was lying on the floor, dying. "I'll get a towel or something."

She had noticed some blue tarps piled by the loading ramp, and fetched one and laid it over the girl. It was better when they couldn't see her.

"I think we should put her with the others," Callie said. She swallowed. "I don't think we can help her."

Samantha looked at her but just nodded.

They rolled the girl—*her skin is still warm!* Callie realized—onto the tarp, lifted her, and placed her as gently as they could on the cart. They wheeled it outside beside the dumpster and put the girl on the ground, slightly apart from the others.

Neither Callie nor Samantha turned away. They stood there, rain pouring over them deep in their thoughts, torn. It felt wrong to leave her there, still alive, wrapped in a tarp, wet and cold.

Callie put a hand on Samantha's shoulder. "Come on."

Samantha said, "Maybe we should...um..."

"What?" Callie asked.

"Put her out of her misery?" Samantha said, framing it as a question.

Callie met her eyes, then looked down at her hands. "Okay," she nodded. "I'll do it."

Samantha said. "Are you sure? I can--"

"No," Callie said. "I'll do it. Just go out front and let them know it's okay. When they hear the shot."

Samantha nodded and glanced down at the girl with the pink hair, who was struggling to sit up and slipped back inside.

Out front, Taylor and Mia were standing at the edge of the porch, staring across the parking lot. Jake sat behind them, holding his tiger, his eyes closed.

"What's up?" Samantha said.

Mia turned and pointed to the bushes at the far end of the parking lot. "There's something over there," she said.

Samantha stepped forward, grasping the girls' shoulders. "What kind of something?"

"I think it's a tiger," said Taylor.

Samantha stepped from beneath the awning, shielding her eyes from the rain, and stared in the direction Mia was pointing. Aside from the trees and undergrowth, she couldn't see anything.

"Whatever it was, it's gone now." She walked back up to the porch. "Now listen, you two. In a minute you're going to hear--"

A shot rang out, sharp and flat in the rain. Mia and Taylor sprang to Samantha's side.

"It's okay," she reassured them. "Callie had to shoot a big rat."

Once Mia and Taylor were placated, Samantha headed back inside, but not before giving the darkening tree line surrounding them another look.

It took four trips before they had removed all the bodies from inside the store. After the third trip, Samantha stumbled off into some bushes, where she alternated between sobbing and vomiting. Callie stood beside the cart, waiting. She kept glancing over at the blue tarp, where the girl with the pink hair lay.

After a few minutes, Samantha, soaking wet, her hair flat against her head, emerged from the bushes, wiping her mouth. She didn't meet Callie's eyes. "Sorry," she said.

"You don't have to apologize," Callie said.

After they disposed of the final body in front of the door, they repeated the exercise in the restaurant area, including an older man behind the counter, wearing a white apron. He still held a spatula in one hand.

Once the corpses were taken care of, they walked back into the store and opened all the windows. Despite the rain, despite the cold, the fresh air felt cleansing. There was another body in one of the bathroom stalls, so Samantha went to get the cart. By this time, they had it down. In and out, in less than two minutes and they dumped the body with the others. Callie wasn't sure if their efficiency was a good thing or not.

Once the store was aired out, it turned out to be a nice place to stay. There was plenty of room, and the toilets and sinks worked just fine. No electricity, but they were used to that.

And there was so much food: chips and beef jerky and candy and jam and jelly and soda. Taylor and Mia ran around the store with wire shopping baskets, loading them up so much that they eventually had to drag them.

They had a sort of picnic, the four girls, along with Jake and Ryan, sitting on a tarp on the floor, surrounded by plastic containers and boxes of food that Callie's mom would never have let her eat, talking and laughing and eating until Mia began laughing so hard that she *Yarp!* threw up all the crap she had eaten.

That ended the picnic. They scrambled to their feet, screaming and laughing as food and drink splattered across the tarp. It was pretty funny until Taylor began gagging at the smell, but Callie pulled her away and led her toward the front door.

Samantha helped Mia into a bathroom (thank God for the working toilets) and Callie and Taylor covered their noses and mouths with bandanas and cleaned up the mess. They really just rolled up the tarp with all the trash and other stuff and ran it out front and dumped it in a metal trash can on the wooden porch.

Callie turned and headed back in before she got too wet, but when she got to the door, Taylor wasn't with her.

She was standing on the top step, staring across the parking lot.

"Taylor! Come on!" Callie said. "You're getting soaked."

Taylor turned and walked into the store.

Once inside, Callie took off her coat and shook it. "What was that all about?"

"I think I saw something," Taylor said, still looking out at the parking lot.

"The tiger?" Mia asked.

Images of the red pickup truck flashed through Callie's mind. *Oh god.*

She pulled Taylor away from the glass door. "What did you see?"

"I'm not sure," said Taylor. "I think it was a dog."

A dog. She could deal with a dog, as long as it was out there. And she was in here. She scanned the rainswept parking lot and the trees beyond but couldn't make out much of anything farther than three or four feet.

"A dog?" she asked. "Not a person? Or a truck?"

Taylor nodded. "I just saw it for a tiny bit. Look!" She pointed across the road. Callie followed Taylor's gaze. Over the cars, the road—wait... something was moving across the street. A mountain lion. A big one. It walked smoothly, easily, between the pine trees across the road. It turned in their direction, sniffed the air, and disappeared into the trees.

"Do mountain lions eat people?" Taylor asked, face pressed up against the glass panel in the door.

"I'm not sure," Callie said, although she was pretty sure they did (or would, if given the opportunity). "But let's just assume they do." She joined Taylor at the door, and gently pulled her away. "He probably wants to get out of the rain just like we do."

Before going to sleep, Callie and Samantha walked the interior perimeter of the store, closing and locking the doors and windows. The back door could lock with a deadbolt, but the front door could not be locked without a key. And they had no key. The thought of going out back and rooting through the pockets of the dead, searching for a key that might or might not be there flashed briefly through her mind, and just as quickly, she pushed it out.

A search of the back office unearthed several keys, some alone, some on rings, but none of them fit in the front door. After some thought, Callie pulled a short wooden shelf in front of the door and placed empty soda cans on the edge of the shelf so they would fall if anyone opened the door. If anyone came in, at least they would hear. *But then what?*

Callie folded up tarps beneath Taylor and Mia, making a kind of mattress for them. But she and Samantha didn't want to lay on the tarps.

They slept on the floor toward the rear of the store in a circle, their heads on the inside, whispering and talking until, one by one, they fell asleep. Jake lay beside Callie, the leash tied around his right leg and her left. He had his tiger beside him.

Despite the fact they were on a hardwood floor, Callie slept soundly and didn't dream at all.

She woke up, a little stiff. Nice to wake up on her own, without someone else banging or screaming. Speaking of which, she sat up, leaning on one arm, and checked on Jake; he was there beside her, face slack, still fast asleep. No disturbances during the night. When he was asleep, he looked like his old self, she thought, gazing down at him, so calm and peaceful.

She thought back to what Samantha had said. What if Jake never got better? Was all this worth it? *Maybe he would be better off*— she stopped it there. She was taking him to Grandma. That was the plan. *But you haven't heard from Grandma in days.* That didn't matter. That was out of her control. What did matter, something she could control, was keeping this group (A *group. When had we become a group?*) safe and together and keeping them moving toward San Diego.

Jake clutched the stuffed tiger in his right hand and curled it up to his chest. Callie had handed it to him right before bed.

Yesterday morning, he was holding it when she woke him up and he didn't let go. She took it from him so she could dress him, and he became agitated, reaching out blindly, his hands opening and closing. So she gave it back to him. He clutched it to his chest. He didn't look at it, just held it. It seemed to bring him comfort.

Callie untied the leash, stood up, and stretched.

"Good morning," said Samantha from behind her. Callie turned and smiled. Samantha was sitting on the floor, her back against the front counter. She had the black and white cat on her lap. "Look who I found sitting outside the front door crying to come in."

"Wow," said Callie, kneeling and scratching the cat's neck fluff. "The girls will be so happy."

The cat pushed his head into her hand, cat-speak for, "Pet me, please."

"Should we keep him? I mean, bring him with us?" Samantha said.

Callie shrugged. "Why not? What's one more?" She stroked the fluff beneath his neck. "If he wants to stay with us."

"He will," Samantha said. "He's come this far."

Callie went to the front door, picked up the empty cans and set them aside, pulled the door open, and stepped onto the wooden steps. The driving rain continued, showing no signs of letting up. The parking lot was a sodden mess, all puddles, and mud. She scanned the area across the road. No sign of dogs, red pickup trucks, or mountain lions.

Callie stepped back inside. "We should probably stay here until it stops." She looked at Samantha, hoping for agreement. Callie knew she was the de-facto leader, mainly because she was the oldest, but also because she was the one with a clear goal. Not just survival. But to get to San Diego and her grandmother.

Hope. She was leading them to hope. But it helped to have Samantha give her opinion. Especially if her opinion agreed with Callie.

"I was thinking the same thing," Samantha said.

The girls woke up in a little bit, and as predicted, were thrilled to see the cat. The two of them scoured the aisles, looking for cat food, and finally settled on chopping up some Vienna sausages. But the cat didn't like them. All was not lost, however, as Ryan loved the greasy sausages and held out his meaty hands for more even after they were gone.

They spent the day eating junk (Callie kept an eye on Mia), playing cards at one of the tables, napping, taking turns holding the cat, and talking. Callie found a brand new Mariners hat. She had lost her other one somewhere and was happy to find a replacement. All in all, it was a really good day, the best that Callie could remember, at least since It.

The rain let up for a little bit in the afternoon, and she

took Jake out for some exercise, walking around the covered area by the picnic tables.

The sun came out on the third day, a Thursday, Callie felt. Thursday was a good day. Thursday was a day of promise, of hope. The next day was Friday, and then the weekend. Thursdays were all right.

A few clouds lingered in the crystal blue sky, stubbornly refusing to vanish, but they were white and wispy and posed no threat.

Callie got the girls up early to help pack. Two days of sitting and waiting were enough. She was getting restless. And a little nervous, to be honest. No word from Grandma. She checked her phone, turning away so the others wouldn't see. One bar. No messages. She pulled up her contacts and found Grandma. She texted, "almost to highway 101. be in California in a few days." She paused, and added, "Jake is doing good love you" She thumbed the power button and slid her phone into her jacket pocket.

"Sam, can you change Ryan?" she asked, walking over to Jake, and sliding his backpack over his arms. She turned him around and fastened the chest straps.

"No problem, "Samantha said, picking Ryan up. He began squirming, as he was doing more and more. He didn't want to be picked up so much. Samantha had said just last night that he looked like he was ready to start crawling.

Callie wasn't quite ready for that yet. The more mobile he became, the harder it would be to keep track of him. Once they got to Grandma's, then he could crawl. Heck, he could walk for all she cared. But crawling should maybe wait. But at least she had help, she thought, watching as Mia and Taylor fawned all over Ryan.

Callie got them all out on the front steps, and everyone loaded up and was ready to move. They were in good spirits: well rested, well fed, and ready to get moving. The younger girls were literally bouncing with excitement.

Samantha had stroller duty, and Taylor held Jake's leash. Callie squinted up at the sun. Her hat.

"Oh, hold up on a second," she said, "I forgot my hat." She dumped her backpack on the top step and headed back inside and found her Mariners cap, on the table in the little restaurant area. She pulled it down over her head and detoured over an aisle and grabbed two tubes of sunscreen off a shelf. She lathered up her face and back of her neck. Her mother would be so proud.

Callie opened the front door and stepped onto the porch.

And froze. Her eyes tracked left, right up, and down, trying to make sense of what she was seeing.

Taylor sat on the wooden porch, her eyes wet with tears. She held a hand to her cheek.

Mia and Samantha stood off to one side, in front of the stroller. Mia looked terrified, but Samantha was scowling, angry.

Jake stood at the bottom of the stairs, in the muddy parking lot. Cody stood behind him, one hand grasping Jake's collar. In his free hand, he held a pistol up to Jake's head.

37

"Don't hurt him," Callie said. "Please, don't hurt him."

"I'm going to hurt him," Cody said. "I'm going to hurt all of you."

Callie took a step toward him, then hesitated. "What do you want?" she asked. She kept her voice soft, non-threatening. "Our food? Take it." She pushed her backpack to the top of the steps and nudged it down with her foot. It rolled over once and slid to a stop on the bottom step.

"I don't want your food," Cody said. He said "food" like it was a dirty word. His voice was hoarse and raw, and he looked terrible. Worn out and battered. His hair was matted and filthy, there were dark circles beneath his eyes, and a long angry red scratch crossed his forehead. He wiped his mouth on his shirt. "I want my brother back," he said. "But you bitches killed him."

"Good," said Samantha. "I'm glad he's dead."

Callie risked a look at her. Samantha stood beside the stroller, one hand reaching down into the pocket. "He deserved to die. And so do you."

She had been through so much already. But she was

staring at Cody, her gaze fierce and strong. No sorrow for Simon. No shame. No fear.

Cody stepped forward and tightened his grip on Jake's neck. Jake's eyes bulged and he gasped, opening and closing his mouth. A line of drool dripped from his lower lip. Cody raised the gun and aimed it at Samantha.

"You're first," he said.

"Stop it!" Callie said, moving down the steps without realizing it. "You're hurting him!"

Cody's eyes flicked to Callie and he grinned. "I told you, he can't feel anything," he said. "Watch." And he slammed the gun into the side of Jake's head.

Jake's eyes blinked and he sagged. His knees buckled. Cody released his hold and watched as Jake tumbled over, striking his forehead on the fender of a car with a solid *thunk!* before bouncing off and landing face down in the mud.

Cody stepped forward and stuck the toe of his boot beneath Jake and rolled him over onto his back. He placed a heavy boot on Jake's throat.

He pointed the gun at Samantha. "Let me see that gun! I know you have one. Now!" He moved the barrel of his pistol down until it pointed squarely at Jake's head.

"Okay!" Samantha held up one hand and with the other, reached into the pocket at the back of the stroller. She came out with the gun.

Cody pivoted and straightened his arm pointing back at her. "Throw it down here."

She kept it away from her body, holding it with her fingers, and swung her arm forward, launching the gun off the porch where it splattered into the mud.

"So what now?" Callie asked. "You going to shoot us all?"

"Maybe," Cody said, all smug and confident. Callie

hated him more than ever. He was every bully she had ever met. More powerful and self-assured than she could ever be. But at least she had her friends. Her family. He had nothing, now. He was alone.

Alone...

"What about Eden?" Callie asked.

Cody's smile faltered.

"You can't create your new Eden by yourself," Callie said. She walked toward him, hands held in front of her. The muddy ground was sticky, and she was afraid her shoes were going to get sucked right off her feet.

Something caught her eye several cars behind Cody. A flash of tawny fur. A dog? Had he brought one of his dogs?

She focused on the boy holding a gun on her brother. "What are you going to do, Cody? If you kill us, you'll be all alone."

Cody's eyes narrowed. "Shut up! You're messing with me. Hell, we found you. We—I can always find more." But he sounded more confident than he looked.

"What about this?" Callie said. She spoke in a quiet, reasonable tone. *Keep him calm.* "I'll go with you. Willingly. Back to your house, or whatever. You let them go." She tilted her head in the direction of the three girls on the porch.

"No! Callie, no!" cried Samantha, as Callie had known she would.

Taylor shouted Callie's name and began sobbing.

But Callie didn't turn. It would be too hard, and she didn't know if she had the strength to go through with this.

Cody's eyes flicked back and forth between the porch and Callie, then he nodded at Jake. "What about him?"

Callie fought back tears. "Just leave him. They'll take care of him."

They will. I know they will.

Cody smirked. That stupid, cocky, smirk. Callie wanted to slap it off his stupid face.

He lowered the barrel of the gun until it was pointed at Jake. "I could take care of 'im right now. How's that sound? Would you like that?"

Before Callie could answer, she heard footsteps behind her, pounding down the steps.

Cody raised the gun.

Callie turned to see Samantha rushing toward the gun sticking out of the mud. Callie's breath was cut off as Cody wrapped his arm around her neck and pulled her against him. A cold circle of steel pressed into her temple.

Samantha stopped in her tracks, slipping in the mud and landing on her butt. The gun lay several feet in front of her.

Cody began backing up, dragging Callie with him. She could feel her heels making grooves in the mud as he pulled her away from Samantha.

She was off balance, scrambling to stay on her feet and catch her breath at the same time. She looked down and saw Jake looking at her, then she glanced up at the front porch of the store. Taylor and Mia stood watching, silent.

Wait. Jake was looking *at* her. She glanced back down at him. He met her eyes, then he looked away, over her shoulder. At Cody? Or was he drifting off again?

A sudden movement from behind her.

Jake looked at her again, his eyes focused on her now, and opened his mouth.

"Call...eee," he croaked.

Callie stared at her brother, shock and surprise mixing with the fear that had been coursing through her just minutes before.

And then all hell broke loose.

Something solid hit her, hard, spinning her away from Cody, and throwing her to the ground. She hit with a loud "Whuff!" as the air was knocked out of her. Mud filled her mouth, her nose, and her eyes. She pushed herself up, gasped, and spat, trying to find her voice, reaching up and clearing the mud from her eyes, crawling toward Jake, turning to see why Cody had shoved her away, all at the same time.

A scream filled the morning air. Not a human scream. Loud, shrill, and angry. She turned toward the sound and would have screamed herself if she still had a voice.

The mountain lion was crouching on top of Cody, snarling, huge teeth bared, and green eyes narrowed into angry slits. It was huge, easily five feet long, not even including the tail, which was whipping back and forth over Cody's feet.

Cody lay on his back, one arm beneath the big cat's neck, straining to keep its massive jaws away from his own throat. His free arm pointed straight out, the fingers clutching mud. Callie followed his reach and saw his gun, several inches out of his reach.

Cody slid his eyes sideways and met hers. "Help me," he muttered, the strain of keeping back the mountain lion evident in his weakening voice. "Please."

The mountain lion snarled, deep in its chest.

Callie got to her feet.

She looked down at Cody. "Go to hell," she said.

Her eyes never leaving the mountain lion, she backed up to where Jake lay in the mud. The mountain lion lunged forward, and Callie turned away

There was a scream and a crunch. The scream stopped and became a thick, fluid moan.

Callie reached down and grabbed Jake by the arm and yanked him to his feet.

His eyes whirled around, taking in everything at once. But his body was limp, and he could barely stand.

She didn't try to process this. She ran, half pulling/half dragging Jake, and waved an arm at the other three girls, all watching wide-eyed.

"Get inside!" she cried. "Go!"

Taylor and Mia ran for the door. Samantha came to Callie and ducked beneath Jake's other arm and together they got him up the steps and into the store.

Callie and Jake collapsed on the floor behind the counter. Taylor and Mia stood, holding hands, against the glass refrigerator doors.

Samantha shoved the stroller against the wall, then ran over to the restaurant section, grabbed one of the tables, dragged it to the door, and shoved it against the frame. She stood at the door, looking out.

Jake looked into Callie's mud-streaked face and put a shaky hand on her cheek. He closed his eyes.

Callie wrapped her arms around Jake and wept.

38

Samantha sat atop the table all afternoon, watching and waiting. She had cleaned the handgun and kept it close by.

The mountain lion didn't stay for dessert. After an hour or so, he dragged what was left of Cody through the parking lot and into the trees across the street.

Callie used some wet tee shirts to clean Jake up. She wiped the mud off his face. He had an ugly welt on the side of his head, and she cleaned it as best she could. Then she changed his shirt and pants. Mia stood by with a bucket of soapy water, occasionally handing Callie a damp rag.

Callie didn't leave Jake's side for the rest of the day.

Samantha stood by the front door peering through the glass.

"His truck's out there," she said.

Callie blinked at her. "What?"

Samantha motioned out front. "His truck. The red one. It's out there."

Callie shrugged. "So?"

"So we know it works. And maybe you can drive it?" Samantha said. "Think of all the stuff we can fit in it."

Callie hadn't thought about driving. She was getting accustomed to walking every day. But with all this rain...

"Look, I know you don't know how to drive now, but think about it." Samantha returned to her post at the front door.

Callie didn't respond.

"You could go slow," Samantha said.

Mia came around the counter with a bag of chips and a bottle of water. "Are you hungry?"

Callie smiled. "Thanks, sweetie." She was hungry. She hadn't eaten since a quick breakfast. That seemed like ages ago.

Mia gazed at Jake, still out cold. "How is he doing?" she asked. "Is he still sleeping?"

Callie nodded. *I hope he's just sleeping, she* thought.

Eventually, she had to pee, so she made a pillow out of some sweatshirts, placed it beneath Jake's head, and got up. Her right leg was asleep, numb and useless, and she staggered around for a minute, holding her knee and cursing, much to Taylor's amusement.

Callie took the opportunity to clean her face, which she had forgotten was still covered with mud. She ended up washing her hair as well, using hand soap and then toweling off with souvenir tee shirts.

She came out wearing a sweatshirt with a big red heart with the word "Oregon" emblazoned across it and a pair of baggy sweatpants. She joined Samantha at the door.

"Anything going on?" she asked.

Samantha shook her head. "All quiet. How's Jake?"

Callie frowned. "I'm not sure. He's still asleep."

They were quiet for a moment, listening to the sound of the two younger girls arguing over a hand of Go Fish. The cat jumped onto the table between them and made his way into Samantha's lap.

Callie said, "He said my name."

Samantha turned to her. Then she looked at the cat. "What?"

Callie stared into the darkness outside. "Jake. He said my name. He knew me."

"What are you talking about?" Samantha said.

Callie told her about the moments just before the mountain lion attacked. "He knew me. I know he did."

"Why? Because he hit his head? It ...knocked something loose?"

Callie shook her head. "I don't know. He saw I was in trouble. Maybe that's what it was."

"You're sure? He said 'Callie?'" Samantha asked.

"Yes," Callie said, sliding off the table. "He said my name. I don't care if you believe me or not. I know he said it." She went back to Jake and stretched out beside him.

"Look, I'm sorry." Samantha stood over them. "I believe you. If you say it happened, it happened."

Callie turned over, facing away. She put one hand on Jake's shoulder. She fell asleep like that.

Jake woke up the next morning. He was groggy, and he didn't say anything, but he was changed. Definitely better.

His eyes were focused and seemed more aware. He looked around and even smiled at Callie.

The day after that Jake stood up and walked around. He used the counter to pull himself up to his feet. He stood and gazed around at the store, his head jerking from side to side, bird-like, at the windows, all the items on the shelves, and at Callie. He walked on unsteady legs over to Samantha, who watched him with something like suspicion and gently patted her shoulder.

He approached Mia and Taylor, who slowly backed away. Jake walked down each aisle, reaching out and touching some items; candy and snacks, occasionally stopping and picking up a knick-knack or souvenir trinket and examining it. His fingers were clumsy, and he dropped several knick-knacks while trying to put them away. He watched them fall but did not try to pick them up.

Callie followed close behind him, just watching, letting him explore, stooping to pick up the fallen objects and place them on shelves.

Taylor and Mia trailed her, observing Jake with great interest (and a little bit of fear).

Jake stopped at the end of the aisle and stared out the front window. He approached the counter and walked until his hips bumped against it.

Callie, who had just placed a snow globe holding an idiotically smiling cartoon mountain lion (what are the odds?) on a shelf, moved behind him.

"Jake?" she said. "You okay, buddy?"

He spun around so fast that he startled her.

Mia, behind Callie, gave a little shriek.

Jake searched her eyes with his, his hands reaching out but not touching her, seeking understanding. He screwed his face up in concentration. "What...happen...?" he said, his voice a horse whisper. He ran a hand along the side of his face and tugged at his overlong hair as if trying to pull the memories from his head.

Callie took his arm and led him to the remaining table in the restaurant. She sat him down in a chair and pulled another over and sat across from him. She reached across the table and took his hands in hers.

"Can you understand what I am saying?" she asked.

His face screwed up in concentration. "Yuh," he said with an effort. It came out almost like a shout.

She spoke slowly as if she was talking to a young child or elderly relative suffering from dementia. She told him everything. About the horrible sound, the TV, finding Ryan, the call from Grandma, the fire, planning her route, the Clown Man and Samantha, Cody and Simon, and Mia and Taylor.

At some point during her telling of the story, the other girls gathered around to listen. Samantha, silent and catlike, perched on top of what had once been a refrigerated reach-in cooler.

The little girls, legs crossed, sat on the floor, looking as natural as if they were back at school during library time, listening to the librarian read a particularly engrossing tale. The cat prowled around them, rubbing up against arms and backs, allowing himself to be petted, but not held.

Callie spoke for what felt like hours, and when she had finished, she stood up and pulled a plastic water bottle from a shelf and downed most of it. Without thinking, she put the cap back on it before handing the bottle to Jake. He struggled to open it, and when she reached over to help him, he turned away, holding the bottle close to his chest. His fingers fumbled over the cap, but eventually, he got it open and drank, spilling only a little. Callie glanced over at Samantha and raised her eyebrows. *See?* Samantha smiled and gave a brief nod.

Callie went around the front counter and returned with her backpack. She reached in, rummaged around, and came out with her map of Oregon, and a pen. She unfolded the map and spread it out over the table. She drew a thick line along the route they were currently on, to show him the route she had planned.

He nodded, his eyes following her pen, but she wasn't sure how much he understood. He was trying, though. She could see it in his eyes.

"When we get to highway 101, we can stay on that all the way through California. It's going to be hard, and it will take a long time...."

By the time they finished talking, the little girls were asleep on the floor. Samantha covered them with blankets and with a brief wave of her hand, went to make her own bed. Callie let Jake change himself, which he was able to do, despite her desire to reach out and help him. *He's getting better*, she told herself, as he struggled to pull one of his socks off. *Let him do it.*

~

The nightmare again.

The beach. The cold air. The silent waves crashing on the beach. Her feet in the sand.

But wait—something was different. Jake was here. He stood beside her, staring out at the ocean. But this was Quiet Jake. His eyes opening, his mouth moving, the darkness surrounding her, smothering her, like a living thing. And then... the shape. The immense, malevolent shape at the horizon.

Jake started forward, into the surf. Callie cried," No!" and grabbed Jake's arm.

He continued on. She dug her heels into the sand and pulled. It made no difference. She slid around in front of him and placed her hands on his chest. No effect. He was as inexorable as the tides he was walking into.

He was pushing her closer to the water. Her feet went under, and she gasped. The water was so cold it was painful. Needles of cold shooting through her feet, her calves, her knees.

He continued forward, pushing her deeper and deeper, past her knees. Her legs were frozen, the incredible cold sharp and burning.

Sobbing, she stepped aside and scrambled to the shore. She sprawled on the sand, gasping, and watched Jake march into the sea, that black foul sea, and there was nothing she could do about it.

When he was shoulder deep, Jake turned to her and gave her a sly smile. And then he was gone beneath the black waters.

39

Callie awoke with a start, jerking to a sitting position. Her hair was damp with sweat, and she pushed it out of her face. Her heart was hammering at the inside of her chest as if trying to break out.

She pushed aside the hair that was plastered to her face with sweat. She was hot, despite the chill in the air. Odd, that she should be hot. Except... except she wasn't. She reached down and touched her feet and ran her hand up her calf. Her skin was cold. Ice cold. Goosebumps covered her legs from the knees down.

What the hell?

It was still dark, the rising sun just a dim promise beyond the trees. The store was wreathed in shadows.

She turned to see if she had woken up Jake.

Callie gave a low, strangled moan

Jake was gone.

～

She stood on cold and numb feet, one hand on the counter, heart pounding.

No, no, no.

She limped to the center of the store, peering into the shadows of the far walls and corners. Shades of gray and dark blue throughout the store gave everything a flat, featureless cast.

She scooped up a flashlight, turned it on, strode to the back of the store, and checked the bathrooms. Both were empty.

"Jake!" she called, not caring if she woke up the others. She stood in the center of the store. "Jake!"

If he heard, he didn't answer.

Mia did, though. She popped her head up from her makeshift bed in the cookie and snack aisle and said, "Callie? What are you doing?"

Samantha sat up. "What is it?" she said.

Callie saw a dark, metallic shape in her hand.

Ryan began crying.

Callie struggled to speak, fighting back the tears and hysteria that had been her constant companion these past few weeks. She swallowed and spoke. "Jake's gone. I don't know where he is."

"I heard someone walking around a little bit ago," Taylor said. "I thought it was you."

"No," Callie said, looking behind the counter in the restaurant. "I just woke up." Maybe he went outside," Mia said.

God, I hope not, Callie thought, her eyes moving toward the front door. But where else could he be?

She went to the front door, her panic increasing when she saw that the alarm cans and bottles had been moved aside. She turned to Samantha. "Did you set up the cans against the door?"

Samantha nodded. "Of course."

Callie pushed her way through the front door and stepped onto the porch.

The air was cool and damp; a thin fog hugged the road and tree trunks across the street. She spared a glance across the way, where the mountain lion had disappeared with Cody's corpse.

"Jake!" she called, peering through the dim morning light. "Jake!"

Was it the dream? Did that thing in her dream call him? And what did it mean when he went underwater?

Once again, Callie was left with more questions than answers.

She stepped to the ground, the moist earth oozing between her toes. Still muddy, but not like yesterday.

The front passenger door of the car closest to the front steps hung open. "Jake?" Callie said and peered inside, saw that it was empty, and closed the door. A plastic shopping bag sat in the trunk.

And over there. A black overnight bag rested on the roof of a little black sports car.

Who did this? she wondered, and then she saw Jake, rifling through the trunk of another car. A powerful wave of relief washed over her, and she ran to him, not feeling the gravel that cut and poked her feet.

He stood at the rear of the car, two suitcases at his feet, holding a backpack.

"Jake!" she called. "What are you doing?"

He looked up at her voice and smiled. "Hey, Callie," he said, his voice thin and raspy.

"Jake," she asked, "Are you okay?"

He looked like he wanted to say something and stopped. He ran a hand over his eyes and lowered his head. Without looking at her, he said, "They're dead, aren't they?"

"Who?" she said. Her voice was soft, and she hoped, soothing. She knew who he meant. She had grown accustomed to her parents' deaths, but this was all new to him.

"So... Mom and Dad? They're..."

Callie nodded. "They have to be. I called them and called them. I waited at the house for a week, and they...they never came back."

He looked down at the backpack in his hands. He fiddled with a zipper. When he looked up at her his eyes were wet. "Thank you," he said.

"For what?"

"For taking care of me. For not... for not leaving me." He met her eyes, then looked away. "It can't have been easy."

She gave a little laugh. "No, sometimes it wasn't."

"And all this." Jake motioned at the shop, the other girls, watching from the porch, yawning, stretching. Samantha held Ryan.

"It's amazing." He paused and swallowed. "Mom and Dad would be so... proud of you..." His voice trailed off. He wiped his eyes with his sleeve, cleared his throat, and tossed the backpack onto the ground.

"How do you feel?" she asked.

He thought for a bit before replying, "Good, good. A little foggy, but way better. Like waking up from too much night-time cold medicine."

She nodded. "You look better. Do you remember anything?" She was torn between wanting to know and being afraid of upsetting him. But the need to know won out.

Jake slammed the trunk, the heavy, metallic clunk

echoing in the still air. Such a foreign sound in such a secluded spot.

He tilted his head, thinking. "Yes and no. I... remember being..." His forehead furrowed as he tried to come up with the right word. "Not called, but summoned, I guess, to go somewhere, and wanting more than anything to go. Like that was all that mattered. Other than that..." he shook his head.

"Do you remember what was calling you?" she said. *If he says something in the ocean was calling him, I'm going to scream.*

"I'm not sure," he said. "Just...something big. And old."

"Old?"

"Yeah." He shrugged. "I'm not sure how else to say it." His voice had an edge to it now.

"So what are you doing out here?" she asked. "Why are you getting all the suitcases?"

He dug into his pockets and pulled out a set of car keys, pushing the remote button with his thumb. A white pickup gave a feeble beep and the tail lights flashed. Jake nodded and headed toward the pickup.

"I was thinking about your plans, and you're right." He turned and gave her a look of appraisal, his eyes roving over her, then nodded in approval. "It's a good idea. If we drive along the coast, we're way more likely to find food and supplies and places to sleep. And we can travel about a few hundred miles a day, so it should only take—"

"'A few hundred miles a day?" said Callie. "What are you talking about?"

Surprisingly, Jake smiled. That smug smile when he knew something she didn't know what Mom and Dad were getting her for Christmas, or conversely, that she was in big trouble but was not yet aware of it.

"What?" Callie said.

"He can drive us," said Samantha, moving over to them. She looked at Jake. "That's what you mean, right?"

Jake nodded. "I don't see why not." He motioned at the cars around them. "We have all these cars to choose from if they start. A couple of them have dead batteries."

"I know which one we should drive," Samantha said.

Callie returned to the porch, walking carefully on her sensitive feet. She sat on the bottom step and scraped the mud and pebbles from the bottom of her feet.

Taylor sat down beside her and balanced Ryan on her lap. He squawked and held out his arms for Callie, who took him eagerly.

"Hey, little guy," she said, nuzzling his fat little neck. He giggled. She hadn't been spending enough time with him lately. It had been so hectic. But now, things seemed to be looking up.

She watched as Jake and Samantha climbed into the red pickup, which just a few days ago had been such a source of dread, but now represented hope.

The engine started, and Jake drove around the parking lot for a bit and turned down one of the rows of cars. He and Samantha hopped out and grabbed the discarded suitcases and bags and tossed them in the back. They repeated this several times and Jake drove over and parked at the bottom of the steps. He cut the engine and hopped out.

It's about half full," he said. "We're going to have to siphon some gas,"

Callie had no idea what that meant, but she nodded.

He smiled at her. "But it should get us where we need to go."

The sun rose and drove the moist air and fog away, and the group took advantage of the pleasant morning.

They opened the bags and pulled out anything they could use: extra clothes, batteries, rain gear, tools, whatever they thought might come in handy.

Taylor and Mia loaded up several cardboard cartons with bottles of water and snacks, while Jake found a length of plastic hose in the back of the store and began the unenviable task of siphoning gas out of one of the other cars. This involved sticking the hose into the fuel tank and then sucking on it until the gas began to flow through the hose. He coughed and spat but eventually, he was able to fill a bucket, and then, using a funnel, he managed to pour most of the gasoline into the red truck's fuel tank. Callie watched at first, disgusted, but then fascinated.

"How did you know how to do that?" she said.

Jake took a swig of water, swished it around in his mouth, spat, and said, "I watched a YouTube video one time. You never know."

The sun was high in the afternoon sky by the time the truck was loaded. Jake sat behind the wheel, Callie had a shotgun and held Ryan. She knew it was wrong; they all knew it was wrong. But none of the cars had baby seats. And Jake had promised to drive *very* carefully until they found one.

Mia, Taylor, and Samantha sat in the back, taking turns holding the cat.

Jake turned to Callie. "You ready?"

Callie nodded. "Yup." *We're really coming, Grandma*, she thought.

Jake glanced up in the mirror at the girls in the back seat. "You guys ready?"

"Yes," cried Taylor and Mia.

Jake pulled out of the parking lot. And turned right onto the highway, heading west.

The red truck traveled down the winding road, eventually passing a sign reading: "Highway 101 17 miles" before turning around a bend and disappearing.

As the pickup rounded the turn, two figures emerged from the greenery along the road. The taller one, an older man, his clothing stained and torn, watched as the truck made the turn. His unnaturally large eyes shone with a bright, vivid green. A narrow, too-long gray tongue licked dry, cracked lips, and he shuffled after the truck.

His companion was a young woman wearing a worn cocktail dress. Her dark hair was long and stringy and hung over her face. There were bald patches on her skull.

Her eyes glowed with the same green fire, and she raised an arm, revealing a taloned claw where a hand should be.

ABOUT THE AUTHOR

Jeff DePew has been writing stories and screenplays for almost twenty years.

He was a contributing editor for 13Thirty Books and is a regular contributor to the "Never Fear" horror anthologies published by Invoke books. His work tends to be dark, although he does occasionally blend horror and comedy. Jeff currently lives in Henderson, Nevada with his wife Mary Beth and his children, Joseph and Annabelle.

His collection of short stories, Something *is out There*, was published by Surtr Books in 2018.

Jeff would like you to know he is a licensed paranormal investigator, a red belt in Taekwondo, a titled Lord of the Principality of SeaLand, has a Doctorate in Occult Studies from Miskatonic University, and according to a certificate (for which he paid good money) on his office wall, a member of the Illuminati.

www.ingramcontent.com/pod-product-compliance
Lightning Source LLC
Chambersburg PA
CBHW061131200626
46817CB00016B/742